# THE VISCOUNT'S LIST

# Books By Lorin Grace

## American Homespun Series
*Waking Lucy*
*Remembering Anna*
*Reforming Elizabeth*
*Healing Sarah*

## Bradford Brides
*Rescuing the Sheriff's Heart*
*Bending the Blacksmith's Heart*
*Converting the Preacher's Heart*
*Healing the Doctor's Heart*

## Heirs & Heroes
*The Viscount's List*
*The Colonist's Petition* (coming)
*The Gentleman's Agreement* (coming)
*The Duke's Directive* (coming)
*The Captain's Letter* (coming)
*The Earl's Inheritance* (coming)

## Stand Alone Titles
*A Little Clean Fun*
*Love in the Valley*

## Artists & Billionaires
*Mending Fences*
*Mending Christmas*
*Mending Walls*
*Mending Images*
*Mending Words*
*Mending Hearts*

## Hastings Security
*Not the Bodyguard's Baby*
*Not the Bodyguard's Widow*
*Not the Bodyguard's Boss*
*Not the Bodyguard's Princess*
*Not the Bodyguard's Bride*
*Not the Bodyguard's Angel*

## Hastings Legacy
*Too Much in Common*
*Too Far to Sea* (coming)

## Misadventures in Love
*Miss Guided*
*Miss Oriented*

## Spellbound in Hawthorne
*(with Maria Hoagland)*
*Taste of Memory*
*Sprinkle of Snow*
*Hint of Charm*
*Dash of Destiny*
*Stir of Wind*
*Essence of Gravity*

*Heirs & Heroes*
BOOK ONE

# THE VISCOUNT'S LIST

# LORIN GRACE

CURRANT
CREEK PRESS

FOR THE READERS WHO
WON'T LET ME STOP.

# ONE

May 9, 1810

Stewards don't belong in the schoolroom.

Yet, Mr. Rhodes stood in the doorway, clearing his throat and straightening his limp cravat.

It was rude to stare. Phil bowed her head over her French book and waited for her governess, who helped her youngest sister on the far side of the room, to notice the steward's presence. Although the man spent several hours a week in the house, the children rarely saw him and, less frequently, spoke to him. And he never, ever traversed the stairs to the floors above the small office near Father's study. Across the room, her twin sisters stopped arguing over their sums. Although they differed in appearance, George and Jane's wide eyes and opened mouths matched in every feature.

Mr. Rhodes cleared his throat again. "Pardon the interruption. Sir Lightwood requires Miss Philippa's presence in the study."

The governess's head popped up, her face registering the same surprise as the twins for a long moment before she returned to her prim demeanor. At the governess's nod of dismissal, Phil closed her book, allowing each page time to float into place and her heart to stop pounding as she took a deep breath. Father hadn't spoken to her in several days and then only to tell her to not run in the garden.

She followed the steward out of the room and down two flights of stairs. The last time she had been called to the study was when she helped her older sister, Alex, put a snake in their old governess's bed. As punishment, father had sent them both back to the nursery for a week with only porridge to eat. The maids hadn't tended the deserted nursery since Rose graduated to the schoolroom. In the interim, spiders had taken up residence in the windowsill. Phil spent each night terrified the eight-legged monsters would climb into her bed. Soon after, the horrid governess left, and their current governess replaced her. If Father had listened to Mother's complaints about the governess, the snake wouldn't have been necessary to rid the house of the spiteful old spinster. However, Phil had done nothing of that sort of mischief again.

Phil slowed her steps. Her chest tightened, making breathing difficult. The only time her father had announced good tidings was the day of William's birth. Phil cataloged all of her misdeeds in recent weeks. None to concern her father came to mind. With each descending stair, she turned over the possibilities in her mind. Was Father upset with her lack of progress in the schoolroom? With Alex and Mother away, she hadn't been paying as much attention as she should to her lessons. Had their governess complained? Why not send a footman or a maid to the classroom?

The heavy study door stood open. Philippa followed the steward into the space Sir Lightwood occupied when not in London. Deep walnut-paneled walls and heavy furniture matched the oppressive smell of coal smoke filling the room. The chimney refused to draw properly, despite all of Father's haranguing the staff, making the room unpleasant after the long winter months. The open window did little to help.

Father stood behind his massive desk buttoning his greatcoat, a sure sign he was leaving again. "Philippa, you are the lady of the house now. It's your responsibility to see to the funeral arrangements. Send a message to the coffin-maker. You'll need to prepare the house. I'll be back in the morning. I want your brother laid out in his new suit. Have your mother's maid choose her dress and Alexandra's."

"Mother is dead?" Phil clutched the back of a chair to steady herself. She must have misunderstood. "Alex? William?" Her mother and two siblings had been visiting Mother's father, the Earl of Whitstone, for the last fortnight. Grandfather had taken a great liking to young William, and Father had encouraged the visits. They were to return today.

"How many times have I told you to call your sisters by their full Christian names? Calling each other men's names isn't proper. William was the only son I had, not Alexandra." Until William's birth seven years ago, father had used the masculine version of their names often enough. Father adjusted the fingers of his right glove. "Your sister still lives, or did when the courier was dispatched, but I doubt she will survive the night."

If a full breath could enter her lungs, she would scream. Mother and William couldn't be dead, nor Alex in danger of joining them.

Father crossed the room in three steps. "Inform your sisters and see they are dressed appropriately when I return with the bodies. I expect to be back by mid-morning tomorrow at the latest."

His quick footsteps echoed through the tiled corridor until the front door shut behind him. As businesslike as ever. Did he not care? Had he no feeling?

Philippa remained standing behind the chair, afraid if she let go, she might fall to the ground. Lady of the house? How could she take her mother's place at father's command?

The housekeeper hurried into the room, followed by the butler. She guided Philippa around the chair. "Sit down, child. Take a breath. Would you like tea?"

"What happened?" Phil addressed the steward, struggling to keep her voice even.

"A message arrived a quarter hour past. There was a carriage accident not two miles from The Willows. According to the earl's missive, Miss Alexandra is with the best doctor his lordship can find." Mr. Rhodes didn't repeat the fact her mother and brother were dead.

A simple visit to her grandfather's estate should not end in death.

Phil closed her eyes, forcing the tears to stay hidden. Funeral and mourning arrangements had not been part of her education. Beyond knowing she needed to shroud the parlor in black and cover her mother's portrait and have black dresses made for her and her sisters, Philippa was ignorant. An ache started behind her eyes and moved to her temples and squeezed her head. How would Mother act? Mother, a genuine lady in deed and title, would not descend into tears in front of the servants. After a steadying breath, Phil opened her eyes and spoke as calmly as she could. "I'll need your guidance. I'm afraid I don't know what my father expects of me."

The housekeeper exchanged looks with the steward and butler. "I'll serve tea in the green parlor. I'll ask the governess to bring your sisters down. Take the time you need to explain. In my experience, a good cry will help."

The butler bowed more deeply than his usual nod. "With your permission, I will gather the staff and inform them of Lady Lightwood's and young William's passing. We will pray for Miss Alexandra's recovery." Except for the governess, even the smallest stable boy most likely had heard of the tragedy already. The staff always knew everything first, even if they feigned ignorance. Still, prayer would be appropriate. Another thing Phil had neglected to request. What would she do without Alex? Phil realized the butler awaited her reply. "Thank you. I wouldn't have thought about informing the staff."

Father's pronouncement that she should take charge weighed heavily on her shoulders, preventing her from running from the house to her favorite bench in the garden to cry in private.

"Besides your governess, is there anyone you would like in the parlor when you talk with your sisters?" asked the housekeeper.

"I think it's best if our governess does not attend to us." Jane, the youngest twin, only spoke in her presence when asked to or when fighting with George. This governess was kinder than the last, yet still not understanding of Jane's quiet nature.

The housekeeper ushered Phil into the parlor. "I'll return in a moment with tea. Do you have your handkerchief?"

Phil pulled one out of her sleeve and nodded. No words could pass the lump in her throat.

The housekeeper closed the doors most of the way, leaving Phil alone to compose herself.

A sob escaped her mouth before she could contain her emotions.

Mother.

William.

Alex.

Life without her dearest sister would not be bearable. A fortnight alone in their bedroom had been an eternity. Alex couldn't die too. What of all the secrets she had to tell? Edward had returned home on leave and had inquired about Alex after Sunday service. The twins and Rose would never care.

Voices drifted around the gap of the door.

"I don't know what he is thinking. Miss Philippa is not yet fifteen. He should have told his daughters himself. And to place the poor girl in charge." The housekeeper's voice carried a tone of anger reserved for when the butcher delivered a poor cut of meat or when William tracked mud through the entrance hall. Phil clamped her hand over her mouth. There would be no more muddy, little-boy footprints.

"The entire staff will help the young Miss. I've taken the liberty of sending a note over to the vicar," said the butler. Her father's instructions hadn't included contacting the vicar. Something Phil should have thought of herself. How was she not to make a muddle of everything?

A door shut and footsteps clicked on the uncarpeted tile in the corridor. Mr. Rhodes's voice was soft, causing Phil to strain to listen. "You best move on. The Misses Lightwood need our support, not our speculation."

"Yes," answered the butler.

Three sets of footsteps echoed as the staff dispersed. Philippa closed the door and blinked back tears. Now was not the time to cry. She needed to wait until she told her sisters.

# TWO



Mr. Rhodes appeared at the morning room door. His gaze flickered to Alex before landing on Phil. "Sir Lightwood requests Miss Lightwood's presence in the study."

*Demanded.* Father never made requests. The poor steward. Father sent the person closest to him again. It wasn't the steward's place to do errands, not when the household employed two footmen. Whatever thought crossed Father's mind couldn't wait for the butler or a footman to answer the bell. Mr. Rhodes stood up to everyone except Father. No one countered Father's wishes when he was in residence. Only a baronet, Sir Lightwood carried on as Phil imagined a king might—an extremely corrupt one at that, judging by the household account books she was forced to balance.

Phil stood. "Which one of us does he want?"

"I'm not positive. Sir Lightwood said 'my daughter'—" The steward let his voice trail off.

"Was he upset?" asked Phil.

"Not in the least. He seemed quite pleased." Mr. Rhodes nodded, as if assuring himself his improbable declaration was true. He left without waiting for them.

Alex nudged Phil. Sir Lightwood avoided all contact with his crippled daughter. Sometimes Phil envied not being noticed. "You should go."

"Not without you. You are Miss Lightwood, not me. Father needs to recognize you. I will not usurp your place." Phil rose and waited by the door for Alex to join her.

"I will only anger him again." Alex leaned on her cane, bracing herself to stand.

"No, I will." Phil and her father clashed often over the four years since the accident that changed the family forever. Starting the morning he berated her for falling asleep while sitting vigil in the parlor next to her mother and brother's coffins, Father had never ceased to find fault in all Phil did. The week after Mother and William were laid to rest, Sir Lightwood lectured Phil for exceeding the household budget. Not only had she been unaware of the budget, but every extra expenditure had been related to the funeral. Phil maintained the error was Father's fault for putting a fourteen-year-old child in charge of her mother's funeral and running the household. Not a week went by when he hadn't found one fault or another. Fortunately, Father spent more time away from Kellmore Manor than not, and Phil was now an expert on keeping his ever-tightening budget. "Besides, Mr. Rhodes says Father is pleased."

"Still, Father may be upset over something I've done or haven't remembered to do." Since Alex's return to health, they shared the household responsibilities, and things had run somewhat smoother, except for Rose's education. Deprived of a regular governess, their youngest sister chafed under her sisters' tutelage.

Phil held out her arm. "Together or not at all."

Linking her arm through her sister's, Alex tapped her cane. "Shall I leave this here?"

Phil studied her sister's face. Tightness around Alex's eyes and their dullness showed she was in more pain than she'd let on. Today, the cane was a necessity. "No. If he separates us, then you may need it."

They reached the open door of the study and entered together. The steward announced them. "Miss Lightwood and Miss Philippa are here."

"I only asked for Philippa." Father didn't look up from his desk. "Rhodes, you may leave."

Phil and Alex stood behind the chairs in front of their father's desk.

Father folded a paper and looked only at Phil. "I've decided it is time for you to marry. Lady Healand has offered to host you for the Season in London, which is only right considering she is your mother's only sister. You leave Thursday. She claims all of Lent is required to prepare your wardrobe."

Phil glanced at Alex before answering. "I will not go."

Father's head jerked up. "Not go? It is your duty to marry well. As long as the earl lives, I cannot receive the entail and our fortunes will not improve. You have three other sisters to find husbands. They are counting on you to make a good match."

Grandfather's death would not be a boon to his grand-daughters, as father would spend through whatever small inheritance they received as well. "I have four sisters, and one is older. If I am to have a Season, Alex should as well."

"Why? No one will marry her. Men with titles need an heir, and men with money want a beautiful woman to host parties in his home. He doesn't want a woman who makes him flee to his mistress on his wedding day."

If this had been the first-time father had spoken so crudely of his oldest daughter or referred to his mistress, one of them might have gasped in shock. Being less than discreet about his own liaison with a certain notorious French widow, Phil had no doubt the entire ton knew.

Phil lifted her chin and stepped forward. Alex put a hand on her arm to stop her. "Phil, I don't mind. I'll stay here."

The cane tapped on the floor as Alex limped toward the door.

"No!" Phil raced to block her sister's way. "Please, Alex. I won't enjoy a single moment if you are not with me."

The legs of Father's chair scraped on the floor as he pushed back from his desk. "Philippa, stop this nonsense. You are not a child anymore."

"You treat my sister like she is a servant, not your oldest daughter. The scar on her face is hardly noticeable. She is as beautiful as Mother."

Father pushed back from his desk. "Philippa …"

"If you want me to go to London, Alex comes too. I refuse to be out before my older sister is. That is her right."

"What is the point? She can't go to balls. A woman who can't dance cannot catch a husband." Father didn't even cast a glance in Alex's direction.

"Balls are not the only part of the Season. No one plays or sings better than Alex. She is intelligent and helps to keep your house running. She'd make a fine wife for any man. Besides, she deserves a bit of fun."

"Who will teach your sisters?"

"Alex and I rarely spend any time teaching now that George and Jane are finished in the schoolroom. They are teaching Rose. George speaks French better than either of us, and there isn't a subject Jane hasn't mastered." Not that Rose paid any attention to either of them. The youngest needed a firmer hand than her older sisters could give. Especially when father was slow to interfere.

"If you have not been teaching your sisters, what have you been doing?" As little time as Father spent at Kellmore Manor over the last four years, it was a wonder he even knew they had taken over for the governess.

"Visiting your tenants, caring for the house, and economizing. Exactly what you charged us to do." Phil struggled to keep her voice at the proper tone.

"I don't have the money to outfit you both for the Season." Not surprising. Father's expenditures in Town had grown exponentially as his gambling increased.

The tap of Alexandra's cane sounded behind her. "Phil, go without me. Father is right. A Season is a pointless expenditure."

Philippa spun to face her sister. "Alex, you deserve one Season. You are Miss Lightwood, not me. My coming out before you will reflect poorly on the entire family. I understand the ton is not forgiving about breaches of protocol." She aimed most of the speech at her father.

Their father sat back in his leather chair. "If I allow you both to go. You must stretch the funds without damaging Philippa's chances for marriage. Her dowry isn't as large as other debutantes'."

"Ten thousand pounds is more than respectable." Phil had never worried about the dowry.

"Five."

"What?" the sisters asked in unison.

"Each of you has five thousand." Sir Lightwood's expression remained impassive.

Alex sat in a chair. "We each have ten. You've told us that for years."

"I've had to make certain changes to support our living."

Phil exchanged a look with Alex. Whatever happened to the money, they'd be powerless to recover the funds. "We'll make do."

"I'll write to your aunt. She can expect you both. You are dismissed."

Alex clutched Phil's arm until they reached the sitting room. "Why did you do that? Father is right, there is no point in giving me a Season. Who would marry me?"

Phil traced the scar between her sister's left eye and ear. "It is a small scar. You are not disfigured."

Tapping her cane against her leg, Alexandra produced a hollow drumming sound. "This is far bigger than a scar. A man returning from war may enter society with a wooden leg, but not a woman."

Phil settled into her favorite chair which had once been her mother's. "How do you know? It is so easy to hide your wooden friend under your skirt. A man can't hide it as well. Dozens of women could hide peg legs under the petticoats. And think, no woman of the ton has such a perfectly turned ankle."

The sisters burst into laughter at the joke, referencing the process the woodcarver used to make the prosthesis.

Alexandra lifted her skirt. "I do like this one. Grandfather even ordered carved toes. They might impress a suitor more than my ankle."

"If you would try to dance, you have one advantage over me. You won't feel it when someone steps on your slippers."

"And I won't know when I step on their toes. If I go with you, absolutely no balls for me. My refusal to dance can only hurt your chances."

Phil grasped her sister's hand. "We can work that out with our aunt. Please come."

Alex sighed. "After getting Father to agree, I have little choice."

Phil threw her arms around her sister. "Thank you. We will have the best Season."

# THREE

I didn't plan on sitting in Parliament for another dozen or more years." Viscount Michael Endelton unconsciously touched the spot where a black armband no longer circled his arm before sitting in the chair formerly reserved for his father when in Town. It was hard to think of the study as his space now. A hint of pipe tobacco lingered about the desk his father had used for so many years. "I loathe the return to session after Easter. I do not know how to act."

"The joys of being a second son, I plan on never attending. Although with the state of things, I believe my wife would have preferred I had chosen the law or the church." Lieutenant Edward Godderidge sat in the chair opposite and smoothed his uniform coat.

"Then my sister could not admire you in your fine coat. I am sure it is the only reason she married you." Michael still was not sure how the yearlong marriage to his sister affected his relationship with his best friend, but it had.

"She may not admire them so much when I am aboard ship."

"You received new orders?" asked Richard Kenworth, Duke of Aylton. As Michael's cousin, he was always welcome in Michael's study, even in one of his darker moods. Which, based on his colorless gray waistcoat, was the case today.

"I have yet to hear, but Deborah is determined to pretend as if the harbor stands empty and I am to only work in the office looking at maps and planning. But I fear we will only have a few weeks for her to enjoy the Season. Our skirmish with the Americans is not going our way and then there are always the French. The admiral has yet to decide when I should return to sea now my arm is healed." Edward's knee bounced up and down, a sign his convalescence had kept him caged on land far too long.

"I warned you of Deborah's willfulness long before you sought her hand." Michael's warm smile reflected his feelings for his elder sister.

Richard grunted as he often did when spousal matters were brought up.

Edward ignored the duke. "My friend, you are the one who should be warned. My wife has declared she will see you wed by the end of the Season. I dare say she has your entire evening planned for Richard's ball."

"Not my ball. It is all the duchess's doing." It was no secret the duke and his wife didn't get on. "I urge caution in matrimony. And steer clear of desperate fathers. They are worse than marriage-minded mothers. When it comes to understanding people, especially women, you are more obtuse than the average gentleman."

"Not everyone looks for dark motives in every action." Or so he'd been told dozens of times when his sister tried to explain the differences between Richard and himself. He never understood women. Or people in general. Humans acted so inconsistent with what they said. His sisters insisted the fault wasn't with people.

"Come now, Richard, if the new Lord Endelton would remember to smile, he'd be well enough off."

Michael could smile, yet a grin would not solve his problem. Finding a wife meant braving the crushes of balls and talking to women at soirees. "Smiling isn't my problem. The difficulty is choosing. There are so many women. How am I ever to know which one to court? It is worse than one of Mother's teas when she has the cook make ten different cakes, and I can't possibly have them all."

Edward went to the desk and pulled out a sheet of paper. "With the Duke's helpful insight, I am sure we can come up with a short list of women whom you might court safely. Would ten be too many?"

Ten? Far too many to choose from. "As you've pointed out, my sister is taking care of the matchmaking. Why not let her choose? She knows me better than anyone."

"The last Season you attended, you were only the Honorable Michael Endelton. This Season you are Viscount Endelton. Hence, there will be more women, and their mothers, seeking you out."

"I still startle when someone addresses me as Viscount or Lord Endelton. Every time a servant says, 'my lord,' I search for my father to answer." Not that it should make any difference. He was still the same person. The title made him more awkward around others, not less.

Edward's pen scratched on the paper. "Prepare yourself for the name of Lord Endelton to be bandied about as often as seagulls' cries at the dock. Deborah says she has two balls, a soiree, and a night of musical entertainment lined up for you already. No doubt every debutante will hasten her fanning in your presence and call you by your title repeatedly, leaving no doubt they are not talking of your father. What do you think of the Simesson's daughter, your grace?"

"New money. In need of a title." Richard shook out a newspaper and muttered something in dire tones, which both men ignored.

"Adding her to the list."

"Lady Christina?"

"Father drinks in excess. Far too jovial for me."

"Everyone is too jovial for you." Edward dipped the pen in the well. "There. Ten names. My list should keep you the entire Season."

Michael raised his glass to Edward. "You should not look so smug, for you shall also have to attend those events with me and be expected to dance even more than I, and none of them with Deborah."

"There is the rub. A man finds an agreeable dance partner, marries, and is never to dance with her in public again." Edward sighed dramatically.

A tap came on the door. The men stood as the subject of their conversation entered the room. "Are you two discussing me again? One would think my husband and my brother could find another topic of conversation." Deborah reached for her husband's hand, then paused and nodded her head at the duke. "Your Grace, I didn't realize you were here."

"Never mind me, you know those two don't. And don't 'your grace' me. I've been your cousin my entire life." Richard waited for Deborah to be seated before taking his newspaper to the other side of the room.

"I didn't expect you back so soon." Edward pulled his chair as close as possible to his wife's.

"Your mother and I spent over two hours shopping with Isabel. That is not 'soon,' especially when the shops are full of other mothers dressing their daughters to impress the ton."

"And my sister? How did she fare?" asked Edward.

"I'd say Isabel would be the most beautiful debutante of the

Season, if we had not met with two of her childhood acquaintances who are in most respects as handsome and kind."

"Anyone we know?" asked Michael, mostly curious if his sister had indeed started a list of prospective wives.

"Give me a moment. You know how terrible I am with names. They were sisters. Their names sounded manly."

Edward's brows creased together. "Alex and Phil?"

"Those are the names your sister used, but your mother called the one Miss Lightfoot, no Lightwood, and the other Miss Philippa." Deborah turned to her brother. "I intended to introduce you to them at the duke's ball."

"It is not my ball." Richard's protests fell on deaf ears. A ball at his Mayfair residence was his ball, despite his grumblings.

"You're sure you met Alexandra Lightwood?" asked Edward.

Deborah's eyes narrowed. "Is this yet another of your past loves I am to learn about?"

Edward tilted his head and looked at his wife so longingly, Michael coughed. "I'm still here."

The newspaper ruffled. "So am I."

"Why don't you leave?" asked Edward.

"Because this is my house," answered Michael.

The duke grunted.

Edward grinned. His amiable nature was in complete contrast to the duke's. "You should both stay. My wife and I can leave as soon as she takes a turn at matchmaking."

Deborah beamed at her husband. Michael was puzzled at how easily she forgave him. Or was she teasing? "Dearest, tell him about the Lightwoods. You know them better than I do."

Edward leaned away from Deborah. "Our families associated often when we were children. The Lightwoods lived near to Leadon Hill. Alex, Phil, and I had our first dancing lessons together, along with my siblings. The last time I saw Phil was the week her mother and brother passed. I haven't seen Alex for longer. I cannot envision either girl grown."

"Hard to picture them as women with such names," said Michael.

Deborah laughed her high, tinkling laugh. "I assure you, they are women. And I consider myself fortunate that my husband has not seen them for so long. I don't know that I would have caught his eye." She smiled at Edward. "Do you think one of them would suit my brother?"

"They are both far too good for him. But there is a chance they could settle for his title." Edward pulled his wife closer. Next, they would ask for a couch to be brought in. Michael pushed aside the thought to focus on the conversation.

"Any woman who wants a viscount for his title is desperate." Richard muttered quietly enough for everyone to ignore.

"Your sister seemed most fond of the Lightwoods. Perhaps we can introduce them before the ball." Deborah tapped her chin. "Would your mother host a small dinner for old friends?"

Edward shrugged. "She may. Lady Lightwood was one of mother's fondest friends."

Finally, Michael placed the name. "Lightwood? Any relation to Sir Felton Lightwood?"

Edward sighed before answering. A sure sign he knew Sir Lightwood's reputation. "He is their father."

Richard lowered his paper. "Too bad for the daughters. What man would want to align himself with such a family? No need to introduce Michael."

Deborah sat forward on the settee. "What do you mean?"

"Sir Lightwood is not a gentleman of discretion." Edward could hardly tell his wife the man flaunted his mistress in public. "They barred him from Whites. He gambles to excess."

"I didn't think one could get barred from Whites for gambling. I've heard men bet on the speed of raindrops on a windowpane."

Richard set down his paper. "If one does not pay their

debts, that is a different matter. Hence, his daughters would be liabilities as marriage partners."

Edward glared at the duke. "Last I knew them, the daughters took after their mother."

Michael tilted his head. Few things upset Edward.

"I have heard their grandfather, the Earl of Whitstone, is much involved in their lives," Edward continued his campaign for the women.

"Even so, Richard says it's not a suitable connection." Michael would not be the one to bring down the family name after all his father's hard work. He trusted his cousin's opinion to keep him from misstepping in his new role.

Deborah's face fell. "Then you don't even want to be introduced?"

"I don't think that is wise," muttered Richard.

"We can hardly avoid the acquaintance with my family connections," said Edward.

"Can you avoid throwing me into their path?" asked Michael.

"Don't be so snobbish, Brother. You are only a viscount of moderate means. If you get a reputation for being prejudiced in your choices, you will never find a wife. As much as I love you, you are not the catch of the Season regardless of what my husband has told you." Deborah crossed the room and pointed to the center of Michael's chest. "True, you cut a fine figure on the dance floor, but marriage-minded mothers will look beyond your charms. And don't you dare let *His Grace* poison you on marriage either."

As Deborah had taught him, Michael mimicked removing an arrow from his chest. "Sister, you wound me with your praise."

"I don't think you should remove any prospect from your list too soon. Especially before you meet," said Deborah.

"You are determined to make an introduction to the Miss Lightwoods?" asked Richard.

Deborah looked at Edward before answering. "I think you should meet them, if only for the practice. You need a reminder of how to conduct yourself in polite society."

"I have been nothing but affable," said Michael.

Edward rose and wrote on the paper. "Yet even now, you wear a look of horror on your face, therefore, I always win at cards. Your every thought shows as clear as words on a page."

Throwing up his hands, Michael paced to the far side of the room. "I can hide my emotions as well as any man when I put a mind to it. I don't see any reason to pretend among family."

"Excellent, it's settled. I will speak with Lady Godderidge about planning a small dinner as soon as possible." Deborah smiled triumphantly.

Richard peered over his paper. "Please don't invite me."

"I said party, *your Grace*, not inquisition. Be sure the Lightwoods receive an invitation to your wife's ball."

"If their grandfather is the Earl of Whitstone, I assume the duchess has already invited them. Titles mean far too much to some people." No doubt he included his wife in that number.

Deborah clapped her hands. "Wonderful. I have a few other names for your list. The sooner Michael can meet all these women, the sooner he can choose his bride."

The list grew from ten to more than a score. Richard stalked over and struck two names from the list.

Michael bowed his head in defeat. It was official, his sister had joined the ranks who believed a single man of means should relinquish his bachelor title as soon as possible. It would be a very long Season.

# FOUR

Phil lay the invitation on the table separating her from her sister. "Stop attempting to decline. It is only a small dinner with our old friends, the Godderidges."

"I should not have come to London with you." With one finger, Alex slid the invitation back to Phil. "You should attend. Isabel was always such a dear friend to you."

"And to you. When we met her out shopping, Isabel looked right at you when she told us we must meet her sister-in-law's brother, Lord Someone."

"Viscount Endelton, but she spoke to you." Alex rubbed the top of her cane. "I didn't think we would meet people we know in Town. I don't want a match out of pity."

"Lord and Lady Godderidge visited last Christmas. They are the one family we don't need to stand upon ceremony with and who won't look at your cane with raised eyebrows, which is all the more reason to go." Phil coaxed her sister even as she guessed at her sister's reluctance. "Are you trying to decline because of Edward?"

"Why would I? Lieutenant Godderidge has been married for more than a year. And I haven't seen him since you know—.

Any girlish thoughts I once shared are of no consequence." Alex resumed her embroidery.

Dwelling on what might have been was as useless as wishing her sister's leg back. Phil wished she could find the words to heal her sister's heart. Words never solved what actions did. Coming to London might prove a colossal mistake for both of them. The ton would not treat them kindly if they learned of Peggy. Phil had thus nicknamed Alex's new leg in hopes of lifting her spirits as she adjusted to what her life entailed after the accident. The wooden prostheses allowed Alex freedom of movement. Dozens of men sported artificial limbs, no thanks to Napoleon, but a woman? There must be a man who could see her sister as more than the sum total of her accident. Unable to answer her sister's question, Phil resumed studying the fashion plates in their aunt's magazine.

Several minutes later, her sister broke the silence. "I shouldn't fear seeing him now, should I? All he ever promised me was a single dance. A promise which I can now release him from with no awkwardness between us." Alex reached for the paper.

"Shall we tell Aunt Healand to accept the dinner invitation?"

"Yes. It is time to renew the friendship. Besides, the Godderidges have the connections to introduce you to eligible men of the best sort. Edward would warn you off of any rakes or fortune hunters," said Alex.

"Our reduced dowries are hardly considered fortunes." Father must have lost in his favorite gambling hells the last few months to lose half our dowries. The very name cautioned men of what might happen inside.

"To a desperate man they could be." Alex bit her lip and turned to the window.

Phil reached across the table and laid a hand on her sister's arm. "We will protect each other. Perhaps it is better father reduced our dowry. It should be much easier to ferret out the men who only want our money."

"In my case, any man who makes an offer is a fortune hunter of the worst sort."

"Alexandra!" Phil leapt from her chair. "Don't say such things. They aren't true."

Alex looked down at her hands. "I should not have said that. I know how much my sour moods upset you."

Phil sunk back into her seat. There had to be a man who would love her sister. Did it matter if Alex couldn't dance? "I hope our new dresses arrive soon, or at least one. Isabel already saw me in my only presentable gown at Christmas."

"I changed the ribbons on the bodice, and with the new shawl, I expect she won't recognize the white gown as it is so similar to many of the dresses the modiste showed us. Not that the Godderidges would ever think less of you for wearing the same dress twice." Alex paused and giggled. "Unless you were to spill soup down the front of your frock."

"I was thirteen. I haven't spilled my soup in years." However, to make Alex laugh, Phil would spill her soup at every meal.

Lord Godderidge's townhouse was twice the size of Aunt Healand's. Lights in the windows signaled a warm welcome. Phil waited for her aunt and sister to exit the carriage before stepping out. The coachman assisted them both up the steps to the front door, leaving Phil to her own means, as usual. She placed one foot on the step and looked down to check for a puddle before jumping down to the walkway.

"Wait!" a man yelled.

Her foot hovered in the air, threatening to undermine her balance. She teetered on the narrow metal step as a gentleman in evening clothes rushed to her side. His offered hand came a second too late, and Phil clutched the man's arm to keep from falling to the ground. He grabbed her waist to keep her upright. Not the dignified unassisted carriage exit she'd perfected over the years, and not the first step she needed to take into London society. Why could it have not been a footman?

As soon as Phil solidly planted her feet on the ground, she let go of the gentleman and stepped away. "Thank you, I —" Phil made the mistake of looking at his face, and further words caught in her throat. There was something about his kind smile that momentarily froze all of her faculties.

Alex and Aunt waited in the doorway. Phil nodded at the man and hurried up the stairs as fast as was prudent. To her dismay, he followed them to the Godderidge's door.

Servants took the women's wraps and his hat. The unbalanced lady's sister held a cane which must belong to the woman Michael assumed to be their mother. The lady he had caught as she stumbled out of the carriage glanced briefly at him, her cheeks pinked. He'd never practiced appropriate things to say after awkwardly rescuing a woman, so he pretended indifference as his sisters had coached him to do.

Michael followed them to the parlor, where he hoped for an introduction. Lord and Lady Godderidge greeted each of their guests with their daughter Isabel by their side. Lady Godderidge hugged both of the younger women. Not a normal society greeting, even for an informal gathering. Isabel did the same, whispering in their ears and looking pointedly at him. Michael had the sudden desire to flee. He wasn't fond of having attention paid to him.

"Endelton, so glad you could attend." Lord Godderidge's greeting pulled Michael's attention from the women. The distraction didn't last long as the gentleman nodded in their direction. "Have you met Lady Healand and her nieces?"

"I haven't had the pleasure." A smile met his practiced response.

"I will introduce you." Lady Godderidge laid her hand on Michael's arm.

"Lady Healand, may I introduce Lord Endelton? His older sister married our Edward, and we consider Lord Endelton one of our own."

Lady Healand nodded. "Pleased to meet you. May I introduce my nieces? Miss Lightwood and her sister, Miss Philippa."

Both women nodded. Deborah had not understated the sisters' beauty. Miss Lightwood had a small scar which did not distract from her fair complexion. Her younger sister's eyes were one moment gray, then almost blue when she turned her head to him. Michael wished to study them longer to determine their color.

Miss Philippa smiled warmly. Her eyes sparkled in the lights. Gray? No, definitely blue. "Allow me to thank you again for your assistance at our carriage. I am not normally so inept."

Michael searched for the proper thing to say. "I am afraid I may have startled you."

"I was not paying attention."

He must say something. It was his turn. Yet he wasn't sure what topic to discuss. He stood awkwardly for a moment, trying to come up with something to say about the weather. Deborah had said it was a safe topic.

Lady Godderidge rescued him. "If you will excuse us, I must introduce Lord Endelton to a few more of my guests."

The small dinner party included more than a dozen guests besides the family, which, while considered small by London standards, was still larger than Michael expected.

And Lady Godderidge introduced him to every single one. Since Deborah helped draw up the guest list, he should not be surprised—all the women were on the list, including the Lightwood sisters, who Richard scratched off.

Miss Simesson was at the top of the list. Michael decided he should learn all he could about her this evening. Working through the list methodically was the logical way to determine who on the list would suit and who would not.

Lady Godderidge did her best to not make the evening seem like the marriage brokerage it was. Thus, Michael found himself sitting between two women, neither of which were seeking husbands for themselves.

On his left sat Lady Healand, who despite being the Lightwood's aunt, spent little of the conversation touting either of the girls' talents, preferring to dabble in political matters. Mrs. Simesson's incessant dialogue focused on her daughter Eliza's many charms, which would have been more than enough if spread among four or even five daughters. Michael minded little, as he wasn't required to speak. His three sisters combined didn't possess half the talents Miss Simesson was purported to have mastered. How odd.

The daughter in question sat on the opposite side of the table two spaces up, between two men who alternated in attracting her attention. She was pretty enough, her pale hair pulled up on her head in a fashion not unlike Deborah's. Michael was careful not to look at her too long, lest anyone take note of his interest.

Growing tired of Mrs. Simesson's description of Eliza's paintings, Michael addressed his next question to Lady Healand. "What of your nieces' accomplishments?"

"I find it works better for a young man to discover those for himself. Although I dare say you will find them eager to put the other forward, which I find an endearing quality in sisters. They remind me of my own sister, their mother."

Lady Healand took a bite of the sauced beef, effectively ending the conversation.

In three short sentences, Lady Healand had succeeded where Mrs. Simesson had failed, piquing interest in the single women in the room under her care. Well done. He must remember that tactic. The fewer words, the more interesting. A single attribute rather than a list. Michael wished he was surer of the status of the Miss Lightwoods on his list. Richard's opinion landed decidedly against them while Edward was in favor of the youngest and more reserved in his opinion of the elder.

At length, the meal concluded, and the women left the room. The elder Miss Lightwood leaned on her sister and limped. She wouldn't be the first lady to twist her ankle as her sister nearly had exiting the carriage. Apparently, the sisters shared their lack of gracefulness.

Edward tapped him on the shoulder, indicating they should move into the library where Lord Godderidge handed out the port. Needing a moment of quiet compilation after Mrs. Simesson's endless monologue, Michael sat near a window apart from the others.

Edward joined him. "I saw you watching the Lightwoods leave the dinner. Was there something to your liking?"

"The elder sister is starting the Season with a turned ankle. The younger woman fell out of the carriage when she arrived. You didn't mention they were prone to accidents." Michael winced in sympathetic pain.

Edward stared into his glass for a long moment. "Both sisters were always nimble. Miss Lightwood's limp is of a longer duration."

"I don't understand."

"It is not for me to explain. Her injury is severe. Please be kind to them. Mother is anxious the ton might not accept them because of Miss Lightwood's limp."

"More of a liability than the father?"

Edward nodded and took a long sip from his glass.

Shame, Miss Lightwood was handsome enough to tempt him to add her provisionally to his list. If the ton found her objectionable, Richard would be against a match, so there was no point. The duke scratched out their names. One could deal with an errant father with provisions of the marriage settlement. The opinions of society were not so easily managed. "Why are these women so important to you?"

"I once made a promise I can't keep." Edward looked to the window before answering.

A suspicion and a memory came to mind from their time as youths at Harrow. "Does my sister know you once favored Miss Lightwood?"

"I see you remember."

"It took me a moment to put the names together. Miss Lightwood being your friend Alex. You had me quite confused back then, you know. Calling girls by boys' names."

"It was how they referred to themselves. Thank you for not saying anything in front of my wife." Edward set his half-empty glass on the table. "However, I told her the entire story the other night."

"What was there to say? When you were fifteen or so, you contemplated what a relationship could be like when you were both older. There is nothing to tell there, right?"

"Correct." Edward finished his port in one gulp. "It looks like Father is ready to join the ladies. I believe my mother has the card tables set up. She devised some means to rotate after each hand, so everyone gets to sit one round with everyone."

"Is this for my benefit or your sister's?"

"Both."

Michael sighed. "Considering my list, I am not sure your mother succeeded."

"The list is in jest. You should put it out of your mind."

"But Richard seemed to think the list a splendid idea, to keep me from going wrong."

"Michael, I'm afraid you put too much store in our opinions. In the end, yours will be the only one that matters."

Marriage seemed far too risky of a matter to leave to his own opinion. Especially when he'd been told so often his view of people wasn't normal.

# FIVE

ady Godderidge assigned the women their places before the men finished their port and joined them, explaining that after each hand, the men would rotate tables and the ladies would remain. Phil's heart swelled knowing her mother's friend planned an activity where Alex could remain seated, leaving no reason for anyone to stare at the limp that became more pronounced when her sister was nervous.

Phil found herself seated next to Miss Simesson as they waited for the men.

"Which do you prefer, whist or piquet? Lady Godderidge instructed each table to choose what game is to be played. I'm frightfully bad at both." Miss Simesson twisted the finger of her glove back and forth.

While she preferred the more challenging piquet, she would not force Miss Simesson to make a poor showing. "I often play with my sisters. You choose the game. Both are enjoyable."

"I choose piquet." The decision came quicker than Phil expected, considering Miss Simesson claimed not to play well.

"You're positive? Whist is easier and the scoring more straightforward."

The grin on Miss Simesson's face resembled the expression on Rose's when she convinced the cook to give her an extra treat or her sisters to end classes early. "I am certain."

"Is this your first Season?" asked Phil.

"Yes. Are you being presented at court?"

It had been an option, since both Mother and Aunt had been presented years ago, however Alex fell over mid-curtsy more often than not. In the end, they'd made the practical choice to use their dress allowance for something they could wear again and forgo the experience of a court worthy gown and crinoline. "Not this year. Are you?"

"Mother found the perfect sponsor for me. I can hardly wait." Miss Simesson's nose tipped up ever so slightly.

So, she paid for the privilege of being introduced to the Queen. The Simessons must be more desperate for their daughter to wed a title than Sir Lightwood. For the first time, Phil sensed the amount and type of competition she might face in this game of catching a husband. Would that she had the luxury of finding love as her aunt did.

As the men entered the room, Lady Godderidge assigned them to their tables for the first round. Edward sat opposite Phil as her partner. His brother-in-law, Lord Endelton, partnered with Miss Simesson. Phil nodded at both men. No warmth came to her cheeks as they were apt to do over every minor embarrassment. Hopefully, the viscount would forget her fall ever happened. With his slightly mussed hair, lean build and tall frame, he would be highly sought after. He had also been kind, which Phil valued more than looks.

"Tell me, Phil, do you still cheat at cards?" asked Edward, as jovial as she remembered.

Did their old friend have no sense? Beginning the conversation with this could only taint her in the eyes of all at the table. Defending herself would be worse.

A gasp came from Miss Simesson. "Phil?"

Edward reddened. "You must forgive me, Miss Philippa. The moment I saw you and your sister, I drew my mind back to our younger days. I meant no disrespect."

The corner of Lord Endelton's mouth inched up, otherwise he kept his face a mask. He would be difficult to play against.

Phil tapped her fan on her palm. "None taken. After all, it took me several moments to recognize you without mud on your person. And I have not cheated at cards for years. I only did because you taught me."

Edward laughed. "Touché, Miss Philippa. What is our game?"

"Piquet." Miss Simesson moved the cards in front of her partner.

Lord Endelton dealt the cards. True to her word, Miss Simesson was as terrible at cards as she claimed. Hand after hand, she laid down her cards out of turn or didn't follow the play. Phil worked to keep a polite smile in place. Edward raised his brow when Miss Simesson picked up another mislaid card.

Turning to Phil, Miss Simesson blinked her eyes rapidly. "I told you I could not play well."

Phil tilted her head in disbelief. "Which is why I advised you to choose whist."

"You said piquet was easier." Miss Simesson waved her fan viciously in front of her eyes.

Denial flowed through Phil's veins. This woman wanted her to argue. Three years of rearing her younger sisters had taught Phil the futility of such a move. Meanwhile, the fan Miss Simesson held increased its speed. Phil worried her opponent might injure herself, which would serve her right for the ruse she tried to play. Phil placed her hand on

Miss Simesson's arm, pulling the fan away from the danger zone. Miss Simesson's fluttering froze. Phil took advantage of the moment. "It is a simple enough thing to fix. We can rearrange the cards for whist."

"Or perhaps you would prefer loo?" offered the viscount.

"I'm quite good at vingt-et-un." Miss Simesson smiled as if she shared some secret with the viscount.

Across the table, Edward gathered the cards. If there were points given for monopolizing the men at the table, Miss Simesson won. Being married, Edward wasn't her target. Phil glanced at the viscount. If he was so easily taken in, then he wasn't someone she would be happy with. Any husband she or Alex found needed to see through their father's subterfuge. The light cleft in his chin could not make up for a weak mind.

Pity. She'd hoped with his kindness, he'd be a match for her sister.

The third rotation of cards commenced with Michael partnered with the elder Miss Lightwood. Beside him, Edward partnered with his mother.

Lady Godderidge beamed. "Oh, this should be the best match of the evening. I may have a chance of winning with my son as a partner."

"Mother, it may not be fair as we have played together so often."

Miss Lightwood shifted in her seat. A flash of pain crossed her face and was quickly masked by a half smile. "Having firmly trounced your mother and her last two partners, I see no problem with the arrangement unless Lord Endelton objects?" She nodded in Michael's direction but didn't meet his eyes.

"No objection whatsoever."

"Edward, deal for piquet if you will." Lady Godderidge handed her son the cards.

Edward, in turn, handed the cards to Michael. "I believe you could use the advantage. Luck has not been with you tonight."

"Did Philippa lose?" Miss Lightwood's attention focused on the table on the far side of the room.

"The game went poorly, but it was not your sister's fault. Miss Simesson seemed most determined to lose." Edward's answer differed from Michael's perception of the game.

Michael paused in his deal. He had thought Miss Simesson to be the victim. She insisted Miss Philippa had chosen the game, and Edward had accused the woman of cheating. Not wishing to disparage Miss Lightwood's younger sister, he continued the deal. Lady Godderidge played the first card. By the third round, it was obvious Miss Lightwood was skilled at the game.

When the final card was laid, Lady Godderidge conceded the loss to Lord Endelton and Miss Lightwood. "What a delightful game. I wish we had time for a rematch. I didn't expect to lose with my son as a partner."

A smile lit Miss Lightwood's face. "I would advise you not to play against George and Jane. They are the true experts of the family."

"How are your sisters?" Lady Godderidge asked. "I haven't seen the twins in ever so long."

"They are well. George—" color bloomed on Miss Lightwood's cheek. "I mean *Georgiana* has brought Mother's gardens back to order, and Jane has been learning Greek."

"And your youngest sister?" asked Edward.

"Rose is determined to grow up twice as fast as she should, if only to not attend to her studies in the schoolroom. She was quite put out that she could not have a Season yet, despite being only ten years old." Again, Miss Lightwood's smile didn't touch her eyes despite her light tone. "I suppose, like all of us, she is too excited to meet the next phase of life to enjoy the one she is in."

A mantel clock chimed.

"It is time for me to end the games. It has been delightful to see you again, Miss Lightwood, Lord Endelton." Lady Godderidge stood, and her son escorted her away.

Michael retook his seat. "Thank you for the game, Miss Lightwood. I was afraid I would go all evening without winning a hand."

"I am sorry your earlier games did not go your way. Philippa is more skilled than I at most games."

"Really? Edward said she cheated."

"She doesn't. She hasn't in years. Not since we ordered the cards in the deck and Edward and his brother caught us. Phil was only twelve. It is hardly fair to hold such an old offense against her. It was not as if Edward and David were blameless. They taught us how to stack cards with their own cheating."

"Your association with the Godderidges goes back some years?"

"One of my earliest memories is of Lady Godderidge's nursery. The boys were teasing Isabel, Philippa, and me. I don't remember specifics, only that our mothers were not pleased. Here is my sister now." Miss Lightwood turned her attention to the woman approaching behind Michael.

Michael stood. "Would you care to join us?"

Miss Philippa nodded in greeting but didn't take the offered seat. "Lord Endelton, I hope you fared well with my sister as a partner."

"We were fortunate enough to have won our match."

"I'm glad." Miss Philippa slipped around the table and removed a cane from behind a planter near the wall. "Aunt insists we leave now."

Miss Lightwood frowned slightly. "Lord Endelton, may I impose on you for a moment? I require assistance."

"I—" The sound barely crossed Miss Philippa's lips as she moved to her sister's far side and handed her sister the cane.

Miss Lightwood extended her gloved hand toward Michael. He held out his own. Instead of taking his hand, Miss Lightwood clasped his arm above the wrist with surprising strength. Michael instinctively reciprocated, supporting her as she slowly rose. Miss Philippa moved the chair out of the way, giving her sister room to balance. Miss Lightwood froze in place for a moment before releasing Michael's arm.

"Thank you." The appreciative words came from Miss Philippa, whose eyes never left her sister's progress. Miss Lightwood nodded with a tight-lipped smile. Their aunt stood by the parlor door, talking to Lady Godderidge. Slowly working their way across the room, the Lightwood sisters joined her.

Miss Simesson and her mother appeared at Michael's elbow. "Such a pleasant evening." The mother pushed her daughter forward.

Miss Simesson fluttered her fan. "Thank you for understanding about our game."

Her mother patted her daughter's arm. "You poor dear. I can't believe that woman tricked you."

Michael glanced at the retreating Miss Philippa. Which woman was to be believed? A year away from the ton had dulled his senses. How had he thought choosing a wife would be easy?

# SIX

hil arose early and slipped slowly out of bed as to not awaken Alex. They hadn't shared a bed more than a handful of times since the accident. Alex often had trouble sleeping, and any movement of the bed woke her. A maid had already added a log to the fire, warming the room. The dressing room door stood ajar, and light seeped out from the crack. Phil entered and found their long-time maid sitting in the corner, hemming a dress. Silently, she closed the door.

"Good morning, Green."

Green was more than a common ladies' maid, not that the good ones were common at all. Green's father had been an apothecary, and the skills Green had learned in her father's house were of immense help to Alex. "Did Miss Alex sleep well?"

"She didn't wake me in the night, and I am determined not to wake her now."

"I have your dress ready for you, Miss." Green wasted no time in helping Phil prepare for the day. The loyal ladies maid worked for their mother and remained with them even after father had cut some of the servants' salaries. Phil long suspected her grandfather, Earl Whitstone, supplemented Green's wages.

Phil exited the narrow servants' door leading from the dressing room. The above stairs maid glanced her way and quickly turned back to dusting. Aunt's staff was slowly adjusting to Phil's unusual method of exiting her bed chamber.

Aunt Healand sat at the table in the breakfast room, her tea cooling. "I'm surprised you are awake so early. I am sure I heard giggling far into the night."

"My apologies. We didn't mean to keep you awake."

"None needed. It brings back fond memories of your mother and me during my first Season. Your grandfather threatened to send us to the attic more than once."

"You had a Season with Mother?"

"A short one. Your grandmother insisted we both be presented at court as she had been. Even then, my father despised London. Still, he only comes when there is a vote in the House of Lords he is especially keen on. Our real Season took place in Bath."

"Mother never mentioned her Season." Over the last four years, Phil concluded there were many things her mother never told them.

"Even in the crush of the Assembly rooms at Bath, your mother shone. She was ever so popular and rarely sat out. Your father arrived halfway through the Season and offered for both of us, for me first, since the earl's complicated entailment would fall to him. When I demurred, your mother, being much more practical than I, accepted the offer for the good of her children. I think she knew I had my heart set on another. Being the oldest, I should have made the match." Aunt frowned.

"Mother didn't marry for love?" She suspected not.

"No, only I did. I'm not sure which worked out better. Had your uncle and I managed to have a child who lived more than a few days, I wouldn't be so lonely now. But we had twelve wonderful years together, despite our impoverishment. Everything you see around you and my house in Lyme is my father's doing. Even my title exists only because I am an Earl's daughter. Your mother had children that surrounded her with love, even if her husband did not." Aunt sighed. "There must be some wisdom in choosing a husband. Somewhere between all heart or all mind, an elusive place exists where heart and mind can agree."

"How does one get such wisdom? I fear Alex and I will be lucky for any offer." If the few men at last night's dinner party were any indication, any interest the sisters aroused would be hard won.

"That is a question few are able to answer. As far as your chances, they are looking up. We've received an invitation to the Duchess of Aylton's ball. I suspect we are late additions to the guest list, since the ball is only days away." Aunt handed Phil the card.

Phil studied the invitation. "When did it arrive?"

"This morning which has me greatly puzzled."

"Why?"

"I have not spoken to Lady Endelton since she returned to Town. We have corresponded a few times since her husband's passing. The lot of being the first widow in our circle, every friend of my youth becomes a friend again once they, too, lose a spouse."

"What would Lord Endelton's mother have to do with an invitation? We only met him last night."

"Lady Endelton's older sister is the Dowager Duchess of Aylton. It could be a coincidence that it arrived this morning, as the only other explanation is that the viscount asked his cousin, the duke, to include you. I see no other connection which would have garnered an invitation. It is unlikely he had time to make such a request of his cousin. I can only suspect Lady Endelton made the request some days ago."

Phil's nose wrinkled at the thought. "Lord Endelton could not have been impressed with me last night. First, I fell out of the carriage, then Edward accused me of being a cheat. Perhaps he was more taken with Alex than I thought. He would be a splendid match for her."

"A splendid match in need of an heir. Alexandra's injuries may prevent her from being a mother. If she is to marry, it will be to a widower who already has an heir and a spare." Aunt raised her teacup to her lips and set it down without drinking. "Spare me the long looks. Men are much more practical than women about these things. As is your sister."

"But I can't leave her to Father's whims for the rest of her life."

"Are you sure she would be better off with a man? Besides, she will have you and your sisters to visit."

"But if that man loved her…"

"From my view, love is wonderful, but love without money or status is difficult. If it was not for being an Earl's daughter, I would be making my way as a mediocre governess or a pitiable paid companion. As for your sister, I have it on good authority my father has her future well in hand. When he leaves this mortal life, she will not be left destitute."

"How do you know?"

"I have said far too much already. Your grandfather is keenly aware of the plight of all of you girls. I dare say he will live to see his hundredth birthday just to make sure even little Rose is properly taken care of."

Over seventy, grandfather claimed to be the oldest Earl in all of England. Phil had read of people celebrating their hundredth birthday. "Our grandfather is uncommonly kind."

A grunting sound came from Aunt as she ate her scone. She coughed a moment before regaining her composure.

Phil waited for her aunt to comment.

"Now about the Duke's ball. Do you think you can convince Alex to attend? It will be a crush, but being seen there will help launch both of you into the Season."

Phil's curiosity was not to be satisfied. "I can try."

"Deborah, please." Michael despised begging, yet found himself reduced to it once more to obtain his sister's help. "I need your opinion. Edward believes I read last night's card game situation all upside down and backwards and have cast the wrong woman as the villainess."

His sister wore a plain frock, not meant for entertaining. "Don't be so dramatic. Neither woman is evil. Although I dare say Miss Simesson lacks creativity in showing herself at her best. Claiming Miss Philippa tricked her into thinking one card game was easier than another is absurd."

"How so?" Michael leaned forward.

Deborah yawned. "You really should come back at a more decent hour."

"I can hardly ask you questions during your visiting hours, and it is nearly noon. We were not out late."

"Just because Edward and I returned home at a decent hour doesn't mean we received enough sleep." Her slow smile sent her brother reeling.

"Sis—um—er—you shouldn't—er" Michael couldn't find words, and his sister laughed.

"Serves you right, showing up here before I finish my morning tea. Women are not as much of a mystery as you seem to find them. Then again, you often don't seem to understand men either." Deborah sighed and set aside her tea. "According to Edward's version, Miss Simesson attempted to garner your sympathies while setting your mind against the other woman at the table. How old were you when you knew the difference between whist and piquet?"

"I'm not sure. I was still a lad."

"Precisely. I could play both games passably by the time I was fourteen. Either Miss Simesson's education is sorely lacking, or she wished to garner your sympathies. From the cut and cost of her dress, I'd be surprised if she hadn't the best education possible, from dancing masters to tutors."

"Then she lied?"

"Undoubtedly."

Michael pondered for a moment. "Why would she risk me thinking poorly of her?"

"Perhaps she thought her tears would blind you to the obvious ploy. I understand most men will go to great lengths to keep a woman from crying."

"It wasn't obvious to me."

Deborah clicked her tongue. "How is it you can be so brilliant with numbers and farming techniques and all manner of academics, but when it comes to people, you misunderstand them so?"

Michael threw his hands up. "Why is it you insist I don't understand people?"

"Because you don't. Remember the disaster of your first year when you came to London?"

Heat crept up Michael's neck. He'd spent a fortnight courting a woman who courted someone else, and according to his sisters, she expressed her disinterest in several ways. "We will not talk about her."

"Or what about when you wouldn't leave Julia alone with Sir Radcliff?"

"Our sister was supposed to be chaperoned."

"He was trying to propose. You nearly ruined it. That's why mother asked you to go to the observatory and get her whatever it was."

"It all turned out well." Michael stopped fighting his sister. The real question was why did he keep missing what others found to be obvious? Julia told him if Sir Radcliff hadn't proposed, she would have slit Michael's throat in the middle of the night, which seemed a rather severe punishment.

Deborah shook her head. "I am not sure how to help you. No wonder cousin Richard is so cross with you."

"He isn't mad at me. He is mad at the duchess."

"True. However, he is afraid you'll be duped. He didn't see his betrayal coming, and he is wise when it comes to judging people."

"How could he? He was asleep." Most likely drugged, since Richard never drank in excess and, unlike his father, he never philandered.

Deborah held up her hand. "We are not talking about Richard. Examining his situation won't help you. People are not something you can learn from a book."

Michael crossed his arms. "It would be much easier if you could."

"I suppose Shakespeare had something to say about the human condition. Or I have a few novels you might read."

"Novels? You aren't serious?"

"Some of them are quite insightful and written by women." Deborah poured herself another cup of tea.

"I would be lost before I began."

"True. Your proposal would be much like Mr. Darcy's first one. I don't think he understood people either."

"Who is Mr. Darcy?"

"A character in *Pride and Prejudice*, published last year by A Lady. Julia and I laughed ever so hard when we read it."

"It's a novel?"

"Of course."

"It would be much easier if you would tell me if a woman were being duplicitous." Michael needed real help, not novels.

Deborah giggled, then laughed, bending at the waist in an attempt to stop. She paused, her eyes wide, and sprinted from the room.

Edward entered the sitting room. "Whatever did you do to my wife?"

"I'm not sure. She laughed at a perfectly reasonable request, and she left."

"What did you ask her?" Edward sat in the chair his wife vacated.

"To help me understand women."

Edward laughed until tears leaked out of the corners of his eyes. After several attempts at regaining his composure, his friend spoke one feared word. "Impossible."

# SEVEN

As anticipated, the Duchess's Ball was a crush. Soon after entering, Aunt Healand found a seat in a corner with several other women her age, passing judgments in hushed tones. She'd introduced her nieces to the other women and sent them off to circle the room, if possible.

"This was a terrible idea. I shouldn't have come." Having given up her cane for the evening, Alex clung to Phil's arm.

Phil searched the edge of the room for a chair for Alex. "I promise this will be the only ball. The house is as grand as our aunt promised. All we have to do is be seen."

Alex leaned close. "Since our aunt has abandoned us, there is little else we can do. I suppose her plan is to have a young gentleman come to her seeking an introduction."

Phil looked over her shoulder. "Considering she hasn't introduced us to anyone our age, I am not sure how I would survive without you."

"Isn't that Isabel?" Alex nodded to the dancers moving down the floor.

At last, someone familiar. "Perhaps she will know others our age."

"We'll wait until the set is over and speak with her."

"In the meantime, what are we to do? We can't stand here." Phil looked around the crowded room.

Alex's grip loosened on her arm. "There is a bench near the far wall next to the window."

"It is not cushioned." Phil's teeth touched her lips. She'd promised herself to stop biting them when she worried, as it sometimes caused her lips to bleed. Alex's hip had been bothering her for weeks. Despite using her aunt's superior coach, the trip to Town drained both of them. Phil suspected the London dampness was not good for her sister, though she never complained. A cushion or a pillow would be better.

"Perhaps something else will open up." Alex tugged on Phil's arm to lead her to the open bench. The set concluded as they neared the bench. Progress through the crowd slowed to a shuffle.

Someone tapped Phil's shoulder. Without releasing her sister's arm, Phil turned to see. "Isabel."

"I am so happy to see you here. I was quite afraid I would have no one to talk to other than Edward's friends."

"What is wrong with my friends?" Edward stood behind them with his wife by his side.

Phil and Alex exchanged greetings.

"Nothing is wrong with them other than they speak mostly of you." Isabel tapped her fan on her brother's chest, hitting one of the gold buttons of his uniform.

Several gentlemen appeared behind Edward. Isabel hid the lower half of her face behind her fan and exchanged a smile with Phil and whispered, "Now we shall find you a dance partner."

After several rapid introductions, one of the new arrivals asked Alex to dance the next set.

"I am sorry, sir. A slight mishap makes it impossible for me to dance tonight. I shall be content to watch from the side." Alex spoke the line they had agonized over earlier. Once a woman refused a partner, she could not dance the entire evening. This, of course, was Alex's goal, as dancing on her wooden leg wasn't an option.

A man in a blue brocade waistcoat claimed Edward's wife for a dance first. A Lord P—something that sounded like pudgy over the din of the crowd but couldn't possibly have been since it described him so well, led Isabel to the floor.

Lord Endelton joined Edward. Phil silently willed Edward to ask her to dance this set. There was something unsettling in Lord Endelton's look. Since he'd obviously found her lacking at cards, there would be no reason for him to ask her to dance.

"Miss Lightwood. Miss Philippa." He nodded, but said no more.

Edward addressed his friend. "Miss Lightwood has already declared she isn't dancing this evening. I was about to assist her in finding an advantageous spot where she could watch the dance. Miss Philippa would enjoy a set, if a partner could be found."

It took a moment for Lord Endelton to respond to his friend's not-so-subtle hint. "Miss Philippa, would you dance this set with me?"

Phil nodded and laid her hand on his offered arm and took her place on the dance floor. Obviously, she owed Edward more mud balls. The viscount dismissed her at the dinner party. Undoubtedly, he had no intention of dancing with her if he had not been forced to. However, if one was to suffer through an unwanted dance, there were much worse dance partners. The viscount was neither too fat nor too thin, his slightly unruly hair wasn't unkept, and there was no unusual odor emanating from his person. All in all, he was rather pleasant looking. Her fate could be much worse.

"I am surprised your sister is in attendance tonight," said Michael.

"Why should she not attend? We received an invitation." What did he know, or had he guessed from helping Alex at the card party? And wasn't he supposed to say something about the weather or the size of the crowd? A gentleman should know they weren't supposed to ask personal questions.

"There is no reason she shouldn't. I was merely surprised she would with her limp." He turned as the dance steps led him away.

It took almost as much concentration to keep her face impassive as it did to recall the steps she hadn't practiced in years. They came back together again. "You presume to know much about my sister."

"Not much. Only little enough to suspect dancing is not her favorite pastime." He did not refer to the help Alex required to leave the card party.

"Whatever you know, or think you do, I would thank you to keep your suppositions to yourself. She came at my request and—" a turn to her side partner forced Phil to end her thought mid-sentence. The turn also brought her to a spot where she could see Alex through the crowd. Only her sister wasn't on the bench they had hoped to obtain. Instead, she stood near a column supporting the upper balcony quite alone, ignored by the sea of people around her. How selfish Phil had been to ask her to attend. As bad as dancing with an undesirable partner was, it would be worse to stand alone set after set without someone to converse with. It was ungentlemanlike of Edward to abandon her, but it was not his fault, it was Phil's. She'd talked her sister into coming. After this dance, she would feign a headache so they could leave.

Lord Endelton returned to her side, blocking her view of Alex. Phil strained her neck to catch another glimpse of her sister. He was too tall and his shoulders too broad for her to even see a bit of the pillar. Her efforts were not unnoticed, and he turned his head momentarily. "Your sister appears to be content."

Heat rose in Phil's cheeks. She hadn't intended to be so obvious. "Thank you."

"She is the eldest, is she not?"

"Of course." Silly man, that is why Alex was Miss Lightwood, while she was simply Miss Philippa.

The next few steps drew him away, then back again where they reached the bottom of the figure and would have to wait there to dance again. Phil dreaded moments in country dances when it was necessary to wait to return to the floor when all remaining was conversation. "She is a lucky sister indeed. Few have younger siblings as devoted as you."

"Isn't it normal to be concerned about another's welfare?" Phil searched for a change in subject before he could answer. "Is it always so damp in London this time of year?"

Lord Endelton's brow dipped for a moment. "I believe it is. I thought Gloucestershire received more rain than London."

"How did you know I lived in Gloucestershire?"

"I have been friends with Edward Godderidge for most of my life. I even visited their manor one wet August not three years past. I believe it was the year his brother, David, took possession, and Sir and Lady Godderidge took up residence here and at the property near Hastings."

"It does rain often, but somehow the damp in London is different, it lingers."

"All the smoke, I assume. The city isn't as clean as the country." They reached the top of the figure, and he led them into the line of dancers.

"Do you live in Town year-round?"

"I spend as little time as I can here. Which, now that I have taken my seat in Parliament, is much more often than I wish."

"Where do you make your family home?" asked Phil.

"West of Oxford, where the Cotswolds begin."

"Lovely. We drove through much of the area on our way to Town. Do you share my need for trees and hills?"

Lord Endelton stepped away as the dance dictated, and Phil temporarily partnered with the man on her right.

"I do not know if I have a need for the trees as much as a deep fondness. Hyde Park is enough when I am in Town. Do you like the park?"

Surely he wasn't hinting he might take her for a ride. "My sister and I prefer to walk in the small park across from my aunt's home, though we can easily count the fifteen trees it boasts."

A chuckle escaped Lord Endelton's lips. "Can you name the varieties as well?"

Phil wasn't sure if she should respond truthfully or not. A sharp cry pierced through the noise of the room. Few heads turned, and everyone continued as they were. Phil, however, froze. She knew that cry. Alex. Frantically, she looked to the column where she last saw her sister standing. There was no way to see over the crush. The dancer behind her pushed Phil out of the way.

The dance.

Her partner.

What was a proper way to leave the floor?

She spun, looking for Lord Endelton. He was not where he should be in the form. Worse and worse. Phil took a step backward and ran into a human wall that hadn't been there a moment before.

"May I escort you from the floor? Your sister seems in distress."

She grasped his arm, a lifeline in the sea of her confusion. "You can see her?"

Lord Endelton nodded and parted the crowd.

No one in the vicinity paid attention to Miss Lightwood. If his dancing partner hadn't stopped dancing, Michael wouldn't have either. As they drew nearer, he wasn't sure if he had been right to rush Miss Philippa off the floor. Miss Lightwood held her fan higher than normal and looked as waxy as the candles shining brightly over her head. At last, they reached the column where she stood, or rather, supported herself upright.

Miss Philippa released his arm. As near as he could tell, the two didn't speak. Miss Lightwood simply pointed down. Miss Philippa covered her own gasp. Michael couldn't help but look at the floor. Impossible. Miss Lightwood's right shoe peeked from underneath her gown. But rather than a glimpse of the toe, it was her heel. Unconsciously, he turned his own foot. Even the most talented of ballet dancers in the theater or contortionist couldn't turn their entire leg backward.

Miss Philippa and Miss Lightwood spoke in hushed tones.

"He tripped over Peggy. I told him I was well."

Michael noticed beads of perspiration glistened on Miss Lightwood's brow. Obviously, she lied. Who was Peggy, and why hadn't she stayed to assist?

Miss Philippa bit her lip and deliberately dropped her fan. Michael moved to block anyone who might trip over her as she retrieved it. When she stood, she held out her gloved finger to her sister. Blood stained the tip. "We must leave."

The next dance, a waltz, was announced, and the surrounding area thinned of people. Michael looked for Edward and saw him deep in conversation with Richard on the other side of the room. "How can I be of assistance?"

Miss Lightwood lowered her fan. "If you could find our—"

"No. Help her exit the garden door just there." Miss Philippa nodded toward the doors to the garden, which had been flung open to provide cool air to the warming room.

"It is too far." Miss Lightwood must be very injured to think the distance of less than eight feet was too great.

Michael turned to Miss Philippa. "How do we best do this?"

"If Alexandra may lean on your left arm and I assist her on the right—"

Miss Lightwood blinked back tears. "I cannot take a single step."

Michael studied the surrounding crush. Most of the crowd seemed intent on seeing who danced the waltz with whom. Only three or four people stood between them and the door. "With your permission, I could carry you out. I don't think many people will notice.

"No." Miss Lightwood barely breathed the word.

"Yes." The firmer reply came from Miss Philippa.

Was this one of those times when a woman protested when she meant to accept? Michael searched the crowd again. He needed Deborah to guide him.

He looked between Miss Lightwood's ever paling face and Miss Philippa's earnest one. Half of a consent was enough. Michael scooped Miss Lightwood off her feet and strode to the door. She was much lighter than he'd expected. Miss Philippa followed. Once they were outside, the younger sister directed him to a bench where he set Miss Lightwood down.

Miss Philippa touched his arm. "Thank you. Would you mind staying a moment while I —" She bit her lip.

"Assess her injury?" Michael turned his back to the bench, hoping to block the view of anyone looking out of the window. Trying not to listen to the sisters was more difficult.

"I think Peggy is broken…

"It is only twisted, and the buckle broke and cut you…"

"It feels like more…"

"I need to take Peggy off."

"Not here. It will ruin your chances." Miss Lightwood's voice grew fainter.

"How can I be worried about that? Look at my gloves. You are cut badly."

"I'm sorry. I didn't —"

"There." Something clattered on the stone path. "You are free. Hold your hand here."

"Your dress. I shouldn't have borrowed yours."

"Alex. Now is not the time. I need to stop the bleeding. I don't give a fig for my dress." Miss Philippa's voice strengthened each time she spoke in contrast with her sister's.

"How may I help?"asked Micheal.

"May I borrow your handkerchief?"

Michael held out his handkerchief behind his back. Immediately, the cloth was snatched from his grasp.

"I need to get my sister home and bandaged as quickly as possible. Do you think we can walk around the house? Can you carry her that far?"

"What, are, you, doing, with, your, stockings?" Miss Lightwood's question was not directed at him. Each word seemed more difficult for her to utter.

"Hush. I need to tie this in place."

Michael cleared his throat. "It is not as far as you think. How will you find your carriage?"

"I don't know. I hope a footman can help us. I must send one for my aunt. You may turn around now."

Despite the conversation, he wasn't prepared to see Miss Lightwood reclining on the bench, a dark stain on her pale dress. Miss Philippa was now gloveless. He couldn't make out what she held partially concealed behind her back. "We should find some footmen in the front. If you hurry, I'll keep up."

Miss Lightwood lifted her arm. "I am sorry to trouble you. Please take care, so I don't ruin your handsome waistcoat."

She was easier to carry this time. Michael walked as rapidly as he could. As he rounded the house, he spotted his own coach and hurried to it.

"This isn't our aunt's," said Miss Philippa.

With no footman around he asked a lady to do work she shouldn't. "It's mine. Open the door."

Miss Philippa completed the task as Michael's driver ran up along with another man. "My Lord, are you leaving?"

"Yes. You there," he called to a passing footman wearing the Duke's livery. "Inform Lady Healand her nieces have departed in my care."

"Yes, my lord." The footman ran to the house.

Michael set Miss Lightwood down as gently as possible on the seat. "Driver, do you have a blanket?"

Miss Philippa climbed in after her sister, still carrying the odd contraption. "We didn't mean for you to interrupt your ball. We can find our coach and driver."

"Your sister has fainted. I believe she is best off if we get her to a place where she can be properly attended. Where is your aunt's home?"

"Russell Square."

"My home in Grosvenor Square is much closer. With as busy as the street is still, we'll save at least a half hour." He took the blanket from the driver. "Home."

The door swung shut. Miss Philippa spread the offered blanket over her sister. "It is bad enough the two of us are in your coach. We cannot go to your home."

"My mother and younger sister are in residence. I assure you, your reputation will not be marred." According to his mother three people were always a safe number.

Miss Lightwood groaned. Miss Philippa helped her sister into a reclining position, all the while kneeling on the floor of the carriage. Helpless, Michael sat in the corner of the rear-facing seat.

Miss Lightwood tried to sit up further. "Phil don't fret. It is best this be attended to. You should explain Peggy."

Miss Philippa grasped her sister's hand. "Is there no other way?"

"Please, Phil. They will know soon enough."

"Very well." Miss Philippa sighed and turned her attention to Michael. "Four years ago, Alex, er—Alexandra was in a carriage accident with our mother and younger brother."

Michael nodded.

"Since the accident, she has needed Peggy to walk." Miss Philippa drew the odd form out of the shadows. "When the man tripped over Peggy tonight, he twisted the brace portion."

Michael had seen men with false legs, usually due to fighting in the war, but never a female. Even in the dim light from the coach lantern, he could see the leg was well carved.

"Are you admiring my finely turned ankle, my Lord?" Mirth laced Miss Lightwood's quiet voice.

"I-um—" Michael lifted his gaze to meet her eyes. "I didn't mean to stare. My apologies."

Both of the Misses Lightwood smiled. The elder continued, "I told you Peggy would capture a man's attention."

Miss Philippa lifted the prosthesis out of the way. "I showed you this because I don't think it would do well for your mother or sister to meet Peggy. Also, to beg for discretion. I mean, for my sister to have the opportunity to make a match of her own. A rumor could hurt her chances."

"Phil, I am only here to accompany you. Not find a husband." Miss Lightwood waved a dismissive hand at her sister.

The coach turned. Through the window, Michael recognized the park of Grosvenor Square. "If you leave the apparatus in the carriage, I'll have my coachmen smuggle it into the house. As for my sister, I can keep Moriah away, but I can't guarantee my mother will not fuss."

"Will she be much shocked? Is she inclined to vapors?" asked Miss Philippa.

"No, but I will have a word with her while you see to your sister. Our housekeeper is levelheaded. I'll ask for her to attend to you instead of one of the maids." The coach drew to a stop. Despite his coachman's efforts to assist, Michael carried Miss Lightwood into the house himself with Miss Philippa trailing behind.

# EIGHT

Only when the footman held out his hand for Phil's wrap did she realize she'd left hers at the ball along with Alex's. Would Aunt know to retrieve their things or to find the two of them at Lord Endelton's? She would have asked, but the man in question was busy giving directions to the butler and a maid.

"—the green bedroom, she will need towels and hot water. Inform my mother, if you will."

Phil hurried to catch up with Lord Endelton, worried he might drop Alex, yet the man didn't even seem winded as he ascended the stairs. He paused on the landing. "Miss Philippa, if you would open the door to the second room on your right?"

The dim light from the corridor kept Phil from stumbling into a chair too close to the door of the darkened bedroom. Lord Endelton seemed to know it was there and maneuvered around the obstruction and Phil on his way to deposit Alex onto the bed.

A maid with a lamp hurried into the room after them. "The housekeeper will be here directly."

"I'll leave you two. If you need anything, ask. Would you like me to fetch a physician?" He addressed the question to Phil.

"May I have a few minutes in private to make a determination?" Phil wouldn't call a physician unless Alex's life hung in the balance. A cut was not life threatening.

Lord Endelton nodded and shut the door behind him.

The maid remained near the door, holding the lantern.

"Will you set the lamp here on the table?" asked Phil, unsure whether to dismiss the girl.

Alex moaned.

"Are you of a robust constitution?" Phil continued.

"Yes, miss." The maid's head bobbed.

"Then if you would, please help me move my sister into a better position."

Phil kept the blanket the coachman provided over Alex's lap and leg as they rearranged the pillows. Someone tapped on the door and the maid went to open it. A woman, presumably the housekeeper, entered carrying a stack of towels. A footman followed her with a steaming bowl of water. The housekeeper sent the maid and the footman from the room. "I'm Mrs. Ivy. Lord Endelton asked me to assist you with whatever you need."

"I'm Philippa, and this is my sister Alexandra. May I have a towel? I don't want to soil the lovely counterpane."

"Heavens, where did this old thing come from?" Mrs. Ivy removed the coachman's blanket.

Phil positioned the towel under Alex before lifting her soiled skirts and petticoats. Phil's stockings held the handkerchief Lord Endelton loaned them in place above the spot where Alex's knee should have been. To her credit, Mrs. Ivy didn't flinch or gasp at the sight.

"It looks like the bleeding has stopped. Mrs. Ivy, is there someone who has experience stitching a wound?" asked Phil.

"I have sewed a cut many a time for the staff. Wouldn't you rather a physician do the job?"

Alex shook her head. "In my experience, a housekeeper's sewing is usually better."

"Let us look. A stitch may not be needed." Mrs. Ivy dampened a cloth before untying Phil's stockings from her sister's limb. She cleaned away the blood, murmuring comforting words as she worked.

To Phil's relief, the cut didn't start bleeding again.

Alex touched the skin above the cut. "Do you think it will hold?"

"With proper bandages and a few days of rest, I don't believe you'll need a stitch at all."

Alex sighed with relief. "Can you bandage it? Then we can be on our way."

Mrs. Ivy shook her head and tsked. "I can bandage it right away, but I advise against leaving this bed for at least two days, or you'll surely start bleeding again."

"But—" Phil objected at the same time as her sister. She allowed Alex to continue.

"We couldn't possibly impose."

"The Lady of the house will see it my way." Mrs. Ivy finished wrapping Alex's stump and gathered the bloodied clothes in a towel. "I'll inform Lord Endelton you have no need of a physician and see if I can borrow one of Miss Moriah's nightgowns. I'll send up some of my willow bark tea."

Phil waited to speak until the door closed behind the housekeeper. "Father will be furious if he hears. We aren't far from Aunt's home."

Alex closed her eyes for a long moment. When she opened them, two tears had escaped. "I am not up to another journey tonight, no matter how well sprung the carriage is. Perhaps, we can leave in the morning."

"I didn't realize how much pain the cut caused you."

"It isn't my stump. It is my hip."

Phil spied the still-warm water. "I can make you a warm compress."

"Please."

The water wasn't as warm as Phil hoped. She dampened one of the clean towels and wrung it out. It was still warmer than her hand, though. She helped Alex set it in place as a tap sounded on the door. Phil opened the door to find Lord Endelton and a woman who must be his mother.

"Lord Endelton. Lady Endelton." Phil bobbed a quick curtsy.

"Do you mind if I come in and meet your sister?" asked Lady Endelton.

There was only one way to answer the Lady's request, so Phil opened the door wider. She was about to close it when Lord Endelton beckoned her out. "A word?"

Torn between leaving Alex alone with Lady Endelton and snubbing the Lord, Phil stepped into the corridor.

"Mrs. Ivy says Miss Lightwood is to stay here for the time being. I've dispatched a message to your aunt, both at her residence and at the ball, in case she didn't learn of our departure. Are you sure you don't require a physician?"

"No. Your housekeeper bandaged the wound well. I fear your handkerchief is ruined." Lord Endelton glanced at her feet. Fortunately, only the toe of her slipper peeked out from under the hem of her gown.

Remembering her lack of stockings. Phil winced. This interview needed to end.

"Would you like a tray sent up? We left before dinner."

Phil covered her mouth to hide her reaction with her hand, only to realize it was ungloved. Her blood-stained gloves remained in her reticule. Mortified, she hid her hands behind her back. "My apologies. I didn't think. Whomever you promised the dinner dance to—I ruined her evening as well as yours."

"I hadn't committed myself to a dinner dance."

At least some other woman wasn't cursing out her lack of escort on their account. "Mrs. Ivy has ordered tea for my sister. A tray won't be necessary."

"What if I told you I'd already ordered one for myself from the leftover cold chicken from my mother and sister's meal, and I had it on good authority there was more than enough to share?"

Had he heard her stomach rumble? "Then we would be thankful. We will strive to make our stay as brief as possible to not continue to impose upon you and your household."

She turned back to the door, hoping to intercept the conversation between Lady Endelton and Alex before it went too far. A touch on her arm sent a shock through her, but not the kind that occurred when Rose scooted around on the parlor carpet in her stockings. It was something else, more of being very aware that her arm existed and that he was there.

"Do not hasten your departure on our account."

A glance over her shoulder revealed his sincerity.

"Thank you, my Lord." Something other than concern for Alex propelled Phil's retreat into the bedroom, although she couldn't name exactly what.

Breakfast had yet to be laid out. Michael went to his study and waited for news of his guests. Although they had remained quietly in their room, he'd been unable to sleep as the younger Miss Lightwood kept invading his mind. A phenomenon he couldn't reconcile himself to. She had flaunted propriety several times last evening for her sister, giving little care to herself. He doubted she'd even realized how much of her hair had fallen from its confines by the time of their last conversation. His own sisters would have refused to be seen in such a state. As much as he loved his married sisters, admittedly Deborah and Julia had spent most of their time competing during their shared Season. There had been little peace in the house for anyone, least of all mother, who constantly had to settle fights over ribbons and other trivial bobbles.

He admired Miss Philippa's loyalty, even if he thought society dictated he was supposed to find it quite the opposite.

A footman tapped on the door. "Sir, this parcel has arrived for the Misses Lightwood, along with a note for you."

Michael took the note. The size of the bundle suggested it might contain clothing to replace the gowns they'd worn to the ball. "Have a maid deliver the package to our guests."

*Lord Endelton—*

*Thank you for your care of my nieces last evening and your note letting me know of their destination. Unless otherwise advised, I will send a coach at noon to retrieve them.*

*Please give my regards to your mother.*

*Gratefully,*

*Lady Healand*

Noon, a well thought-out time. Late enough to allow the women to awake naturally, yet before the time when callers would be out, thus avoiding potential gossip.

The footman knocked on the door again. "His Grace Richard Thomas Kenworth, the Duke of Aylton, is here."

There was no need to announce his cousin's full title, Richard visited often enough. "At this hour? Show him in."

Michael barely had time to stand before his cousin strode through the door.

"Yes, at this hour. I assumed you would be awake after being so thoroughly duped last night. Mother has not stopped with her fits of vapors since learning you left unchaperoned with two young ladies and was seen carrying one of them. Of all the boneheaded messes to step into, I thought you had more sense than to have some young miss snag them at my wife's ball." The famous Aylton temper surfaced in rare form this morning.

"I've never known your mother to suffer from vapors."

Richard crossed his arms. "She should have been. The point is, they duped you."

"I wasn't duped into anything. Miss Lightwood is injured. My housekeeper tended to her and assured me my actions fit the situation."

"Your housekeeper? Miss Lightwood is here? Please tell me not Mr. Felton Lightwood's daughter. I shall lose all respect for the intelligence you have shown, especially in debates in parliament."

Michael gestured for his cousin to have the more comfortable of the seats in the room. "Would you like me to ring for some food? Breakfast is likely to be ready."

"I don't want food. I need an explanation and proof there was no scandal at our ball last evening."

"I left the ball with two women, sisters, and so therefore not unchaperoned. Miss Lightwood and her sister Miss Philippa did not attempt any of the tricks and beguiling those of their set want to try to secure a husband of title. While I danced with Miss Philippa, a man stepped on Miss Lightwood's foot in the crush."

"Being trod upon is not uncommon. In fact, it is quite expected from time to time."

"True. However unintentional, the injury to Miss Lightwood was severe enough to warrant an immediate departure, as she bled profusely."

"Why not simply send her to the retiring room? My staff could have seen to the girl."

"Miss Lightwood stood next to the garden door. It was much easier to escape outside than to carry her across the ballroom. She was far from well, and her sister and I deemed immediate removal the best course of action."

Richard's shoulders dropped. "Who suggested your carriage?"

"I did. We came across it looking for Lady Healand's. Knowing it could take some time to locate the lady and her coachman, I decided to take my own. It was my idea to bring them here, as my residence is closer to yours."

"Of all the stupid, irresponsible blunders… I will not see you forced into an imprudent marriage." Rumors abounded about the duke's own hasty and unhappy marriage that had yet to mark its first anniversary. Michael knew some of them to be true. The purpose of last night's first-of-the-Season ball was no doubt to discourage gossip by showing the duke and duchess in their best light.

"No one has mentioned marriage."

"Mark my words, they will. It is only a matter of—" Richard cut his sentence short at the appearance of Michael's mother in the doorway.

Both men stood.

"Your Grace." Lady Endelton inclined her head. "I wondered whose voice I heard. I shall leave you two to your argument."

"Beg your pardon, Aunt Endelton. I didn't mean to disturb your peace." Richard's contrite bow was almost believable.

"What did you need, Mother?"

"I only wanted your opinion on a matter of my guests." Mother raised her eyebrows to convey extra meaning.

"Richard is aware of our guests. If it is not something too private, you may ask in front of him."

"The Misses Lightwood are adamant they leave immediately and asked for a note to be delivered to Lady Healand as soon as possible. Mrs. Ivy is concerned because she believes Miss Alexandra is feverish and should not be moved. Can you convince Miss Philippa staying is no imposition?"

"What is your opinion of Miss Lightwood's condition?"

Mother twisted her handkerchief. "Mrs. Ivy is correct, a day or two of rest is required. If she were my daughter, I wouldn't want to take any unnecessary risk."

Michael caught Richard's eye before asking the next question. "What are the risks to their reputation and ours?"

"Reputation? How could there be any slight on either under the circumstance?" Mother looked from one man to the other, with one of those motherly glares meant to put sons in their place.

Richard tugged on his cravat.

"Send Miss Philippa down, and I'll talk with her, but mother, the final decision will be theirs. Lady Healand has sent word that she will send a carriage at noon unless she receives word otherwise."

"Very well. Breakfast is ready. Your Grace, you are welcome to eat with my son if he has forgotten to invite you." Mother closed the study door behind her.

"Do you still believe I am being duped?" asked Michael.

"Although I find it hard to believe someone could be injured so grievously at a ball, your mother's concern is genuine."

"Come eat with me. Our cook's buns are among the best in Town. If you don't stay, they shall force me to dine alone, as Mother usually eats in her room and my sister comes down when she pleases."

"I can hardly refuse such an offer."

A warning note in his cousin's voice caused Michael to turn his head. He wasn't sure if Richard meant the food or something else.

# NINE

The raised voices downstairs quieted. Phil assumed the participant of the disturbance had left. She could do little but return to her aunt's as soon as possible. Hunger and a desire to allow Alex an undisturbed bit of sleep before they left propelled Phil to the main floor of the residence. Once Father learned of last night's mishap, he would be as furious as the visitor had been. Alex would likely be called home. The journey to London had been so straining on her. Phil didn't think of what her own fate would be. Father had been so adamant she make a good match. He might attempt his own match or try to force Lord Endelton into marriage over some twisted version of last night. Phil could not allow the man's kindness to be returned in such a way.

The breakfast room was not empty, as Mrs. Ivy informed her it would be. Lord Endelton sat with the Duke of Aylton at the end of a long table. She attempted to back out of the room before either noticed her. Lord Endelton's voice stopped her in the doorway.

"Miss Philippa, come in and eat with us. You met the duke last night, I assume?" He and the Duke stood.

"Your Grace." Phil curtsied and backed up a step. "I can return later."

"How is your sister?" Lord Endelton took a step in her direction, making leaving without answering impossible.

"She is well enough, we can return to our aunt's."

"Mother said she thought your sister should remain with us for a time." His words countered the argument she'd heard coming through the walls earlier. The fact the duke had to be the other person whose voice they heard made leaving all the more imperative.

"It isn't necessary, I assure you. It would be best if we left."

Lord Endelton pointed to the sideboard. "You shouldn't leave before trying one of the cook's buns. Even his Grace agrees they are among the best he's ever eaten."

Phil avoided looking at the duke as she made her way to the sideboard. She had little choice but to stay, at least for a moment.

"Why do you think you should leave?" asked the duke.

A question from his Grace was so unexpected, Phil needed to grasp her plate with both hands to keep it from tipping. She looked from one man to the other. The Bible claimed the truth would set one free. In her case, the truth would get them booted from the house in short order. Perhaps it would be best. She set her plate down on the sideboard. "Our father is not the most scrupulous of men. If he were to learn we were in your home under your protection, he would take your kindness and twist it to his own means. As much as I wish nothing more than my sister to find a match with a kind man, I cannot allow you to be forced in such a manner."

The duke's eyes narrowed. "Why your sister and not you?"

There wasn't a suitable answer to the question not leading to more. Phil formed several responses in her mind. "She is the eldest, is she not?"

"If it was only a matter of your sister's health, would you accept our invitation to stay?" asked Lord Endelton.

Phil dropped her head to break eye contact. Even the short drive over cobbled streets might further injure Alex. And though her sister denied it, she felt feverish to the touch. There had been some seepage from the wound in the night.

"Should she stay?" asked Lord Endelton a second time.

"Yes." Her soft answer seemed to echo around her. Phil raised her head. "But we cannot. Someone may have seen our exit last night and assume—" She took a deep breath. "My sister and I are of the same mind. We should leave with all haste. Surely you agree, your Grace." Phil hoped she had not misread the duke's expressions or misheard the loud conversation.

"My opinion doesn't matter much here. I am aware of your father's reputation and don't deny there is some cause for your fear. Your Grandfather is Earl Whitstone, correct?" asked the duke.

"Yes, our mother's father."

The men exchanged looks. Phil couldn't read their reactions.

"Miss Philippa, you should eat." Lord Endelton gestured to her abandoned plate.

A near smile grazed the dukes's lips. "He is correct. His cook's buns are worth an early morning excursion. Do sit and eat, please."

The duke was more welcoming than she expected, or he wanted her to sit so he could do likewise and continue eating. Adding a boiled egg to her plate, Philippa headed for a chair at the far end of the table.

"Come sit with us." Lord Endelton pointed to a seat at his end of the table. The duke's formidable gaze made her wish she could ignore the viscount's invitation.

A footman refilled the duke's cup of tea.

"I am still curious on one point. How could your sister have injured herself to such a degree at a ball? As the host, I am most concerned we may have been negligent."

Phil swallowed the single bite she'd managed, not tasting the food. "I assure you it was none of your fault. My sister was injured many years ago. Unfortunately, a misstep caused a new problem. It is my fault. I unwisely asked her to accompany me to your ball. There is no blame on you or your guests."

The duke frowned and added cream to his cup.

Phil ate silently, unsure if she should start a new conversation.

A clatter in the corridor drew everyone's attention. A girl of fourteen or fifteen skidded into the room. "I knew I heard you! It's been so long since you visited."

"Moriah." Lady Endelton appeared behind the girl, her lips thinned in disapproval.

Moriah bobbed the forgotten curtsy. "Your Grace, we are honored by your presence."

The duke raised a brow. "Manners after all these years? I won't recognize you, cousin."

Cousins? Aunt Healand mentioned as much. The connection explained the duke's early morning visit, as well as his concern.

The girl moved to the duke's side and did her best to loom over him. "I heard you yelling earlier. You don't practice your manners either."

"And did you hear why I yelled?" His eyes flicked in Phil's direction.

"Of course. Michael's imprudence at your ball."

Phil winced at Moriah's confirmation of what she and Alex had only assumed.

Moriah continued, "Only you are wrong. I saw Miss Lightwood through the door. She looks quite ill."

Phil froze mid-bite.

Lord Endelton coughed. For a moment, Phil thought he might be choking as his face turned red, but he took a sip of tea and the color receded.

Lady Endelton tapped her daughter on the shoulder. "You forget yourself."

Moriah nodded but did not look contrite.

"Miss Philippa, may I introduce my youngest daughter, Moriah?"

Moriah's face reddened like her brother's had. "Oh, beg your pardon, I didn't notice."

"Nice to meet you. If you will excuse me. I'll go to my sister."

"Mrs. Ivy is sitting with Miss Lightwood. Despite what Moriah says, your sister's condition hasn't changed since you left her. Please finish your breakfast." Lady Endelton sat down with a cup of tea.

"I am finished, thank you. My compliments to your cook. This is the most delicious bun I've ever eaten." She must escape this room and the house as soon as possible. The duke's opinion was likely shared by others. She could feel every pair of eyes on her back as she exited the breakfast room. If only she had not stayed to eat or Lord Endelton had deemed the extra miles to Russell Square worth the risk. If she had insisted. If only she hadn't pestered Alex to attend the ball.

She'd mounted the first step when Lord Endelton's voice interrupted her thoughts. "Miss Philippa, a word, please."

She pivoted on the step. With the added few inches, their eyes were at the same level. The brown in his she'd noticed earlier was ringed with golden flecks. Warm and safe as tea in her mother's favorite cup. She stared for a moment before realizing the inappropriateness and dropping her eyes. "Ye-Yes?"

Miss Philippa's soft blue eyes reminded him of a wild fox trapped in a corner. Michel didn't want to scare her. "Please stay as long as you and your sister need. Her care must be your first consideration, despite what you may have heard from my dunderheaded cousin."

Her eyelids flew up, her gaze meeting his.

"Yes, I called a duke a dunderhead. My mother is a more than adequate chaperone, but if you think my presence here will besmirch your character, I can arrange to stay elsewhere."

"You should not need to leave your own home because of us. We are the interlopers."

"No, guests. Promise me you will not leave if there is a risk that moving your sister would harm her further."

She looked down, her eyes hiding behind long lashes. "There are always risks. Such a promise would make it impossible to leave."

Michael sighed. "That is not what— In the breakfast room you said you don't believe she is well enough to move. Will you at least promise not to move her until Mrs. Ivy believes it is safe?"

Miss Philippa bit her lip. "How do I know your housekeeper isn't overprotective?"

"A physician then?"

"No, no doctors. Alex is wary of their dire opinions."

"I see. How can I be assured when you leave, you don't go because you are worried about my cousin's opinion?" Richard's opinions should not be a tool to further endanger Miss Lightwood.

"I would never knowingly bring harm to my sister."

"Then you will not leave this morning?"

"No."

"May I take the liberty of informing Lady Healand her coach is unnecessary?"

"She will come anyway."

"As I would expect, although at a later hour."

"Yes, if you could send a message to our aunt, it would be best." She turned, taking the steps as quickly as her dress would allow.

"Miss Philippa?"

She paused and looked over her shoulder.

"The item you left in the coach is being cleaned by my valet."

Her face pinked, and she bowed her head. He hadn't meant to embarrass her, but the blush became her. He waited until she reached the top of the stairs before turning back to the breakfast room.

Moriah looked up from her meal. "Mother says I should apologize to you and Miss Philippa. Was she truly embarrassed?"

Michael rubbed the back of his neck. "I believe so. She is in an awkward position, and you didn't make it any easier on her."

Lady Endelton nodded at her daughter. "You are excused to pen a note of apology to Miss Philippa and her sister."

Moriah left the room in a silent contrast to her arrival.

Richard harrumphed.

Lady Endelton pointed her butter knife at her nephew. "Neither did you help the situation, Richard. As a duke, your opinion carries more weight than it ought. I know you would feel as poorly if a premature removal caused Miss Lightwood further harm. Neither girl seems to be of the same mind as your wife."

"Upon speaking with Miss Philippa, I admit I may have misjudged the situation." Richard's offering was not a full back track. "However, even she admitted her father could find potential to—"

"Richard!" Lady Endelton's scolding tone caused his grace to jump. "Not every debutante is after a husband by cunning. Assuming every woman is as calculating as—" Mother paused. No one actually spoke of the incident precipitating Richard's hasty and imprudent marriage.

Richard tossed his head back and laughed. Not at all a cheerful sound. "Aunt, if only I could believe you. My wife wasn't the only woman to try such a ruse. She was the only one to succeed. From the day I took my father's title, I've had not a moment of peace as woman after woman paraded herself in front of me. Even at last night's ball, I received a most scandalous offer from one who perceived I was unhappy with my situation."

Mother pursed her lips. "There is no talking to you on this matter. However, if you remember, both your mother and I warned you of your wife and you refused to listen."

"And have you warned your own son?"

"I have no need, since you have every time you see him." Mother took a deep breath and relaxed her shoulders. She dealt with his cousin better than he. "As far as the Misses Lightwoods' presence here, believe me, they did not willingly set some plan in motion that led them to this place. I have seen the elder sister's injury, and I can assure you no woman would ever inflict such a thing on herself, even for your title and money."

Richard rose and turned to Michael. "I apologize for the disruption I caused. I have learned too late to trust our mothers' opinions. If my aunt is correct, apparently trustworthy women, other than our mothers, exist."

"I appreciate your concern. I will be careful, cousin."

"I shall take my leave. It seems as if I have done enough damage for the morning. Aunt." Richard placed a kiss on

Lady Endelton's cheek. "I'll tell mother you found my fears unfounded."

"Ask her to visit tomorrow and I'll tell her myself." Lady Endelton patted the duke's arm.

"If she will wait that long." Richard's laugh lost its sharp edge of earlier.

"My sister is not nearly as impatient as her son."

Michael walked his cousin to the door, where the butler met them with the duke's hat and coat. Neither said anything of consequence. For a moment, Richard looked like he may say more, but he shook his head and left.

Michael retreated to his study, unsure of what to do next; his morning routine had been far too disrupted.

"Peggy is where?"

Phil smoothed the blankets covering Alex, hoping to soothe her fears. "Lord Endelton's valet is cleaning it."

"If I wasn't so tired, I might scream. However did we get into such a mess? Your Season is ruined before it even started, and it is all my fault."

"I fail to see how it is your fault or how it is ruined. Forgive me for asking, but you are always more unreasonable when you are in pain. How bad is it today?"

"Bad enough I'd be tempted to take laudanum if it were available, if only in hopes of getting some sleep. Last night I could feel my foot." Alex stifled a yawn.

Phil ached for her sister. They'd talked about Alex's ghost of a limb often enough Phil knew she referred to the missing foot. "Do you think you can travel to our Aunt's?"

"Mrs. Ivy worries about reopening my wound. I am more fearful of the pain. I don't believe I could handle much more without resorting to drastic measures. You haven't let them call for a physician, have you?" Upon meeting Alex, men who claimed to be medical professionals only did one of three things: offer her laudanum, which Alex refused to take; bleed her, which only made her weak; or forecast a dire future, which wasn't helpful in the least.

"No, Mrs. Ivy doesn't think the wound needs care."

"She's taken excellent care of me. Green would approve."

"Likely Aunt will bring Green when she comes this afternoon."

"You think she will visit?"

"Curiosity will compel her to, even if duty doesn't. She'll want to give a proper report to Grandfather at any rate."

"I hope he doesn't think financing my extra dresses was wasted on me."

"You know better than to think that. Grandfather loves you." Phil smiled her brightest smile. Love and guilt were an odd combination. Where Grandfather's guilt led him to give Alex everything she could need to succeed, Father's guilt would keep Alex hidden the rest of her days.

"He'll be disappointed Peggy's new revolutionary design wasn't as good as my old prosthetic Mr. Potts made. I may go back to using the old one, even if it doesn't have carved toes." Alex closed her eyes.

"Will you be able to sleep?"

"Mrs. Ivy had me drink some of her special chocolate with cream. She guaranteed it would help me sleep like an old lord on the fourth day of parliamentary deliberation." A yawn proved the point.

Phil tucked the blanket around Alex's shoulders and settled into the chair.

"Don't sit there watching me. There must be a library here. Go find a book." Alex's words trailed off.

Phil looked longingly at the other half of the bed. If she didn't think it would hurt Alex, she would climb in and take a nap herself. What little sleep she'd received in the chair last night wasn't nearly enough.

She found the library easily enough, or what she supposed could be a library. There were only two hundred or so tomes in the bookcases. Most of them were newer, with several on agriculture and sheep. They might be useful, but Phil doubted they contained enough details to keep her awake. *Pride and Prejudice* by the author of *Sense and Sensibility*, looked to be interesting. However, Phil hadn't read the first novel, so she returned the book to the shelf as well.

Ann Radcliff's *The Mysteries of Udolpho*, which Phil had read often enough to have memorized several passages, won out over the other choices. She settled into a chair next to the window. After a few pages, her mind wandered. A new agriculture book sat on the table next to the chair. Curious, as the title promised to mix agriculture with chemistry, she opened the book and skimmed a few pages. George did more with the land planning; it might be a book she'd enjoy. She flipped to the title page, and a paper fell out of the book, landing face up on her lap.

Phil stared at the list of names with Alex's and her own scratched out.

# TEN

The small study didn't have enough shelves to hide the book Michael knew he'd left there yesterday. He walked around his desk again. *Elements of Agricultural Chemistry in a Course of Lectures* by Humphrey Davey was simply not there. Michael pinched the bridge of his nose and closed his eyes trying to remember where he last read. Ah, the west sitting room. Despite the paltry number of books on the shelves, his mother insisted on calling the room the library. He'd been reading last night while waiting for news on Miss Lightwood's condition.

Reading had not been a good way to pass the time as focusing on the text proved impossible. What was he to do with the women in the house? Especially women whose names Richard removed from his list because of the reputation of the father.

If Michael was going to help move England forward and effect changes, he needed to be respected in Parliament. Or so he'd been told often enough. His father had hoped the Slave Trade Act passed seven years ago would do more to end slavery than it had. He'd spent his last year urging his fellows that there was still more to do to abolish man's terrible abuse of man. Michael intended to continue his father's legacy. He had to win not just the battle but the war. Being young, others would judge him on every decision. His wife's connections needed to aid him in his fight. Miss Simesson was a much better choice if he couldn't marry a woman whose father had a title and connections.

Michael entered the library. The book in question sat on the table nearest the window. A soft snore interrupted his quest. Miss Philippa's head leaned at an awkward angle, and the book she held threatened to fall from her lap. He recognized it as one of Julia's favorites. He should back out of the room and ask a maid, his mother, or his sister to come wake her. He could retrieve his book first. He stepped closer.

Before he could reach the book dangling precariously, it fell to the floor and Miss Philippa shot to her feet. "Oh. Lord Endelton, I didn't hear you." She looked around her feet. "I was reading."

Michael picked up the book and handed it back to her. "Mrs. Radcliff's work I see."

Turning the book cover right-side up, she nodded. "I'd fallen asleep, hadn't I?"

"Sorry for disturbing you."

"I didn't mean—pardon me for taking your time again." She bobbed her head and took a step away.

"How is your sister?"

Miss Philippa traced a line on the front of the book before answering. "She was sleeping when I left the room. She didn't sleep well last night."

"And neither did you?"

"As you see." A smile teased the corner of her mouth. "I managed to fall asleep reading *The Mysteries of Udolpho*, which, even if I have read it before, is not a book conducive to sleep."

Michael picked up the agricultural book. "You are welcome to continue reading. I found what I am looking for."

"Does the book contain any helpful techniques?" She nodded to the book he held.

"I don't know yet. I have only started."

"If it does, will you tell me? I thought of reading—" She paused. "I suppose I shouldn't admit that, should I? It makes me sound like a bluestocking. I'm not. I want to help our farmers." She looked down again.

"You don't need to explain."

"Of course not. I'm afraid each time we meet, I lower your opinion of me. Is that why my name is scratched out?" She covered her mouth. "Please don't answer. My question is beyond impertinent and none of my business…"

"Scratched out?"

"The paper in the agricultural chemistry book." Her cheeks flushed pink, and she turned her gaze to the window.

Michael opened the book to the paper he had used to mark his place. The list Edward started. It wasn't her fault the book had been laying on the table. He cleared his throat, hoping to dislodge the lump that had formed as it did whenever he was unsure how to explain himself… "My friend wrote this list. Your name—"

She held up her hand. "I told you there is no reason to explain. I shouldn't have been reading your books without permission."

For a moment, he supposed she might cry. His sisters often did for no apparent reason. Instead, she lifted her chin a fraction, all signs of sleep obliterated.

He folded the paper, trying to hide it away. "You are welcome to read all of our books."

Miss Philippa shook her head lightly causing a curl to bob near her ear. "I won't risk finding other lists."

"This is the only one they drew up for me."

"Marriage prospects?"

"Women who might be possible matches." Even he knew lying about the paper she'd seen would be useless.

"I am glad they crossed Alex's and my names off. It means your actions in helping my sister were not calculated to impress me, and I don't have to wonder at your motivations other than your natural kindness." She paused for a moment. "It is good to know we are only to be friends."

"We are friends?" He didn't have any female friends.

"Better than enemies. Especially since you hold the entirety of my sister's secret at your disposal."

"And you have evidence my courtship is calculated." Talking about the list made the hand holding it burn. Michael wished for a roaring fire, so he could rid himself of the paper forever.

"I'd assume many men do the same. Write up a list, I mean."

"Do women write lists?"

"I'm sure some do. If I were to keep a list, it would be men to avoid." She stepped around the back of the chair, adding distance between them.

"Which I have now earned a place on?"

"No person showing kindness to my sister could ever be on such a list, even the worst sort of rake." She shuddered and took a step further from the chair.

"I'd be careful of such information being bandied about, as some rake might try to use her to get to you."

Miss Philippa kept her eyes on the back of the chair and took another step away. "I am not worried. As pointed out this morning during your cousin's visit, my father is a liability on the marriage mart."

"You are decidedly blunt."

"Which is another good reason I am scratched off of your list. I'm afraid we are off of a great many lists like yours and unlikely to have a successful Season. I so hoped Alex would." She took another step away, still focused on the back of the chair.

Most people looked at others when they spoke. His mother spent hours helping him learn to look others in the eye or, at the very least, their nose. "Is there something wrong with the chair?"

She looked up, her cheeks pink. "A spider."

Michael walked around the chair, where a common house spider dangled from a silken thread. "It's so small."

"I know, it isn't reasonable. I just don't like them." She moved another step away.

Pinching the fragile string, Michael opened the door leading to the garden and set the spider down.

"Thank you."

"What were we discussing?"

"The success of Miss Lightwood's Season."

"Oh, yes. What of your Season? Aren't you hoping to be successful also?"

"I have been commanded to do so."

"Commanded?"

"Yes, Father wants me to make a good connection." She circled the chair.

"And you? What do you want?"

"I will settle for someone who doesn't despise me, as long as they are kind to Alex. If she doesn't have a successful Season, I will need my husband's blessing to eventually have her under his roof."

"That could be years and years from now. Why do you care so much for your sister's welfare? I have three sisters and they don't show half as much concern for each other."

Miss Philippa sat in the chair she previously vacated. "Have you ever lost something and only in the loss did you discover how much you loved it?"

"I wish my father back often for his advice. Advice I didn't seek when he lived. Something like that?"

"When my father informed me of my mother and brother's deaths, he also told me Alex would not live." Blinking rapidly, Miss Philippa looked out the window. "When Father returned with the bodies, he brought news that she still languished in agony with little hope of survival. The prayers I prayed and the promises I made—some of which I haven't kept well—God listened anyway. I suspect your sisters have never lost something they loved and then impossibly found it still."

"Few of us have lost the thing or person we love and find them again."

"Father isn't kind to Alex."

"And you can't abandon her."

"Precisely."

The list still burned in his hand. "I have a rather unconventional idea."

The conversation was already wildly inappropriate, yet she could not end it. Something about Lord Endelton reminded her of her brother, and she wished to put her finger on exactly what it was. He didn't quite look at her when he turned in her direction. The fact he'd answered her impertinent question without censuring her was most puzzling. Speaking her mind too much would be the end of her. It would have been better to leave when she first had the chance. Instead, Phil had sat back down and told the man everything. Why had she mentioned the paper with their names scratched out? She could blame it on having woken with such a start or still feeling hurt for being excluded. Lord Endelton had already proved himself as kind and attentive. Nerves loosened her tongue. "How unconventional?"

"It seems you could be a better resource than those who drew up this list. And I, in turn, could make sure to introduce you and your sister to men who are not rakes and would be in a position to overlook your father's deficits."

"Since this is our first Season, and I've met only one of the women on your list, I don't see how my opinion would be beneficial to you in the least." Propriety demanded she find a way out of such a scheme.

"I don't need you to introduce me. I need you to help me discern—. The other night at cards. Miss Simesson's story was all too believable. I thought you were the villain."

Forming an answer without calling him a simpleton caused Phil to pick her words carefully. "Lord Endelton, at what point did you see through her poor playing to the truth?"

"Later, when I talked to my sister. To be honest, if her husband hadn't accused you of being a cheat in the first place, I might not have formed my opinion against you so quickly and assumed you were trying to best Miss Simesson in some way."

"You did not understand that Edward joked?" How could a man hope to do well in the House of Lords if he couldn't even understand when his friends talked in jest? Lord Endelton acted more like her brother than she'd realized. He'd rarely understood a joke and had spent much of his time alone. Mother worried about his future at Eton and had gone to ask her father's opinion on that matter as well as others.

"Not precisely. You had attempted to cheat him before."

Phil blew out a puff of air. "I was a child. I also climbed trees. That doesn't mean I'd climb one today."

"You can climb trees?" Like her brother, Lord Endelton fastened on the point of the sentence holding no meaning.

"I can, but we were discussing why you would need my help to find a wife."

"My sisters tell me often I misinterpret or misunderstand what is being said." He leaned forward, resting his elbows on his knees, a pleading in his eyes that would have given her sister Jane's dog competition.

"You are in earnest?" The statement came out as much of a question as an answer. For some unfathomable reason, Lord Endelton didn't understand the subtleties of conversation or even how odd his request was. Would little William have grown up like this?

"Please."

She searched his face for a hint of guile. He was so similar to her brother, how could she say no to the impractical question? "Tell me how am I to go about this? Befriend women on your list and spy on them?"

"Not spy. Take Miss Simesson. You knew she played a part, and I did not. You didn't need to spy on her. I needed to be warned."

With a sharp call, a bird flew out of the tree closest to the window and soared into the sky. Phil watched until the bird was out of sight, then dropped her gaze to the trunk of the tree where a cat prowled. She noticed Lord Endelton's attention likewise captured by the cat. She waited until he turned from the window. "How am I to let you know? If we are seen conversing often, it may give others the wrong idea."

"You could write me a note?"

"By no rule of society could I write to you. Besides, if our communications are intercepted, a scandal would be created."

"There must be a way to talk freely as we are now."

Another scandal if anyone saw them unchaperoned even with the door open. So far, she'd seen little chance to speak freely. No wonder rides and walks in Hyde Park were an expected part of courtship in Town, there was no way to find a moment of privacy otherwise. "At a ball, it is easy enough. We have only to dance. No one would think anything of it as long as it was only one set, and you varied the timing."

"What about other events? What if we have another dinner?"

"Unless Lady Godderidge hosts another dinner party. I don't know if we will attend one together again. I believe your circles are somewhat different than our aunt's."

"What of the theater or one of those musical evenings?"

"Having been to neither, I am not sure."

"You've never been to the theater?"

"No. And the last musical evening I attended was at Godderidge's home when I was a little younger than Moriah. Our piano master set it up to give us a taste of what it would be like to exhibit our skills in public. I doubt it was much like one during the Season."

Lord Endelton's face fell. "I didn't think this would be so complicated. If you were a man, you could meet me at our club. Perhaps you are correct; this wasn't a good idea. I should not have asked."

"You said your sisters teased you. Can't they help?"

"Julia is entering confinement, and the list you saw was Edward and Deborah's help."

"What of Moriah?"

He focused on some point above her left shoulder. He'd done that several times. If not for William doing the same thing, she might look askance to his behavior. "She isn't out in society yet. And I don't think she understands my inability to do whatever it is I don't understand."

"Hmm. But if something was amiss I thought you should know about, I could invite Moriah to tea. Or if it was more immediate, I could ask you about her health, a type of signal. that I have something to tell you."

"Brilliant. Will you help me?"

How could she not? Somehow, Lord Endelton wasn't like other members of the ton. His differences allowed him to put aside society's rules and be kind to her sister. She must at least try to help him. "I still doubt my usefulness, but I will help you."

# ELEVEN

The agriculture book kept Michael occupied for most of the afternoon. Once he started reading something of interest, he possessed the ability to block out the rest of the world. The talent of being able to immerse oneself fully in a project was under-appreciated by most people. Perhaps they, like his valet who knocked a book to the floor, were envious.

"Pardon the intrusion, my Lord." His valet returned the book to the table. Michael should discuss the man servant's clumsiness. Almost daily, the man dropped something, though so far, nothing valuable like one of his mother's vases. "I think I have discovered the problem with the apparatus you gave me to clean. If you could obtain Miss Lightwood's permission, I believe I could repair it."

"Her permission?"

The valet's face reddened. "The item is rather personal in nature. I believe it would be proper not to make changes unless she approves."

"Very sensible. Is there any particular question I should ask?"

The valet produced a paper. "I've taken the liberty of making a drawing. I am afraid it is not very precise. The addition of a soft leather strap here and another here would protect Miss Lightwood in the chance of another mishap."

Michael studied the drawing. It was as good as some illustrations he'd seen of machines in books. "I see what you mean. Do you have the tools you need?"

"My brother is a saddle maker. I thought to take it to him. He is more skilled than I."

"Will a guinea cover the expense?"

"Most certainly."

Michael pulled the gold coin from his pocket and handed it to the valet before retiring to the pages of his book.

"My Lord?" The valet's voice was louder than usual.

Michael looked up.

"If you would obtain the lady's approval this afternoon."

How had he forgotten he needed to discuss the drawing with Miss Lightwood? "I'll ask permission straight away."

"Thank you, my Lord." The valet continued to stand near the door.

Michael set the book aside and rose. "Do you know where my mother is?"

"I believe she is in the parlor with Lady Healand and Miss Philippa." Michael checked the time on the hall clock. Half-past two. How long had Lady Healand been here, and why had no one informed him? Murmurs of quiet conversation reached his ears as he turned into the east corridor. The conversation stopped when he entered his mother's parlor.

"There you are. I told them you'd be along any moment." Mother's tight smile was one he'd seen often. She'd been waiting on him. Someone must have informed him of Lady Healand's arrival, only he'd been reading and hadn't heard them. Deborah claimed he frequently ignored others when reading. Either she was right, or their family employed the most disobedient staff in all of England.

"Sorry, I was detained." Michael greeted Lady Healand and Miss Philippa. He'd have to wait for an opportunity to talk to Miss Lightwood, and he needed one of the women in the room to accompany him. On second thought, he needed his mother, but his mother shouldn't need to deal with the issue of the broken prosthesis. It wasn't very proper. Miss Philippa would know, but she wasn't a suitable chaperone into a bedchamber. He needed Deborah to visit. Since she was married, she'd be a much better chaperone. Oh why must interactions with women be so complicated?

Taking a seat near his mother, he sipped from the offered cup of cooled tea. Mother must have been waiting on him for a while.

"I just finished telling your mother how much I appreciate your quick actions last evening and your diligence in alerting me. I'd hoped to remove Alexandra to my townhouse today, but it isn't possible. Your mother informs me there is no imposition, but—" Lady Healand allowed the sentence to hang in a particular fashion people used when they wanted to ask a question but for some reason couldn't.

"It isn't an imposition at all."

A nod from his Mother indicated he responded correctly.

Lady Healand stood. "If you would please direct me to my niece, I should visit her before I leave."

Miss Philippa set aside her tea.

"Finish your tea, Miss Philippa. I'll show your aunt up. Your maid, Green, was it? Should have settled in by now." Mother led Lady Healand from the room.

Left alone with Miss Philippa and Moriah, Michael sipped his lukewarm tea and waited for one of them to speak. The silence grew. Michael finished his tea.

Moriah set aside her cup and saucer. "When are you taking me to the theater? You promised you would."

"Is there anything you want to see?"

"I don't care. I want to go and see all the people I've been reading about in the paper. I want to know who Sir R is and Miss W." Moriah bounced forward in her seat.

"I thought Mother told you not to read the society pages."

"All of my friends do. I have to read them, or they'll think I don't know anything. Do you read the papers, Miss Philippa?"

The teacup wobbled as Miss Philippa set the saucer on the table. "I don't keep up. What is the point? Even if I managed to decode the initials, the stories are probably exaggerated. Some may be humorous, but others are hurtful. My mother taught us to be careful about what we believe about others, especially if we don't know them. Within reason, of course."

"What kind of reason?"

"For example, if someone is rumored to be a rake, one should take caution not to be unchaperoned around him."

"Well, of course, that is why we have chaperones in the first place, isn't it? And how are we to know who the rakes are if we don't read the paper?"

Miss Philippa smiled the kind of smile Deborah did when she explained something to him, again. "I am positive your brother or older sisters would warn you off."

Moriah's mouth formed an exaggerated frown. "They'll warn me off everyone. They always do."

"That is because you are fifteen, and it is my job to keep you safe." Michael hoped she would understand he wasn't trying to be cruel.

Moriah set her cup and saucer on the tray. "It is so difficult being the youngest. I suppose I should go practice the pianoforte or something before someone banishes me from the grownups."

Miss Philippa turned her head and coughed as Moriah pranced from the room.

"Are you alright, Miss Philippa?"

She turned to face him, her eyes as bright as her smile. "Quite."

Michael was sure there was something he was missing. From her smile, Miss Lightwood was amused. There was no cause for merriment in his sister's sullen statement. Since it was only Moriah, he decided not to have his new friend enlighten him. He pulled the valet's drawing from his pocket and offered it to Miss Philippa. "My valet believes a small adjustment to the item left in the coach last night will avoid future problems."

Miss Philippa unfolded the paper. She traced a section with her finger and closed her eyes for a moment. "The leather would have to be very soft."

"My valet assured me he can access the tools needed. His brother is a saddle maker. He only needs your sister's permission and —" Heat warmed his ears.

"Would you like me to speak with her?"

"If you would, please."

"I will as soon as our aunt leaves." She folded up the paper, and it disappeared into the folds of her dress. "Well done, by the way."

"What? What did I do?"

"Did you not intend to put off your sister's question about the theater?"

Michael replayed the conversation in his mind. "Not precisely. I want to make sure I am taking her to something appropriate for the outing. I didn't intentionally put her off. She was the one who changed the subject."

Miss Philippa's brow creased. "May I ask you some questions relating to our conversation this morning and helping each other?"

"Of course."

"Do you know why I was trying not to laugh when your sister left the room?"

"No."

"Hmm. When you are summoned, does it often take you more than a quarter hour to respond?"

"I am not sure. Others claim it is so."

"Before you came into this room, what were you doing?"

"Reading."

Miss Philippa nodded. "And you found the book interesting?"

"More intriguing than interesting. The chemical properties of soil and how to change them gives me much to ponder."

"Thank you, Lord Endelton. That helps me to better understand our earlier conversation."

"How? What do I need to do differently?"

"I don't know what you need to do as much as I need to understand." Miss Philippa rose, so Michael did too.

"I'll let you get back to your book." She turned at the door. "And I was laughing because Moriah reminds me of my younger sisters."

"Thank you for explaining." Michael still didn't understand, but it must be one of those sister things he would never comprehend.

Fatigue rimmed Alex's eyes, but her color was better. Her smile brightened as Phil neared the bed. Green sat in the corner sewing. Phil didn't worry about what their maid might hear, as she never carried tales.

"It seems Lord Endelton's valet has a talent which may help you. He drew these plans to modify Peggy."

Alex pushed herself up into a sitting position and took the paper from Phil. "After last night, I think I should call her Pokey or Brutus."

"Brutus?"

"Et tu, Brute?"

Phil laughed, along with her sister. "Very fitting. You have thought about this too long, I see."

Alex smoothed out the paper. "The valet draws well. I think his modifications would solve the problem of getting cut again. But the leg can still turn. I think the problem is my old Peggy had a wider strap here."

"Yes, I remember."

"Will you ask the valet to replace the lower one with a wider one?"

Green set her sewing aside and came to look. "This drawing looks clever."

"At least it solves the problem of being cut by the buckle." Alex handed the drawing back.

"How did Peggy come to be hit so hard, anyway?"

"Edward left me at a bench. However, a white-haired matron was in need of a respite, so I went in search of another perch. Just as I was taking a step, a man stumbled into me. His foot caught on mine. He apologized and hurried on. I took another step and realized something was very wrong. The column was the closest thing to support me."

"And I shall never beg you to go to a ball again."

"Aunt would forbid it if you did. She says there are other less crowded events we might attend once I am healed." Alex yawned.

"Are you still tired?"

"Green brought me some of her tea. You know how it affects me." Willow bark, chamomile, a hint of lavender and who knew what else made up a tea that soothed her sister.

"I'll leave you to rest while I seek out the valet." Phil left Alex in Green's capable hands.

Where did one find a valet? Likely in the kitchen or the lord's chambers. Finding Lord Endelton would be much easier.

He was in the library in the same chair she'd fallen asleep in earlier. As she approached, he didn't move. The only sign that he was awake was the turning of the pages.

"Lord Endelton?"

He continued to read.

"Viscount?"

Still no response. If Phil hadn't been told he sometimes became so engrossed in an idea he paid no attention to the world around him, she may have left, fearing she'd suffered the cut direct. Her brother had often done the same. A large volume sat on the table. Phil picked it up and dropped it to the floor.

Lord Endelton jumped out of his seat, his own book falling to the floor. "Miss Philippa, I didn't realize—"

"The book must be good to capture your attention so fully."

"Perplexing." He bent and retrieved the book and checked the spine. "May I help you?"

"I need to speak with your valet about his drawing."

"I'll send for him." Lord Endelton pulled the cord on the wall. A moment later, a footman appeared and was dispatched on the errand.

Lord Endelton shifted his weight from one leg to the other, apparently not sure what to do next.

Phil sat next to the large table mostly so he could retake his own seat. "I am sorry to interrupt your reading."

"How long have you been standing there?"

"Long enough if I had not been warned you could be so focused, I would have left quite dejected."

The valet entered the room, saving them from further awkward conversation.

"Miss Philippa wishes to speak to you."

The valet gave a slight bow.

Phil smoothed the paper on the table. "My sister likes your design very much. She wonders if a wider strap would improve the fit?"

The valet pulled a pencil from a pocket and drew over his sketch. "Like so?"

"Exactly."

Lord Endelton left his chair and stood over the table. The valet continued to draw. "I think two smaller buckles positioned here and here would provide more security."

"Yes. Much like her older one. How soon could it be repaired?"

"If his lordship gives me leave, assuming my brother has the leather I need, it will be finished by morning. Is that soon enough, Miss?"

"Yes. Do you know how much it will cost?" Phil didn't have any money with her, but she could ask for some from her aunt.

"His lordship has already provided the funds."

Phil turned to Lord Endelton. "Thank you."

He nodded in response to his valet. "Take all the time you need."

"I've taken the liberty of laying out your clothing for dinner. The young footman has been practicing tying the cravat. He will aid you if I have not returned."

At the Lord's nod, the valet departed.

"Please, what did you pay him?"

"There is no need to pay me back."

"My grandfather will insist upon it."

"Not your father?"

"Grandfather insists on providing for all of Alex's needs related to the accident. He will be distressed to learn her newest prosthesis failed."

"Who would tell him?"

"Our maid is in his employ. As an apothecary's daughter, she has skills to help my sister."

Lord Endelton took a seat on the other side of the table. "I only met the earl once. He visited my father when I was six. I thought he was ancient."

"Recently celebrated his seventy-sixth birthday."

"Remarkable."

"Grandfather is determined to live another twenty."

"And would you like to live to be one hundred?"

"I'm not yet twenty. I can barely fathom such an age."

"Do not take offense. I thought you were older. You don't behave—I mean—I'm not saying this well." Redness creeped up under his collar.

"I think I understand. I was put in charge of our household the day my mother died. Not many of my peers have run a household or overseen the welfare of the tenants. Once Alex recovered enough, she took over the teaching and planning. I took the jobs that required running up and down the stairs or visiting around the estate."

"Who is in charge while you are gone?"

"George. I mean Georgiana and Jane, our twin sisters. They are sixteen and more than capable."

Lord Endelton nodded. "The experience will help you secure a husband. Some, like Rich—I mean, some men find the woman they married have no experience with anything other than flirting."

"Which is a skill necessary to secure a husband. One I am lacking in."

"How do you know?"

"If I were skilled, the duke would have remained here, guarding you like a faithful bulldog to keep you safe from my influence."

"But we are friends, so you wouldn't flirt with me, anyway." His face was all seriousness.

Phil was unsure of how to correct him. The reason she wouldn't flirt with him had nothing to do with the newly formed friendship and more to do with the fact she wasn't one to force herself where she wasn't wanted. "I should return to my sister and tell her the news."

"Will you come down for dinner?" There was a hopeful look in his eye. As yet, she hadn't worn out her welcome.

"Yes, I will."

# TWELVE

For the second day in a row, Michael arose before the rest of the household, including his valet. Perhaps this morning he could finish his agriculture book without interruption. Last evening, Mother had insisted he stay around after dinner for a game of cards since Miss Philippa made a foursome. For the first round, he'd partnered with Mother mostly so he could see if Miss Philippa cheated. She hadn't, and she and Moriah won. When he partnered with Moriah, Mother and Miss Philippa won. Again, there was no cheating. He suspected if he had partnered with Miss Philippa, they would have made the winning team, however after two rounds, Miss Philippa excused herself to go to her sister.

Very disappointing, as he had no way to prove his hypothesis, because if Miss Philippa wasn't an extremely skilled player, he must be a very poor one. And he had never considered himself unskilled before. Unfortunately, he'd spent the time he should have been reading last evening trying to analyze her card skills to no avail. He was unable to remember most of the plays; however, her laugh and the sparkle of her blue grayish eyes remained in the forefront of his mind. Another conundrum to ponder. At first, he'd thought them a pale blue. Last night they'd been grayer, like a cloud not quite yet ready to rain. She really was the most perplexing woman.

Michael turned the page of his book back. What had he read? Was it something about rain? Yes, there was the line. The reference distracted him as he'd thought of Miss Philippa's eyes. That was one of the problems with women. If you weren't careful, they snuck into every part of your life. He'd watched it happen with both of his sisters' husbands. Even Richard's wife had invaded his life, though he was loath to admit it. His cousin spent most of his time trying to keep the duchess out of his affairs.

And why should he think of Miss Philippa? She was not on his list. It made no sense to ponder on her at all. He simply must put her out of his mind.

Michael returned his focus to the text and finished several pages before his valet interrupted him.

"My lord, I need to return to my brother's this morning to complete the work on the item."

"Of course."

"I should be back in two hours. Is there anything you need before I leave?"

Michael looked down to check his cravat and for crumbs. "No, I believe all is in order."

The valet nodded and left the room.

The smell of fresh bread reminded Michael he had yet to eat. Hence no crumbs. Experience told him he should set the book aside or he may have to wait until later for sustenance. Mother had been strict with the staff since his boyhood on the subject of missed meals. A rule which irritatingly enough only applied to him and not his sisters. They never became so engrossed in a book that they missed two meals and tea on the same day.

Setting aside his book, he went in search of sustenance.

The house was much quieter than it had been the morning before. Phil descended the stairs to the breakfast room. Alex still slept, so ordering a tray would have been an unnecessary burden for Lord Endelton's staff.

A maid set a plate of buns on the sideboard as Phil entered the otherwise empty room. The possibility of conversation caused her to come down from her room. There was such a thing as too much isolation. Until coming to London, she hadn't realized exactly how little time she spent in solitude each day.

Filling her plate, she took a seat where she could gaze out of the window and see if anyone entered the door. An unopened newspaper lay on a silver tray. Phil could only make out the headline news about the troops in Canada. It would be so much better if men would stop fighting all these wars.

She longed to open the paper, if only for a distraction.

Footsteps in the corridor alerted her to Lord Endelton's approach.

"Good morning." They said in unison.

Lord Endelton appraised the food on the sideboard. "Are we the only two who have been down?"

"I haven't seen anyone else."

"My mother and sister do not typically arrive early. Thus, they miss out on cook's buns when they are warm from the oven."

"Are they your favorite part of the meal?"

"Quite. I would have her serve them every day, but mother refuses to put them on the menu often. Two days in a row is unusual."

"That may be our fault. Alex and I both expressed our enjoyment of them."

"Then you are welcome to never leave if I can eat cook's buns each morning with my coddled eggs."

"Then we may disappoint you. My sister is much improved this morning. I believe we will be able to return to our aunt's this afternoon."

He sat opposite of her at the small table and picked up the newspaper. "And I have beaten Moriah to the paper."

Phil didn't speak as he perused the rest of the front page, then set the paper aside with a sigh.

"My older sisters tell me it is rude to read the paper when I am in company."

"Don't let me interrupt your morning routine."

"I usually read it after breakfast. My father always read it first. I cannot yet believe it is my prerogative to read the paper before others."

Phil lowered the teacup she'd sipped from. "Providing Moriah hasn't found the paper first."

"Precisely."

A rush of feet on the stairs caused them to look to the door.

Moriah slowed her steps as she entered the room. "Michael? Have you finished with the paper yet?"

"I haven't even started, and Mother said you were not to read the papers."

"Mother said I wasn't to read the gossip pages. I was looking for the pages about the theater. Since you are not inclined to choose, I must select the show." Moriah tossed a bun and an egg on her plate.

"I was going to have Mother choose."

"She'll choose something not exciting at all. Like dusty old Shakespeare." Moriah plopped down into a chair between them.

"Since you are not yet out, she will want to approve whatever we attend, anyway."

"Will she have to come with us?"

"I believe it is appropriate she attend."

Moriah crossed her arms. "Then it will be no fun at all."

"I wouldn't let Mother hear you. She'll decide you should wait another year."

"But I've already waited my entire life." Moriah's lip jutted forward ever so slightly.

Phil suppressed a smile. Youngest sisters had the most difficult life.

"Then I fear you will be disappointed. The theater isn't nearly as exciting as you imagine." Michael's face gave no hint he was teasing.

"What is your opinion, Miss Philippa? Will I be disappointed?" Moriah leaned forward in her seat.

"I cannot say, for I don't know what you are expecting, and since I've never been to the theater, I cannot tell if your hopes are too high or too low for the adventure."

Moriah's eyes widened. "You've never been?"

"No. This is our first visit to London."

"Then you must go with us. And your sister. Right, Michael?" Her question caught her brother with a mouth full of food.

Phil had to stop this idea. The invitation wasn't even Moriah's to extend. "Thank you, but—"

"Excellent, Moriah." Lord Endelton cut off her objections. "Do you think Miss Lightwood will be able to attend the function?"

Theaters had stairs, didn't they? "Perhaps in a fortnight."

Lord Endelton nodded. "Our cousin keeps a box. I'll see if he can be persuaded to loan it to us for the evening."

"Oh, Richard never goes to the theater, only the duchess attends. Everyone knows that." Moriah rose and went to the sidebar.

Phil spoke in a low voice. "You don't need to honor your sister's invitation."

"The Duke's box has plenty of room."

"In a fortnight, you could be courting one of the women from your list, and she would not be well disposed if you went to the theater with another."

Lord Endelton paused. "If I explained it was Moriah's wish, she would understand."

"Possibly. Not to mention being seen at the theater with two women you are not courting will not help your cause."

His lordship's brow pinched together. "I do not see how it could hurt. I will discuss the matter with Mother. If she agrees, you and your sister will come?"

While they talked, Moriah returned. "Do say yes."

There was no graceful way out with Moriah's sighs and raptures interrupting every attempt to back out. Phil agreed, for Moriah's sake.

Moriah stuffed a large piece of her bun into her mouth, barely pausing to swallow. "I'll ask Mother what we should see. You won't forget to ask Richard about the box, will you?"

Lord Endelton pulled a paper from the pocket inside his coat and scribbled a note with a short length of pencil. "I have made a memorandum of it. I will not forget."

"You are the best brother in all of London." Moriah flitted from the room, leaving her half-eaten bun on her plate. A pity it would go to waste.

Phil tried again to extricate herself from the imprudent invitation. "Lord Endelton, please, there is no need to include us at your sister's whim."

"Nonsense. It is a good idea."

"Given yesterday's agreement, this is much too public of a meeting. We are to remain only friends." She clasped her hands together under the table to keep them from waving about to express her point.

"Actually, the theater would be an excellent place to introduce you to some of my eligible friends."

Phil couldn't find a way to explain her misgivings. "All the more reason we shouldn't go."

"Why ever not? You said you've never been to the theater. And the duke's box has a perfect view of the stage. So much better than seeing your first play from any other seats. Even I am aware being seen in the duke's box would go far to erase any stigma your father may have caused you."

Fair point. Phil doubted his lordship had any idea how problematic the invitation could become if he pursued a courtship in earnest. She'd have to count on others to bring him to reason "If the duke doesn't object."

"I doubt he will. He is more than happy to loan out his box."

"Then I thank you for the invitation. I will relay it to Alex." Phil stood to leave. Lord Endelton stood a half second later.

Phil curtsied and hurried out of the room.

# THIRTEEN

As Michael penned the last word of his note to Richard, the footman announced Edward's visit.

"What brings you here so early this morning?"

Edward sat on a leather chair on the opposite side of Michael's desk. "Deborah found herself in need of your mother's advice."

Michael checked the clock on the wall. "It's not even eleven yet."

"As you see, it was most urgent."

"I cannot fathom what my sister would want of Mother. An opinion on the latest fashion could wait until calling hours."

The corner of Edward's mouth turned up. "Yes, I believe it could. Deborah's inquiry is of more import."

Michael narrowed his eyes. "Are you trying to get me to guess at your errand?"

"No."

"Then why the funny smile? Have I done something wrong?"

"Not at all." Edward's smile grew.

"Then why do you sit at my desk so early in the morning grinning like a child's puppet?" Michael pointed to his friend with his pen.

His brother-in-law raised his chin. "I am not smiling like a puppet."

Michael folded the note to Richard and melted the end of the sealing wax over the candle. "I beg you to enlighten me. It is bad enough I've had to puzzle out the meanings behind women's words, I do not need your hidden meanings, either."

"Surely, Moriah isn't difficult to figure out."

"No. It is Miss Philippa Lightwood. She agreed to be my friend and help me find a suitable wife, but when Moriah proposed an outing, which would allow me to introduce her to gentlemen. She all but refuses."

"You have an agreement with Phil? I mean, Miss Philippa. How did that come about? You had not been impressed with her at the card party, and you only danced once at Richard's ball."

"The Miss Lightwoods have been our guests since the ball ended."

"Your guests?" Edward's eyebrows rose, and his laughing smile faded.

"Miss Lightwood suffered a mishap after you left her. It was prudent to bring her here. Of course, Miss Philippa joined her."

"Are you insinuating I am in some way responsible for the Misses Lightwood being here?"

He'd never thought of it as Edwards' fault, but it could have been. "I don't know. You were going to find her a seat."

"Which I did. She was nicely situated when I left for the card room."

"Well, that was not the case when we found her injured. Perhaps if she had been sitting, she would not now be convalescing upstairs."

"I don't understand. Can you be more specific?" asked Edward.

Michael swallowed. Edward was a friend of the Lightwoods' and had alluded to Miss Lightwood's injury earlier, but there was no way to know if he was aware of the extent or the prosthesis. "I am afraid confidence doesn't allow for specifics, beyond the fact she was trod upon by someone in the crowd."

"Then why bring them here?"

"My home is much closer to the duke's than Lady Healand's at the slow speed we were able to travel the crowded streets. I felt obtaining proper help immediately was the best course of action."

Edward scratched behind his ear. "And after your tale, you find Phil to be perplexing?"

"Almost as confusing as you calling them by those manly names. I've noticed Miss Philippa uses men's names for her sisters too." Michael rubbed the wax onto the paper and sealed it.

"It is their father's fault. According to mother, he was quite insistent each child Lady Lightwood bore be male, despite his wife informing him they were girls. The oldest, as you have guessed, was named Alexander. The parish priest, of course, christened her Alexandra, because wishful think-ing does not a son make. Philippa was, of course, named Philip and Georgiana named George. George's twin was such a surprise, Sir Lightwood gave Lady Lightwood the task of naming her. Hence how Jane was spared being called Johnathena, Melvina, or some other name of masculine derivative. Then William was born. And since he had his heir, Sir Lightwood gave up on naming the children. So little Rose has the most feminine name of them all. When the girls were young, Sir Lightwood called them by the male derivative name. And they naturally followed suit."

"How peculiar."

"Indeed. Could you imagine what Deborah would do if I attempted to name our child in such a way?"

"She'd have your guts for garters."

"Or worse." Edward laughed. "She has already made me promise I will be sensible with our children's names."

Michael studied his friend's face for a moment. The funny grin on him still reminding Michael of the children's puppet. "Have you had reason to be discussing names?"

Edward's eyes widened. "I am afraid you will have to wait for an answer."

"Is that why my sister must speak to Mother?"

"We've already discussed your sister's temperament. I had best not answer the question."

Michael pondered for a moment, sure his friend had indeed answered his question. He would be an uncle twice over before he could be wed. He turned the note over and addressed it to the Duke.

"Why are you writing your cousin?" asked Edward.

"Moriah has begged me to take her to the theater. I thought it best if I could borrow Richard's box for the evening."

"You will only set her up for disappointment later. She will never have such a fine seat as she will in your cousin's box."

"Would you and Deborah like to join us?"

"I am unsure of our social schedule. When is the proposed outing?"

"Not for a fortnight. I've invited the Misses Lightwood to go with us, and I have been informed Miss Alexandra Lightwood will need to continue convalescing until then."

Edward raised a brow. "Does this have to do with why Miss Philippa is perplexing you?"

"Yes, she seemed quite reluctant to accept our invitation."

"Did you not say she was helping you to find a wife?"

"Not so much to find a wife as to help me understand when a woman was being less than truthful with me."

"Whatever do you mean?" asked Edward.

"The other night at cards. I was quite sure Miss Philippa was the cause of the problem at our first round, when in fact, it was Miss Simesson who was being disingenuous. As much as my sisters have drilled into me, I do not understand people. I thought it was best I find a truthful ally to help me navigate the process as I cannot always count on my sisters' opinions to be at hand."

"And how did you choose Miss Philippa for such a position?"

"She found the list you had made of prospective brides and was bold enough to ask me why her name was crossed out. She didn't even flinch when I informed her it was because of her father's reputation. Thus we made a deal. She would be just as honest with me about her knowledge of other young women. In turn, I would help her find men who have a good character. Who would not be bothered by her father's reputation?"

"Madness. Only you could get in such an odd position."

"Why? She knows we can only be friends and has agreed to be my friend. Wouldn't a friend help me?"

Edward ran his hand down his face and sighed. "Most women would take the opportunity to entrap you. Fortunately for you, Miss Philippa is not most women."

"Whatever do you mean?"

"According to Mother, Miss Philippa is the most responsible debutante she has ever seen. The girl has been running her father's house for the last four years. The reason her card-cheating came to naught so many years ago was because she had to confess. It is her nature to be overly honest."

"Then I did not choose wrong." Michael rang the bell for the footman and handed him the note to be dispatched to Richard.

Edward waited for the footman to leave before talking again. "Choosing any woman for such a role as an advisor was improper. However, since you chose a woman, at least you were fortunate enough to choose Miss Philippa. I hope you do not come to regret your bargain."

"I'm afraid I do not understand."

"And I hope you never do."

Michael stared at his friend for a moment, then changed the topic to the agricultural book he had been reading. Science was ever so much easier to comprehend.

Alex took the book from Phil and began reading the next chapter. A knock at the door interrupted them.

Green answered and returned with a battered leather valise. Faded initials M N were carved in the handle. "His lordship's valet delivered this."

Alex held out her hands for the bag. "I can't wait to see how he repaired Peggy."

Phil leaned in close as Alex removed her prosthetic from the bag. The wooden leg was as pristine as the day Alex first got it. The valet had taken pains to remove any trace of blood from the wood. The sisters inspected the new leather work. The leather was soft and supple.

"Is it too thin? Will it break?"

Green took her turn inspecting the prosthetic, tugging and twisting every bit of it. "No, miss, this is the finest work I've ever seen."

"Lord Endelton said his valet's brother was a saddler." Phil inspected the buckles. Extra care had been taken to smooth any rough edges.

"Do you think I can wear it home?" asked Alex.

The maid frowned. "It would be best if you put no pressure on the wound for a few more days. We can ask your aunt to send my husband with the carriage to pick you up. He will carry you out."

Alex frowned. "Can I not walk from at least the door to the carriage? I don't want to give Lord Endelton's neighbors any fodder for gossip."

Green turned to Phil. "How many steps are there in the front of the house?"

"Three, maybe four."

The maid inspected the prosthetic again. "Only those few steps. And with your sister by your side supporting you."

"How soon can we leave?" asked Alex.

"As soon as Lady Healand can send the carriage," said Green.

Phil rose from her seat on the edge of the bed. "I'll ask for a message to be sent."

She had hoped to find Lady Endelton in the sitting room, but it was empty, as was the parlor. Finally, Phil braved knocking on the open door to the study where she could hear someone talking to Lord Endelton. Both men stood as she entered the room. Thankfully, it was not the duke but their old friend, Edward.

"Pardon my interruption. I was hoping to send a message to my aunt. Alex is well enough to return, and we are in need of the carriage."

"You're certain?" asked Lord Endelton.

"Yes, our maid who has cared for Alexandra for several years has approved."

"And my mother?"

"I was unable to locate Lady Endelton, hence the interruption."

Edward sighed. "She is closeted with my wife and no doubt will be for some time. We brought my father's carriage. If you would like, you may use it to facilitate your return. I have no doubt my driver will return long before we are ready to leave."

"Very kind of you. If it is no imposition, we can be ready to leave within half an hour."

"I'll let my driver know," said Edward.

Lord Endelton nodded in agreement. "Have your maid ring for the footman when your bags are ready."

Phil looked from one man to the other, again glad the duke was not present. "There is another thing. My sister will not be able to walk down the stairs. Usually our maid's husband carries her. Do you have someone who might help her?"

"I carried her up; I can bring her down," answered the viscount.

She doubted he had ever carried someone down the stairs. It wasn't easy finding one's footing when you couldn't see your feet. "Not to be contrary, my Lord, but carrying a person downstairs is much more difficult than up."

"There is a carry we use in the Navy when a person is injured where two men link arms to make a chair." Edward demonstrated half of the position. "Would that work?"

Phil was familiar with the lift as she and her sisters had performed it many times. "Yes. I am sure two footmen could if they are available."

Lord Endelton looked at Edward before answering. "No need for footmen. The two of us are capable."

Phil pursed her lips. Alex would probably prefer footmen, but arguing would be impolite. "Very well. My sister insists she walk between the front door and the carriage. She doesn't want to give your neighbors cause to talk."

"I doubt they are sitting at the window watching," said Lord Endelton.

Edward laughed. "Three doors down, there is a woman almost always sitting at the window when we come."

"I've never noticed." The Lord's brow crinkled. "Three doors down? The dowager countess. She doesn't get out much in society."

Exactly the kind of observation she and Alex wished to avoid.

"Thank you. I must return to my sister now." Phil bobbed her head and hurried from the room. Lord Endelton was entirely too kind. His willingness to help her sister went well beyond what she expected from any member of the ton, including Edward. Perhaps, despite his list, there was a way to convince him Alex was his perfect match, as he was definitely a good match for her sister. And those soft brown eyes were not at all difficult to look at, especially when he smiled.

# FOURTEEN

hat is the invitation for?" asked Alex from where she sat propped up on the settee in the corner of the sitting room.

"A soiree Wednesday night. Do you think you can come?" Phil handed the cream paper to her sister.

"Is our aunt familiar with the house?"

"I didn't ask."

"If there are not too many stairs. I can manage with my cane and a firm arm to hold."

Phil found their aunt in her private parlor, writing at her desk.

"Are you familiar with Lady Milburn's house?"

Lady Healand tapped her jaw. "I haven't been there for two or three years. Other than a vibrant red walled room, I don't remember much. Why?"

"Alex thought she could attend a soiree, if there were not too many stairs."

Her aunt held out her hand for the card. "Ah, she resides in Grosvenor Square. So no more than a few stairs into the house."

Grosvenor Square? Lord Endelton lived there. Phil wondered if he might be behind the invitation. "I'll let Alex know. I think we can safely accept."

"I'll write to her now. There is also a ball on Saturday. I know Alex cannot attend, but you should go. And the Godderidges have invited us to another card evening. Will the stairs be an issue there?"

Although the card room was on an upper floor, the stairs were wide and there should be someone to help Alex. "I believe we can attend."

"There are two more letters for you. They were included inside of mine." Aunt Healand handed Phil the still-sealed missives. The one from grandfather was addressed to Alexandra, while the one from father was for her.

Phil considered tossing father's in the fire unopened. It could not contain any encouraging news. "Thank you. Is there anything else?"

"Yes, we will make calls today. I cannot have you hiding away simply because your sister is unable to accompany us as yet. Wear your green dress, please."

"Yes, Aunt." Phil tried to hide her reactions. Making calls was akin to being on the baker's shelf for everyone to scrutinize. Were you too thin or too brown? And the green dress scratched at the back of her neck every time she moved. Which was probably why Aunt chose it. Phil's posture in the dress was necessarily impeccable. It was the only way to avoid the scratchy spot.

Phil returned to the parlor where she'd left Alex. "We have letters. Should we read them or guess what is in them?"

Alex took the letters and tapped one against her head. "And the great Alexandra will now divine the contents of the letters. Father's requires no imagination at all. He wants to know if you have secured a titled gentleman of no less than ten thousand a year. He will berate me for stalling your progress, likely hinting at calling me home, as Rose is giving Jane fits in the classroom and George is squandering the household budget because they had both chicken and beef last week."

Phil took the letter back and broke the seal. "Not bad. Only father is hoping for at least twelve a year. He wonders why I didn't secure Lord Endelton while we were at his residence. And they had fish three times last week, hence, George is still in trouble." Phil paused. "And worse, Father's friend is seeking a wife. He has offered to Father for me. As he needs someone quote, 'who can keep up with his five motherless children and continue to provide for the expansion of the future of the family,' unquote."

"I can't imagine any friend of Father's being a good husband." Alex was right. Father's friends likely gambled in excess, and an instant family of five children made Phil shudder.

Phil read the rest of the letter. "The friend only has five thousand a year. As such, Father has not yet given him an answer."

"Does Father name his friend?"

"No, but it shouldn't be hard to discover who he might be. There cannot be many widowers with five thousand a year and five children."

"How old are the children?" asked Alex.

"Another detail Father didn't see fit to share." The oldest could easily be ten or older, more than half Phil's age.

"Do you think it is an actual threat? Father could try to scare you into making a hasty match."

"I have had no opportunity to make a match, although our aunt is determined to correct that. I am going to go calling with her this afternoon. She has accepted an invitation to a ball and another evening at Lord and Lady Godderidge's, which, of course, includes you."

"And the soiree?"

"It is at Grosvenor Square, so, only a few steps into the house."

"Have you heard from Moriah about the date for our theater outing?"

In the ten days since quitting the Endelton's home, she had no word from any of the family other than Deborah who had visited with Lady Godderidge. Obviously, she would have to find her own prospects. As for her side of the bargain, she had yet to meet most of the women on his suitable list. "No. My hope that the duke refused the use of his box may have come to fruition. He must have succeeded in warning Lord Endelton off since neither of us are a suitable match in the Duke's estimation. Although I do pity poor Moriah."

Alex cocked her head. "You know, whenever you mention Lord Endelton's name, your voice changes? Are you sure you are unaffected by him?"

"I don't see how it signifies. Lord Endelton was kind to you, and I will always think of him fondly. But I will not pursue him to please Father, especially when the viscount has expressed I would be an unsuitable match for him."

Alex frowned and tapped their grandfather's missive against her head. "The great Alexandra is having difficulty with this one. It contains a bank note or a mention of funds given to our aunt."

"That is not mystical. Grandfather always sends you some little thing."

Alex opened the letter and pulled out a banknote.

"See, I was correct." Phil laughed.

"Hush or I shan't tell you a word." Alex read silently. "I would have never guessed this—Grandfather is interested in hiring Lord Endelton's valet. And he is insisting his gardener name a rose Hannah for mother."

"I doubt Lord Endelton will want to give up his valet. Does he mention the color of the rose?"

"No."

"I hope it is yellow. What of the rest?"

Alex read silently for a moment, then gasped. "Grandfather has finally received a letter back from his cousin in America. The cousin is the one who relinquished the title, and he recently celebrated his ninety-fourth birthday. However, it is unlikely the cousin will return to England, the rigors of the journey being too great." Alex set the letter in her lap. "I wish I could see the original letter from my cousin. I believe there would be much more to the story. Can you imagine a country where one's ancestry doesn't determine one's future?"

"It wouldn't change much for us. We'd still be dependent on our husbands for our livelihood."

"But wouldn't we have more choices?"

"I doubt a wealthy merchant wants his daughter running off with the baker's son any more than Father would want us marrying the farmer's son."

Alex pursed her lips. "In my case, it wouldn't make a difference at all. Regardless of class, I am not marriageable. I am completely unsuited to any type of work other than perhaps being a seamstress. I have only the slightest chance among the wealthy and who among the lower classes would think a one-legged wife would be of any use."

"Don't talk like that. Someone could very well fall in love with you."

"Phil, love has very little to do with it. A man marries because he believes his wife can produce an heir and help improve his station. Not one where father can damage his reputation. Although Father wants a titled son-in-law, you'd be far better off with a merchant or landowner with no title. Even if they had political aspirations, Father's reputation would have little effect on them."

"You have been putting more thought into this, I see."

"At the Duke of Aylton's ball, before my mishap, I was counting the people in the room. Even excluding the women who looked to be over twenty-five, women far outnumbered the men. Among the debutantes, there were few who were not in one way or another considered pretty. And the ones that were not, wore the finest silks and the most expensive jewelry. Some of the men seemed to be less careful in their appearance, which as the minority, they can be. It is much like when we go to market, and everyone has an abundance of carrots and is trying to convince everyone their carrots are the best."

"So now we are no more than carrots?"

"Sadly, yes." Alex set the letter in her lap. "And there are far too many of them for sale."

"That must be the least romantic marriage analogy ever made."

"Probably. However, it proves my point. You can do very little to choose your husband, but anything will be better than whom Father chooses."

Weariness consumed Phil. She was tired of every conversation coming back to marriage. "Did Grandfather say anything else?"

"He is coming to Town. Apparently, there is some issue before the House of Lords he wants to weigh in on. He has instructed Aunt he wants her to hold a dinner with an evening of music in three weeks. He wants us to play."

Phil buried her head in her hands. "Doesn't he know I've hardly practiced in months? At least you'll be shown off to an advantage."

The rooms at White's were unusually full. Michael inquired if his cousin might be found and was directed to a small sitting area far from the windows.

"This is where you've taken to hiding out?"

Richard grunted.

Michael didn't wait for an invitation before sitting. His move elicited another grunt from his cousin. "Tell me, what has you in such a good mood on this rainy day?"

"Against my wishes, the duchess is planning a house party, immediately after the Season is over at Redbridge House." The name belied the size of the duke's country estate.

"And can you not prevent it?"

"It is not easy. She knows the only thing I require of her is to produce an heir. After the house party is over, she claims she will stay in the same house with me for six months."

Michael wasn't sure what to say. His cousin had slipped into delicate matters, which he had no experience with. "Will a house party be terrible?"

"It was at a house party where I was ensnared into marriage. I fear other men may meet the same fate. The duchess' younger sister is not experiencing a successful Season. It is her third." Richard drank a sip of the amber liquid from the glass he held. If Michael was to guess, his cousin's drink contained more water than alcohol. Richard never drank above a few sips a day and often held the same glass for an entire evening without drinking at all. "I have, however, had you stricken from the guest list. If she invites you, refuse any way you can."

"Easy enough. I have promised Mother and Moriah I would take them to Terrace Hall as soon as the session ends. It seems none of us prefer city life."

"I thought Moriah was rather anxious to at least see some of the sites. Or is that not why you asked if you could use my box?"

"My purpose in seeking you out is the loan of the box. You have yet to answer, if I may."

"Will a week from tomorrow suit?"

"I believe so. Moriah has invited the Lightwood sisters, and I will also need to check with their schedules."

"I thought you had finished with Sir Lightwood's daughters."

"I cannot entirely avoid the connection. Edward Godderidge's mother is quite fond of the girls. There are events Deborah simply insists I attend when they're in attendance."

Richard called over a staff member and exchanged his glass for a cup of tea. "There are some days it is more difficult to keep my vow to never drink in excess again."

Michael also ordered a cup of tea to support his cousin.

"Is there no way out of the theater invitation to the Lightwoods?"

"Moriah has her heart set on it." And Michael was rather eager to speak with Miss Philippa again. She was the most diverting woman he'd ever met. He hadn't had a chance to converse with her since they left his home last week. Only intelligence came through Deborah, who'd called upon Lady Healand the day before last and found the sisters both quite delighted in receiving callers.

"And who else have you invited?"

"Deborah and Edward, of course. Oh, and Mother."

"Then there is still room in the box. Perhaps I shall bring my mother and the duchess along."

"Will your wife come with you?" As soon as he said the words, he knew he had misspoken.

"Perhaps not. But I should endeavor to make a gesture all the same. She frequents the box often enough on her own."

Moriah had pointed out more than once the duke's box was the place to be seen at the theater, although Richard rarely attended. Having the Lightwood sisters welcome in the duke's box might help them overcome any stigma from their father's name. It would do well in keeping his deal with Miss Philippa to have her there. He wondered if she had yet found any information about who would make him a suitable wife. "Do you know what is playing?"

"I have no idea. But does it matter? Most do not go to the theater for the production." Richard finished his tea. "I need to speak to a few men about my stand on the upcoming vote. Would you like to come along?"

"In one minute. I need to make a note to tell Moriah the date of our adventure to the theater and to make sure an invitation is sent to the Misses Lightwood." Michael scribbled on his ever-present paper. Some people remembered their obligations. Michael found it better to write them down, so they didn't wake him in the middle of the night with a persistent nagging.

Before he could leave, Mr. Newcomb entered the room and took Richard's vacated seat. "Endelton, good to see you. I see you are out of mourning. Hunting for a wife, too?"

Something about Newcomb's voice caused Michael to want to move away. It had always been thus. When did Newcomb become a member? Apparently, the money his father made opened doors in every quarter. "I am hoping to find one."

"Endelton, you are too droll. Of course it is a competition. Despite the number of potential mates this Season, there are so few women who possess the proper qualities for a wife. Too many have gotten it into their heads they can lead their husband around like a prize bull, bending them to their will."

At Terrace Hall, there was a fair amount of cattle. It was no easy job leading around a bull. Not wanting to prolong the conversation, Michael didn't comment.

"Some don't act like they have husbands at all. I just saw the Duke of Aylton pass by. Now take his wife. If she was mine, I'd lock her up and never let her leave the house, at least not until she produced the heir and the spare. But then men like him get the wives they deserve."

Michael wasn't prone to fighting, but he wanted to defend Richard. "What do you mean?"

"Everyone knows he tried to bed her before he wed her. Who knows how many others he ruined for their husbands?"

Leaping to his feet with hands fisted, Michael tried to form the words to tell the man his information was wrong. Deep down, he knew Richard wouldn't want anything said. He forced his hands to relax and left without saying a word.

Behind him, he thought he heard Newcomb call him a derogatory name. Michael took a deep breath and walked on.

# FIFTEEN

*It is entirely possible to be lonely in a crowded room.* The truthfulness of the thought struck Phil as she kept up with her aunt in the crush of Almack's. Unlike the duke's ball, Aunt Healand seemed determined to introduce Phil to every eligible bachelor in the room. The only explanation was her father had written to her aunt about the threatened marriage offer.

Already she'd been introduced to four men, one of which had asked her to dance the second set. The others had been polite. Phil pictured herself as a carrot being dragged around by its green top from buyer to buyer. A giggle welled up inside, and she quickly hid behind her fan.

At last, Aunt Healand stopped at a group of women, each old enough to be chaperoning their own children. Phil recognized the last name of the first woman she was introduced to from the list in Lord Endelton's book. The next lady also shared a name with the list. As the women talked, they revealed their daughters were dancing the current set. If nothing else, Phil could keep her promise to Lord Endelton and learn something from the women. Sadly, the conversation centered on silks, ribbons, and the difficulty of getting a good maid.

Phil bit her lip. Running her father's house for the last several years taught her most servants, when paid reasonably and treated kindly, were more than adequate for the job, and most even excellent. It couldn't be so different in the city, could it? Aunt Healand's staff was superior, as far as Phil could tell. A fact which her aunt related to the other women, effectively ending the discussion.

The woman with the most elaborate turban spoke. "Lady Healand, I thought you had two nieces with you for the Season."

Aunt dipped her fan. "Yes, I do. Miss Alexandra was unable to attend this evening."

"I heard she required a cane. Could she not get a voucher because of it?" asked the mother of the first woman on the list. Her condescending tone grated on Phil's nerves.

Aunt made a show of looking around the room, knowing that because of her leg, Alex hadn't applied for a voucher. "I see several people with canes, and they seem to enjoy the evening. Obviously the matrons don't give a fig about canes."

"But they are men."

"What of the Dowager Duchess Aylton?" asked Aunt Healand.

The woman's fan moved faster. "Entirely different. She is not here to find a husband."

"Says whom? She has been widowed nearly as long as I have. And I have never closed my mind to the possibility of finding love again."

Phil raised her fan to cover the smile. Oh, to be as free as her aunt in stating her mind.

The large turbaned woman was not to be dissuaded. "The duchess only uses a cane for show, not because she is missing a limb."

Two of the other women's eyes grew wide and one's jaw dropped. Most scrambled for their fans.

Aunt Healand tilted her head. "Listening to gossip again?"

"It isn't gossip. My Christina saw your nieces when they left the Duke of Aylton's ball." The woman lifted her chin.

Phil wondered where Lady Christina could have been. She'd seen no one in the garden. There were places someone could have concealed themselves. But why would one hide in a garden alone?

Aunt Healand raised her brow and turned to Phil. "I thought you said you left through the garden. You didn't happen to meet Lady Christina, did you?"

Surprised her aunt confirmed they left the ball, Phil answered as quickly as she could. "I've never had the pleasure."

Lady Christina's mother grasped the implication and stepped back. "Perhaps my daughter was mistaken. It was dark, and how could she see from such a distance?"

The set ended, and the dancers came to join those on the edge. There was a moment of introductions. The woman who Lord Endelton returned was the infamous Lady Christina. Phil met Miss Brand, another woman on the list. She was shorter than the rest, and her enormous eyes made her look younger than the average debutante.

After a moment of brief, meaningless conversation about the excellence of the musicians, the next set was called, disrupting the conversation.

A man in a bright orange vest with what appeared to be golden threads claimed his dance with Lady Christina. Lord Endelton escorted Miss Brand to the floor. One of the men Phil had been introduced to when they first entered appeared at her side. She allowed him to escort her to the floor while she tried to place his name.

"Do you know Lady Christina well?" he asked.

"No, I only met her this evening." Their conversation ended by necessity as they took their places for the country dance. Much to Phil's dismay, Lady Christina took the place at Phil's left. From the smile on her partner's face, his good fortune did not disappoint him.

Lady Christina hadn't said a word to Phil beyond the required 'pleased to meet you' and Phil was already decided against her. The daughter might not be as terrible as the mother. The music started, and they wove their way through the steps. Her partner didn't talk when given the chance, not even to ask innocuous questions about her favorite dance or the weather. He missed more than one step while paying more attention to the other women in the set, in particular, to Lady Christina. By the time the set ended, Phil counted herself fortunate her toes had only been trod upon twice.

A Mr. Newcomb claimed her next dance. The colors of his clothing were not as bright as some of the men's, but they were of the finest quality. Unlike her other partners, he did talk of the weather and of the dancers before getting to more personal questions. "Lady Healand is your aunt correct?"

"Yes."

"She is the Earl of Whitstone's daughter?"

"Yes."

This time he didn't respond, other than with a tight smile. Obviously, the carrot's pedigree mattered. Her next turn brought her beside a redheaded man. A carrot top looking for a carrot. Phil was suddenly glad her dark blond hair didn't boast a bit of auburn.

Mr. Newcomb rejoined her in the next step. "When at home, do you attend church?"

"Of course." What an odd question. Everyone went to church.

"And do you read the Bible daily?"

Phil owned a small prayer book and a New Testament, but she rarely opened them to read for pleasure. "Not as often as I should."

Mr. Newcomb's eyebrows lowered at her response, but he made no comment as the set ended.

She found her aunt with another group of chaperones. Christina's mother wasn't among them.

"There you are Philippa. Have you met my friend Dowager Duchess Aylton?"

Phil curtsied. "We were introduced at the ball."

"Oh yes, you were with your sister. Do pass on my wishes for her speedy recovery."

"Yes, your Grace."

"You know my nephew, Lord Endelton?"

"We are acquainted."

The women scrutinized her from the toes of the slipper peeking out from under her hem to the little flowers Green had woven around her coiffure. "Are you pursuing him?"

Phil looked the duchess in the eye when she answered. "No."

The duchess stared back until Phil blinked. "That is what my son said. Pardon me for not believing him."

As happened with all awkward conversations, the person discussed appeared.

Lord Endelton greeted all the women by rank, starting with his aunt and ending with Phil. She couldn't help but smile at his stiff correctness.

"Miss Philippa, has someone claimed this set?"

"No."

"Will you do me the honor?"

"Of course." Phil laid her hand on his arm and allowed Lord Endelton to lead her to the floor. Several women glared icily at her.

Phil waited until they took their positions at the bottom of the line to speak. "It seems your dancing with me is cause for speculation."

"I didn't realize. My apologies." Michael didn't understand exactly what he was apologizing for. Only Deborah had told him it was safest to apologize to a woman if she ever thought he was in the wrong.

Miss Philippa gave the slightest shake to her head. "There is naught to do about it now. I considered twisting my ankle, however rumors about my sister are already filtering through the ton. If you carried me from the dance floor, it would go no better for either of us."

"Rumors? I hope you don't think I started them."

"No. You didn't."

At last, it was their turn to enter the floor. He led her through a promenade step and reminded himself this dance was about gaining information. "The gentleman you danced with two sets prior to this is desperate for funds."

"That explains his lack of attention, then. My dowery isn't large enough to tempt him." Her laugh blended with the music.

"Have you found anything out about my list?"

"I met two of the women this evening so briefly, I could not sketch their characters with any certainty." She looked away for part of her delivery.

"You hesitated."

"I met Lady Christina's mother long enough to hope to never be subject to her again."

"Like mother, like daughter?"

"Not necessarily." A crease appeared on Miss Philippa's brow. He wished to smooth it away. "For me, being like my mother would be the highest of all compliments, yet

I don't think I measure up. I have part of my father in me too, although I hope it's not the worst part."

"I have seen nothing of your father in you."

"Have you ever met him?"

Michael took a moment to reflect. "I've seen him, but I don't think I've ever been introduced. What I know is solely based on his reputation, and you are nothing like I would expect based on that knowledge."

"Then it would be wrong of me to set you against Lady Christina based on my interaction with her mother."

Michael nodded, and they danced the next few steps in silence. "As for my end of the bargain, I am also at a loss. It seems most men are something of a scoundrel or they are boorish. I can't see you married to anyone as supercilious as Mr. Newcomb. Although I can find no other faults."

"Please do not make me laugh, too. There are too many eyes on us."

"I didn't mean to make you laugh. I am not sure why you find the lack of integrous men humorous."

"I don't know how to explain."

Michael wished she could. There was nothing in his peers' conduct he could see to laugh about. How his sisters found such good matches was surprising. Richard always placed the blame on conniving women, but had he taken an honest look at his own peers?

They stepped closer together.

"You are frowning. Is something wrong?"

Endeavoring to smile, Michael answered, "Nothing really."

"Then pretend to not be upset."

He needed to change the subject. "I haven't received your reply to the invitation to the theater."

Those gray eyes widened. "We have received no invitation."

"You did not? I thought I—" Michael tried to recall asking his mother to send the invitation and could not. "Oh, I may have neglected—a week from yesterday. I know I was going to ask Mother—"

"As far as I know, our schedule is open. Is your mother here?"

"No. But Deborah and Edward were going to attend, although I haven't seen them tonight either. If you could ask Deborah—" Michael lost his thoughts when she looked up at him. "That is terribly wrong of me, isn't it?"

"It is very perplexing." Her face didn't show any anger, but he couldn't be sure.

What a muddle he'd made. Dancing the wrong dance, forgetting the invitation. And according to Edward, Deborah, and Richard, his agreement with Miss Philippa was daft. The music ended, saving him from any more faux pas for the evening. Michael returned her to her aunt and made his escape. He must find his sister before he forgot about the theater again.

# SIXTEEN

The days passed faster than she could count. Finally, Alex could join her for some entertainment. Even if the singer was tone deaf, tonight would be more fun with her sister. Phil stood near the base of a grand staircase with Alex. The music room in the Milburn's townhouse was situated on the floor above. Phil silently communicated her concerns to her sister. What they needed was some gallant gentleman to offer Alex his arm. Between his arm and the banister, Alex could safely ascend the stairs. Phil's help would be more obvious.

Phil searched for an unattached gentleman. Lord Endelton entered and immediately sought out Lady Christina. There would be no help in that quarter. They hadn't been introduced to the several other men waiting to mount the stairs. Aunt Healand chatted with a gentleman. Phil hoped he might have a son in attendance.

At the butler's invitation, guests moved from the entrance hall to the stairs. Phil and Alex stepped back. Lord Endelton tipped his head in greeting, as did Lady Christina, but neither of them paused. Aunt Healand took the arm of the gentleman she'd been conversing with. A younger man followed them. Their aunt introduced them as Lord Murdock and his son.

The son offered his arm to Phil. She stepped aside.

"My sister is the eldest." Phil said in way of explanation.

He glanced at Alex's cane and his lip curled for a moment. Under his father's withering stare, he offered his arm to Alex. Phil took Alex's cane so her sister could hold the banister, and walked as close as she dared, not trusting the young gentleman to support Alex if she needed it. At the door of the music room, the son abandoned them. Phil and Alex found seats near the back of the almost full room.

Directly in front of them sat Lady Christina and her mother. Lord Endelton was seated with them. Phil hoped the mother wouldn't turn to speak with them.

Lady Milburn stood and introduced the pianist visiting from Italy and his sister, who was singing. A hush fell over the room. For a blissful hour, Phil let her mind wander the images the music brought to mind.

A break was announced, and refreshments provided. Phil breathed a sigh of relief when Lady Christina and her mother exited to the adjacent refreshment area with Lord Endelton.

"I suppose we should go see and be seen." Alex rose unassisted from her chair.

They found their aunt still in the company of Lord Murdock and his son, the latter of the two taking the time to introduce the sisters to his friends. Among them was Mr. Newcomb, the same who Lord Endelton labeled "supercilious" and who danced with her at the last ball. Curiosity kept her in conversation with Mr. Newcomb. What exactly made a man not of the clergy supercilious?

"Have you been to see the lions at the Tower yet?" asked Mr. Newcomb.

"We have not had the pleasure." Alex, who stood closer to him, answered.

"You really should endeavor to go. And of course, you have visited Vauxhall."

Phil took her turn to answer. "I'm afraid we have not been there either."

Mr. Newcomb looked from one sister to another. "You go on outings together?"

"Usually. Don't most sisters?" asked Phil.

"I wouldn't know. I have no sisters." Mr. Newcomb raised his brows as if he had never contemplated such a thing.

Phil wondered where his questions were leading, as he didn't seem to be offering to take them to either place. "Do you have brothers?"

"Three younger ones. They're all in school."

Alex opened her mouth to ask a question at the same time the announcement was made the musicians would continue in five minutes.

Mr. Newcomb offered one arm to each sister to escort them back. Because of the crowd, Phil demurred and stepped back. Mr. Newcomb responded with a raised brow but continued to escort Alex to their previous seats. Many people took the opportunity to sit in different locations, among them were Lady Christina and her mother. However, Lord Endelton returned to his previous seat, accompanied by his mother.

He turned in the chair and spoke in a low voice. "You should have warned me."

"Warned you?"

Lord Endelton scowled. "About—"

Lady Milburn interrupted his next words, announcing the remainder of the program. His mother rapped his knee with her fan, and Lord Endelton gave one more accusatory glare before turning to face the front.

Phil exchanged a look with Alex, who seemed as perplexed as she.

Michael could not focus on the words of the song, so he only caught bits and pieces of Italian, enough to know the women sang of a lost love. Miss Philippa should have been more forthcoming about her objections to Lady Christina. Had he known the woman had witnessed his departure from Richard's ball, he would have been more careful. Instead, Lady Christina's mother had nearly trapped him into admitting Miss Lightwood used a prosthetic. He could only hope his face hadn't betrayed the truth of his knowledge.

The music changed, but his mood did not. Miss Philippa should have been firmer in her objection. And as far as mother being like daughter, Lady Christina shared her mother's knack of pointing out the flaws in others. They had even belittled the Italian soprano for singing in Italian. Italian arias were meant to be sung in Italian. Would they have them performed in German? A thought he had shared with Lady Christina and offended her in some way.

Good riddance. Another name gone from his list. He could have spent the evening cultivating another introduction if it hadn't been for Miss Philippa. Why did any woman agree to help him?

The sharp tap of his mother's fan on his knee reminded him to clap. Around him, people stood. Was the evening over? Michael stood and helped his mother.

"You are still scowling. I was afraid you might scare the soprano with your expression. I'm going to speak with Lady Milburn. I'll meet you in the entry hall to walk home." His mother left him standing between the rows of seats. Behind him, only Miss Lightwood and Miss Philippa remained.

He turned to face them. "Why didn't you tell me the nature of Lady Christina's gossip?"

Miss Philippa's jaw tightened, and she hissed back at him. "Hush, do you want the entire room to hear?"

The room was crowded enough. Michael doubted anyone noticed. Still, he looked around. "She said she saw us leaving and that Miss Lightwood has—"

Miss Philippa's hand on his arm stopped his next words. "I am aware of what she thought she saw."

"Then you knew and didn't warn me?"

"I only heard her mother's thoughts on the matter. Aunt Healand ended the conversation by asking how the daughter saw us if we left through the garden."

"Why would that stop the conversation?"

"Because she could have only seen if she was in the garden. I looked for others around us and saw no one. A single woman in the garden will cause as much speculation as her accusations against Alex—andra." She stuttered on her sister's name.

What did she say? Lady Christina must have been in the garden. What of their deal? Two things which should have been reported to him were not. "You should have informed me of her being in the garden. I don't want to associate with—"

Miss Lightwood pointed her fan at him. "You are jumping to conclusions. Which I believe my sister tried not to do. There could have been any number of reasons for someone to be in a garden. Or she could be repeating what a servant told her. Now, will the two of you stop with this?"

Michael wanted to point out it was Miss Philippa's fault, however, Miss Lightwood's plea gave him pause. "Perhaps everyone is correct, and I should have never asked for your help."

"I believe it was a poor choice on both our parts. Good evening." Phil turned away with her sister in tow.

Michael watched them for several seconds before he remembered the stairs. He hurried after them. "Miss Lightwood, allow me to see you down the stairs."

The sisters looked at each other for a long moment before Miss Lightwood disengaged her arm from her sister's. "Thank you, Lord Endelton."

Miss Philippa followed behind them. Even he could tell she was not happy with him. He hadn't done anything. He'd been honest in his opinion of Mr. Newcomb, for example. And she'd chosen to ignore his advice and have a lengthy conversation with the man. In fact, she had paused to speak with him again.

Yes, it was best if their agreement ended. She had been of no help whatsoever. A tug on his arm caused him to look up as they reached the top of the staircase.

"Would you mind slowing down?" Miss Lightwood's face looked slightly pale.

"My apologies. I was thinking—"

"More like being upset with my sister. Which I understand. We have had our upsets from time to time. I suspect even the closest of friends do. She really wanted to help you."

Michael nodded and paid extra attention to the stairs. Miss Lightwood was the innocent party in all of this. His anger should not cause her any additional harm. They reached the bottom without incident, and Miss Lightwood removed her hand from his arm. It dismayed Michael to realize Miss Philippa still stood near the top of the stairs with Mr. Newcomb. Why exactly that bothered him, he couldn't say.

"Is the invitation still open for tomorrow night?" Miss Lightwood's question reminded him to look away.

"Tomorrow night?"

"The theater?"

"Of course. Moriah will be devastated if you don't come. And I see no reason my disagreement with your sister should curtail your happiness."

"I understand it is very difficult to maintain friendships with the opposite sex during the period of courtship. Or at least the novels I have read give me that impression."

"Are you saying your sister and I would be better off as mere acquaintances?"

"It would be the proper course of action."

Michael felt himself frowning and worked to keep it from showing. "Your sister is one of the few people who seems to understand me."

Miss Lightwood's laugh was not nearly as musical as her sister's. "I believe you understand people better than you think you do."

Miss Philippa and Mr. Newcomb finally descended the staircase. He overheard Mr. Newcomb ask Miss Philippa when their at-home hours were. The man really was wrong for Miss Philippa. He should not be visiting her at all.

Lady Healand finished her conversation and joined their small group. "Nieces, we should go."

Michael leaned close to Miss Lightwood. "Do you require assistance to your carriage?"

"It would be most welcome." Miss Lightwood laid her hand on his arm. Mr. Newcomb escorted Miss Philippa out. Her laughter at something the man said hit Michael like a punch in the breadbasket. She should not be laughing with him. Mr. Newcomb was not the least bit funny.

# SEVENTEEN

Despite her best efforts, the tiny sniffle Phil awoke with refused to turn into a full-blown cold. She would have to attend the theater tonight. If she were very lucky, Lord Endelton would find a reason not to be there. She didn't want to converse with him, knowing he would inquire about Mr. Newcomb, and she would have to concede his correctness in the man's assessment. Not only was Mr. Newcomb supercilious, but he was also terribly boring, as she discovered on their first ride through Hyde Park. However, Mr. Newcomb seemed interested in her. And even without a title, his money should be more than enough to make Father happy.

Green finished with Alex's hair. The new arrangement was quite becoming.

Phil waited to take her turn in front of the mirror. "If I was not your sister, I would be quite jealous. You are truly one of the most beautiful women of the Season."

"Oh Phil, you exaggerate far too much. By the time Green is finished with your hair, there will be very little competition.

But I am glad you think I look well; I've been quite nervous about sitting in the Duke of Aylton's box."

"Why? I doubt the duke will be there."

"Just being in his box will get us noticed. Everyone will look at us."

Phil hadn't thought about everyone looking at them. She'd been so busy figuring out how to avoid Lord Endelton she hadn't thought about the other repercussions of the evening. Drat it all. Alex was correct. "Being seen sitting in one of the most distinguished boxes in the theater will have people at least curious and could benefit our social standing. If our father's reputation irrevocably damaged us, the duke would've never allowed us near his box."

"True. It is a great service Lord Endelton has provided. I hope you can lay aside your anger towards him to thank him properly."

Phil wasn't exactly angry with him. He'd jumped to con-clusions as fast as a rabbit leaping away from the gardener. Though she should have told him about Lady Christina's rumor about Peggy's existence. "Why don't you thank him?"

"Because both of us should. It isn't his fault your helping each other didn't work out. It was doomed from the start. Surely you saw that."

"Of course I did, but what was I to say? I'd discovered I'd been labeled as persona *non grata*, and you were also struck from the list. I couldn't very well tell him he was an idiot."

"Did you think he was an idiot at the time? I thought you thought he was being kind."

Phil thought back to the moments in the library. He had been in earnest, and he clearly hadn't meant to hurt her. In fact, he'd seemed completely unaware her unsuitability as a potential wife was anything but a well-known fact. There had been a genuine sincerity behind his offer. She'd known it was folly and told him as much, but as her host, she had hardly been able to argue. "You know how much he reminded me of our William? I am more upset at myself than him. I should've never been alone in the library with him in the first place."

Green tugged on Phil's hair harder than necessary. "That is why young ladies are to have chaperones. They keep you out of all sorts of trouble."

A knock on the door stopped the conversation. Aunt Healand walked in without waiting for them to answer. "Good, you're almost ready. Lord Endelton's carriage will be here any minute."

Phil turned from side to side to study the maid's handiwork. "Green, how come you never dressed our hair like this at home? I had no idea you had such a talent for it."

"At home, there is no one to see you. Would you have me style it thus for an errand to one of the tenant cottages or to help Miss Georgiana in the garden?"

Green's reply sent Alex into a fit of laughter.

Phil studied her sister. "Are you in pain tonight?"

"No. Why do you ask?"

"You've been laughing quite a bit. And I know the more you laugh, the more you're using it to hide your pain."

Alex threw up her hands. "With a sister like you, who needs a doctor? My hip hurts a bit. But it's nothing bad. The image of you working around the house with curls and pearl pins in your hair struck me as funny. Imagine what hair styles Rose would demand."

Green narrowed her eyes at Alex. "There isn't time for any of my tea, miss. I will have it ready for your return."

"Thank you, Green. You are far too good to me." Alex tugged on her long gloves.

"Come girls. We do not wish to keep Lord Endelton waiting." Aunt Healand rushed them out of the house.

The theater was as grand as Phil expected, and more so. At her elbow, Moriah could barely contain her raptures. They wound through the crowd, greeting people, and making and receiving introductions. The grand staircase had wide, even steps. Alex had no trouble navigating them, barely leaning on Phil's arm at all. The box itself was as Phil dreaded. The amazing view of the stage placed them in the perfect spot to be seen by absolutely everyone.

Moriah pointed to a seat near the front of the box. Phil followed, with Alex a step behind. Though lit, the area around their feet was still dim. A familiar and unwelcome thump sounded in the large box. Phil schooled her face to not wince for her sister. Peggy must have connected with one of the chair legs. There was nothing to be done for now but to pretend nothing happened.

Reflections of single-lens opera glasses flashed as Phil took her seat. Apparently, the popular accessory was used for more than watching the play. Aunt Healand had loaned a pair to each of them. Phil was overcome with a desire to pull hers out and peer back at the audience members in the other boxes.

Alex's hand atop hers stopped her. "You have time to look later. Ignore them for now."

Phil turned her attention to Moriah. "What do you think?"

"Isn't it splendid? So many fashionable people. Do you think the Prince will attend?"

"This isn't an opening night. He has most likely seen the play."

Moriah's face fell for a moment. She turned to look behind her. "Cousin Richard came with his wife."

As had Lieutenant Godderidge and his wife Deborah. The addition brought their number to ten, making the box quite full. The duchess moved to the front seats and signaled Moriah to join her. The duke stayed near the back, talking with Lord Endelton.

Alex leaned closer. "I'm afraid Peggy is damaged."

"Can you walk?"

"I think so, but she seems to be cracked on the shin." Alex tugged at her skirt above her right knee.

"Are you hurt?"

The crowd quieted as the curtain rose.

"No," whispered her sister.

Antonio entered the stage with his companions. "In sooth, I know not why I am so sad." And *The Merchant of Venice* began.

Phil was glad to be acquainted with the play. Aunt Healand told them of sitting through an entire German opera having no idea what the plot was about.

During the second act, Phil surreptitiously looked at the other audience members. Only a few seemed to be intent upon the box in which she sat; among them were Lady Christina and her mother, and Miss Simesson and her mother. It was difficult to see the expressions on their faces, yet something in them caused Phil to lower her opera glasses and wish to scoot back into the shadows.

Intermission came all too soon. Michael blinked at his surroundings. He should come to the theater more often. It was a most enjoyable pastime.

Beside him, Richard grumbled. "I detest intermission."

"Why?"

"You'll see."

Moriah joined them and spontaneously hugged Richard. "Thank you, cousin. This is the most remarkable evening of my life."

Richard's expression softened. "What has been your favorite part?"

"I like the actor who plays Shylock. Although the duchess says he is not nearly as fun at parties as his understudy. Does the duchess always talk so much in the theater? I can see for myself who is wearing the finest silks."

"Perhaps for the last half, you should move next to the Lightwood sisters or your mother and Lady Healand; they seem to enjoy the play much more." Richard's answer didn't satisfy the question. Meaning it was a polite thing people often said.

The first of several guests arrived at the door of the box. The first two men seemed surprised to see the duke and left quickly. Michael wished he could say the same for Mr. Newcomb, who took up a spot next to Miss Philippa and gave his own monologue critique of the play. For her part, Miss Philippa appeared not to mind at all.

Michael glanced again at Mr. Newcomb. He thought he understood his cousin's dislike of intermission. The last two acts passed without Michael's notice. He couldn't figure out why it should bother him Miss Philippa had found a suitor.

Another man entered the box speaking to no one in particular. "I intend to speak to my duchess."

The man stepped into the light. Mr. Duncan Kenworth possessed more gall than brains to appear in his half-brother's box when said half-brother was in attendance.

Richard's glower grew and his hands balled into fists. "Endelton, you had best distract me."

"Can you not tell him to leave?"

"He wants a fight," Richard spoke through a clenched jaw. "I will not give it in such a public place."

Edward joined them standing between Richard and his base-born half-brother. "My wife is enjoying herself immensely. Thank you for including us."

They chatted until the signal was given to end intermission. Mr. Newcomb left the box with a nod of his head to Michael. Mr. Kenworth left with a sneer.

Michael sat through the rest of the play, regretting they contained intermissions.

On the ride home, Moriah kept them all entertained recounting the evening, hardly allowing anyone else to speak. Miss Philippa encouraged his sister by asking questions, the answers of which she must have known.

"Are you courting Mr. Newcomb?"

"Moriah!" Michael's response matched his mother's.

Miss Philippa smiled good-naturedly. "I've only known him for a fortnight."

His sister continued, heedless of her impertinence. "But he came to see you in the box and mentioned he took you to Hyde Park. Men only take women for a drive to tell other men they are claiming someone as their own."

This time Miss Lightwood laughed. "I've never heard of it that way."

Mother had a firm grip on Moriah's arm, but his sister shook her off. "Everyone knows men do it to warn the competition."

"In my case, he has had no contenders to warn." Miss Philippa's admonition wasn't in her usual voice. Michael wished the carriage was better lit so he could see if she was frowning. There should be lines of men calling upon her. She was the nicest woman he'd met, and those eyes…

"Moriah, that is quite enough." The frustration in mother's voice was easier to discern.

Silence filled the coach.

They turned into Russell Square and stopped in front of Lady Healand's. Michael climbed down first and assisted the women.

First, Lady Healand. "Thank you for the wonderful evening."

Miss Lightwood handed Michael her cane before stepping down. Miss Philippa hovered behind as usual. Michael helped Miss Lightwood to the door. Surprisingly, Miss Philippa waited for him before descending.

"I see you've learned to wait."

"Falling on my face in the street doesn't make a good impression on people I meet." She smiled, but in the light of the streetlamp, he thought he saw a tear on her cheek.

"Are you alright?" Michael reached for the tear. It came off on his gloved finger.

Miss Philippa shook her head and hurried to the townhouse.

Michael waited until the butler closed the door before climbing back into the carriage and sitting across from his mother and Moriah who had traded seats to the front facing ones. His sister sat as far into the corner as she could on the seat with her arms crossed. Mother wore the exasperated expression she'd worn all too often when he was younger.

The ride home was painfully silent. As soon as they were in the door, Mother ordered tea and retired to her room.

Moriah hung back and followed Michael to his study. "Mum says I need to apologize to Miss Philippa."

Michael gestured to a seat. "Even I know better than to ask if someone is being courted in front of others."

"But you are her friend and have no intention of courting her."

"That doesn't signify."

"Yes, it does. Talk among friends is always different from in public."

All the rules his mother and older sisters drilled into him needed to be taught to Moriah, but he wasn't the one to educate her. "Friends also don't injure friends."

"I didn't hurt her."

He debated a moment before speaking. "Miss Philippa was crying when I helped her out of the carriage."

"Is that why you touched her cheek?"

Michael buried his face in his hands and groaned.

"Should I go up to bed?" Moriah's voice was tiny.

Michael dropped his arms and stepped closer to his sister. "Mori-ha-ha," he used her childhood name. "You are the best little sister. I love you." He held her for a long moment. He hadn't hugged her in ages. A funny lump formed in his throat, and he stepped back. "Now go to bed. And write an apology to Miss Philippa."

# EIGHTEEN

The footman brought in a vase of hothouse flowers, handing the card to Phil. Another gift from Mr. Newcomb. In the past fortnight, he had not allowed a day to go by without seeing her or sending something. True to Moriah's prediction, most men she'd been introduced to at the balls asked for one set and no more. None appeared during calling hours. Phil handed the card to her sister.

Alex read the card and raised one brow. "I think he's decided on you. Are you willing to accept his suit?"

"I do not know. I have found nothing objectionable about him. And I am sure his fortune will please Father even if his title won't."

"Do you have any feelings for Mr. Newcomb at all?"

Was indifference a feeling? Mr. Newcomb was kind enough. And he danced well. When they touched, it wasn't like when she danced with one of the rakish men who left her feeling as though she had been holding a snail. There was very little to wonder about. She never wondered what he was thinking, not like she did Lord Endelton. "You mean is he my Mr. Darcy? I have yet to see his country estate, so I don't know."

Alex laughed. "You know that's not what I mean."

"I think he is a good enough sort. He has not yet invaded my dreams. Yet, I believe we could be quite comfortable together."

"Then he is your Mr. Collins?"

"If you are going to equate every man to that novel, I will refuse to purchase another one by the author to read to you."

"Can I help it if the characterizations are so perfect? Is Mr. Newcomb a Mr. Collins?"

"Mr. Newcomb is not nearly as repulsive. Nor does he bow and simper to anyone. I think it will be a good fit with Father. Whomever we marry must be able to stand up to him."

"Will you be going to Hyde Park with him for another drive this afternoon?"

Phil read the card once again. "I have no reason not to."

"And if he proposes?"

In Phil's imagination, it wasn't Mr. Newcomb who proposed. "I doubt he has talked to Father yet. As such, I can avoid giving him an answer for now. Anyhow, I doubt he would propose today. Mr. Newcomb strikes me as a very methodical type of man. He often talks about his solicitor and business. I do not see him proposing before coming to a marriage settlement with Father."

The word *acquisition* came to mind. Mr. Newcomb had used the term in a conversation last week about some properties he was inquiring about. Mr. Newcomb wouldn't use the word to propose. Nevertheless, he would acquire a wife—one with the connections in the peerage he craved.

"It all sounds too businesslike."

"We knew our courtships would be, regardless of what the novels we read say. In the end, we'll both make the best matches for our futures." Love wasn't a feasible option.

"Don't you want something more? Before the accident, when we shared the dancing master with the Godderidges, and I would dance—" Alex paused for a long moment. "My heart would pound as fast as horses' hooves racing across the field. My palms would become moist. And when my partner smiled at me, it was all the worse. Have you never felt that?"

Her sister spoke of Edward. If Deborah wasn't so kind and witty, Phil would be disposed to not like her, simply because Alex had been deprived of her first love. Thinking of Deborah naturally brought thoughts of her brother, the viscount. Who else would she think of but Lord Endelton with her sister's question? But if Lord Endelton was to marry either of them, it would need to be Alex. No other gentleman of the ton had been as considerate of her sister's welfare. "I don't recall ever having sweaty palms."

"When Mr. Newcomb speaks, do you notice your heart beating faster?"

Phil could only shake her head. Such a feeling only happened once—no thrice. Each time, Lord Endelton had been near. In the library the day they had made that ridiculous agreement. At Almack's when he had danced with her. And last night, as she'd left the carriage. No, she had to be mistaken about the last one. It was only the shock of him touching her face. The embarrassment of having been caught crying for no reason she could discern. He was so kind, despite being in a disagreeable mood earlier. "I should go find Green; I'll need to wear a different dress on my outing."

Phil left the room and the painful discussion behind her. If Mr. Newcomb would ask for her, she would have him. No one else was vying for her hand. And if Lord Endelton's list was similar to that of other men's, they never would. Since the only other option was to marry Father's choice, the sanctimonious Mr. Newcomb was the better option. He didn't gamble or drink to excess as Father's acquaintance must. While he wasn't what she would call a kind man, he wasn't mean either. The worst part of their time together was she never was able to speak. One question needed to be answered before he proposed. Would he allow Alex to live with them and provide for her if necessary? He hadn't spoken to her sister at all and knew nothing about Peggy. Today at the park, she would try again. No matter how wealthy the man was, she wouldn't agree to marriage unless her potential husband agreed to care for Alex.

When Michael returned home, he was going to give Deborah a lecture.

"Go for a ride in the park in your curricle," she said.

"Best way to talk to a woman," she said.

"Very fashionable," she said.

And despite Moriah's opinion on being seen with a woman in the park meant he was ready to court her, he was not. Miss Abbott was one of the few remaining women on his list, and she had all but begged for a ride.

What Deborah hadn't told him was much more sinister. She neglected to tell him every time he hit a bump with his curricle, the woman at his side, Miss Abbott, would grab his arm, causing him to jerk the reins. Or he was expected to nod at people he passed, carry on a conversation with the woman next to him, and handle the horses at the same time. It was all too much. He would have been much better off with the open carriage and a driver. At least then he could work on making appropriate comments to the inane chatter coming out of Miss Abbott's mouth.

Apparently commenting that a certain woman's hat looked like a dead pheasant had not been appropriate. Most likely, Miss Abbott would refuse any efforts to continue his suit, which he didn't intend to pursue further anyway, beyond the obligatory pleasantries Deborah insisted upon. There really must be another way to find a wife. So far, all of Deborah's suggestions had not helped him in the least.

"Well?" Miss Abbott's question hung between them.

Michael did not know what she had been talking about. Had it been another hat? Or something of real import? Michael took his eyes off of the horses for a moment and glanced at her. The frown indicated she was not happy. Nevertheless, Michael risked asking what he shouldn't. "I'm sorry. Will you repeat the question?"

"I don't think you've heard a word I've said all afternoon. I think it is best you return me to my home."

"Yes, Miss Abbott."

Her frown deepened. Agreeing with her upset her more?

Michael focused on where he drove. They had a quarter of a circuit to go before they returned to the point where they had entered the park. Michael debated the merits of exiting the park sooner and driving around the perimeter. The one thing Deborah had gotten correct was that absolutely everyone would be out this sunny afternoon.

A shiny new curricle came from the other direction. Michael recognized the passenger before he did the driver. Miss Philippa. She would have laughed at his observation about the pheasant hat. She, however, wasn't laughing at all. Instead, she had the most passive expression on her face. Mr. Newcomb was doing all the talking. Miss Philippa's head bobbed like a duck on the water.

Mr. Newcomb slowed his curricle, which was now blocking Michael's path. "Endelton, stay on your side."

The man was right. Michael had drifted out of his lane. "I beg your pardon." He corrected the matter.

"How mortifying." Miss Abbott's words were low enough he almost missed them.

Finally, they reached the park gate, and Michael turned onto the street. Eventually, they stopped in front of Miss Abbott's house.

"Do not bother walking me to the door. It is obvious we do not suit." Unassisted, she hopped out and ran up her front stairs.

Michael drove to the Godderidge's townhouse. The butler showed him into the study, where Edward sat at his father's desk.

"Where is my sister?"

"Deborah is with my mother. Some issue with Isabel's dress and tonight's dinner."

"Oh. That." Michael had forgotten he was expected to attend. "Do you know the guest list?"

"No, sorry. I think Deborah included Miss Abbott for you."

"She'll likely beg off. We had a disastrous ride in the park. I can't believe Deborah suggested a curricle. Which I am returning. One should never ride in a curricle with another human."

"Why ever not? Deborah and I quite enjoy it."

"She probably doesn't yank on your arm each time you hit a bump."

Edward smiled. "Matter of fact, she does. One of my favorite parts of the ride is her clinging to me. That is the point of a curricle ride with a woman."

"However do you manage to drive straight?"

"I trust the horses. Don't tell me—you were holding those reins with a death grip again, weren't you?" Edward shook his head.

"I didn't want them to skit off."

"They won't. They are better trained than you are."

Michael crossed his arms. "I know how to drive."

"I know you do, as long as you are alone."

"I have no problem with my sisters or Mother riding with me."

Edward sighed. "So, how badly did it go?"

"Miss Abbott said we didn't suit and rushed to be away from me."

Edward's brow furrowed. "Well, this is the end of your list. We must find you someone else for a match."

"What do you mean? There are still two women on the list."

"They're both good friends with Miss Abbott."

"And?"

"Miss Abbott will tell tales about her horrid ride in the park, and they will side with her and avoid you. Although I doubt they will go as far as to give you the cut direct."

"Oh."

"Cheer up. There are many more debutantes, several on their second and third Seasons we can introduce you to."

"I've read about societies where a matchmaker facilitates the groom getting his bride. Arranged marriage sounds much easier."

Again, Edward laughed. His friend was quite annoying. There was nothing funny about the situation. "Your sister is doing her best at playing matchmaker."

"It isn't working."

"Have patience, my friend. There will be some fresh faces at my mother's party tonight. Perhaps one of them will suit."

"All I need is a reasonably respectable woman, preferably one I can talk with. I am adding conversation to the requirements. I must be able to converse with her." *Like Philippa.* Michael suspected the problem with the equation of finding a potential wife was him.

# NINETEEN

The carriage rumbled over the street, not unlike her afternoon ride with Mr. Newcomb. The sound of laughter from Aunt Healand and Alex was different in the extreme. Mirth and Mr. Newcomb were complete strangers. When Lord Endelton nearly ran into them, her giggle earned her a reproving look. After that, she didn't bring up the subject of Alex and spent the ride listening to Mr. Newcomb expound on the importance of quality tar in shipbuilding. Could she endure such conversations for the next forty years of her life?

They arrived at the Godderidge's. The liveried footman helped her down from the carriage. And she left all thoughts of Mr. Newcomb behind her. Perhaps there would be someone new to meet tonight.

A strange sense of repeating her own life tugged at Phil's mind and she entered the Godderidge's parlor behind Alex and their aunt. Phil took in the scene as she waited to be greeted by Lord Godderidge. At first glance, the event was the same as it had been the previous month. The longer she looked, the more differences she found. Standing next to her father, Isabel wore a new white dress, this one with a blue sash. Lady Godderidge moved around the room, making introductions. Judging by the few pale-colored dresses in the room, it appeared as if the men outnumbered the women. How odd. Their party arrived late. Could another party have been more delayed?

"Ah, Lady Healand, our little group is now complete." Lord Godderidge greeted their aunt warmly.

Phil looked over the guests. Her eyes locked with a pair of brown ones.

Lord Endelton.

She turned and took a deep breath before greeting Lord Godderidge and Isabel. Her friend leaned closer, "There is a Mr. Tomlins I think you will like."

The words echoed those of a month ago when Isabel had recommended Lord Endelton to her.

"He is standing next to Michael, I mean Lord Endelton."

*Michael.* The name fit him. Phil almost missed Isabel's next whispered sentence. "The man who is joining them is Sir Rothy, a widower with three children."

"Is that a warning?"

Color tinged Isabel's cheeks. "Mother wouldn't invite anyone unsuitable. Shall I have her introduce you?"

Was there a choice? "Of course."

"Come then. Both of you." Isabel looked meaningfully at Alex.

Phil allowed her sister to take her arm.

"Do you think they mean Sir Rothy is meant for me?" asked Alex.

"You don't think he is the man father wrote about, do you?" Phil observed Lord Endelton leaving the group of men. He must have realized she was coming over.

"Father would have mentioned the title, and he wrote five children." Alex's hold on Phil loosened as she dipped into a curtsy. "Lady Godderidge."

"Sir Rothy and Mr. Tomlins, may I introduce Miss Light-wood and her sister, Miss Philippa?"

"Pleasure."

The feeling of being watched tingled in the back of Phil's head. She touched the curl Green had draped over her shoulder when she styled it. Her hair was in place. There was no reason for anyone to be looking at her. Allowing Alex to answer the question, Phil nodded at the appropriate points in the conversation. She itched to turn and see who was behind her. Finally, dinner was announced, and Phil discreetly looked over her shoulder. No one was there.

Michael should not have been surprised the Godderidges included the Lightwoods to their party. Seeing Miss Philippa for a second time in one day did something odd to his heart. Unlike their encounter in the park, she smiled at him for a brief moment when their gazes met. There were more men than women, a problem Deborah blamed him for since Miss Abbott was among those who sent last-minute notes of apology rather than attend. Michael proceeded to the dining room without escorting anyone.

Despite the change in numbers, he found himself seated between two women. A Miss Burke, whom he had been introduced to moments earlier, and Miss Lightwood. The widower, Sir Rothy, on Miss Lightwood's far side, kept up a continual conversation while Mr. Tomlins on Miss Burke's other side spoke so much, Michael was surprised the man finished his soup. Michael attempted several times to ask Miss Burke a question, but before he could get a single word out, Mr. Tomlins had captured her attention again.

"Lord Endelton, is Moriah still in raptures from the evening in the theater?" asked Miss Lightwood.

"It is all we hear about. She is already begging for a second outing. I may have been unwise to take her to an event before her first Season."

"I'm sure after mourning for her father, she was eager to mark its end."

Michael paused his next bite. He never thought of marking the end of his mourning for his father, but he hadn't been as limited as Moriah. "Is that common?"

"I don't know. My sisters would have been happy with a diversion. I am not sure Jane has ever completely put off her mourning for our mother. She still refuses to wear anything but drab grays and browns. But we all found ways to mark the transition."

Nothing wrong with gray. Michael preferred it to some of the bright colors his mother insisted he purchase. Aware he was about to make some comment, he said the first thing which came to mind. "Miss Philippa?"

A smile warmed Miss Lightwood's face. "She purchased a new book."

"And you?"

"I listened to Phil read."

There was something in her smile Michael couldn't match to her words, so he nodded. "Do you advise I should take Moriah to the theater again?"

Miss Lightwood's face pinched. "No, I don't believe I said you should take her again. I only meant I could understand her desire to do something new. She will have her first Season next year, won't she?"

"Mother insists upon it." Michael would like to put such a thing off indefinitely. He was having a difficult time finding his own wife. How could he decide if his sister's suitors were worthy?

Another course was served, and Michael once again found himself listening to the surrounding people rather than participating in a conversation. The loud clatter of silver hitting porcelain followed by a gasp drew his attention. Across the table, Miss Philippa's mouth stood agape. While wine sauce dripped down her dress, the foot man behind scrambled to offer her a cloth. A maid appeared at the footman's elbow.

Miss Philippa held the towel to her chest. "My apologies. I'm afraid I reached for my cup at the most inopportune moment." She rose and followed the maid out of the room.

Next to him, Miss Burke spoke. "It was entirely the footman's fault. He should be released from service."

Miss Lightwood leaned forward. "Mishaps happen to all of us. My sister would be mortified if he were dismissed."

"But her dress is ruined."

"And a spill is the reason to ruin a man's life?"

"He is incompetent." Miss Burke flicked her hand before reaching for her glass.

"My sister said she is at fault," said Miss Lightwood.

"Lord Endelton, would you dismiss him?" asked Miss Burke.

"I see no cause to. Unless it was discovered it was a deliberate act." Michael looked to the empty chair where Miss Philippa's meal had been cleared.

Miss Burke leaned away. "How ever do you run your house if you are so lenient with your servants?"

"Under my mother's guidance, my household runs quite well."

"I'm sure it does." Miss Burke's words were kind, but something about the way they were said came off wrong. Was this the sarcasm Deborah and Julia explained to him?

"My sister is capable of seeing after herself. I am sure I don't need to go after her," Miss Lightwood spoke to Sir Rothy, her words were not meant for him. However, Michael couldn't agree more.

Sir Rothy said something else Michael missed.

Dinner concluded with no other excitement, and the ladies left for the parlor. Lord Godderidge passed around the port.

Michael found Edward at the opposite end of the room. "Would it bother your mother much if I left? It would even up her numbers a bit."

"Have you already decided against Miss Burke?"

"She thought the footman should be let go over a single spill."

"Well, she is the only woman here who could be added to your list."

Michael shook his head. Poetry spoke of courtship as enjoyable. His attempts found little joy in it. "The infernal list should be tossed in the Thames and drowned for all the good it has done me."

"Come now, it isn't that bad, is it?"

"Remember in school when we were asked to write on a topic and whatever the subject was, it became the most difficult idea to explain, and then, the day after the paper was graded, you had a thousand ideas?"

"Yes."

"I must find a wife, and it is the most insurmountable task of my life."

"Then you must be doing something wrong."

"That is what everyone tells me." Michael swirled the liquid in his glass but didn't drink.

"Leaving won't solve this."

"Neither will staying."

Edward sipped from his glass. "Go then. I'll give your excuses to my mother."

Michael slipped out of the library door. As he neared the entrance, Miss Philippa descended the stairs. A lace shawl wrapped around her shoulders and dress front.

"Miss Philippa, how fares your gown?"

"As you see, hiding my dress is the only option for now unless I drag Aunt and Alex away. Because Sir Rothy is showing some interest in Alex, and I am loath to end her evening."

"Do you wish to leave?"

Miss Philippa waved her hand dismissively. "There is no reason I must. I am presentable enough."

"Why don't you answer the question I asked?"

"I did."

"No, you didn't. I asked if you wished to leave."

"And I answered I had no need to leave."

Michael shook his head. Why didn't people answer his questions directly? "But do you want to?"

"Of course I do. We attempted to clean my gown and dry it next to the fire, but it's still damp, and I am not comfortable. Is that the question you wanted me to answer?"

"Matter of fact, yes. Why are you staying?"

Miss Philippa sighed. "I have no other choice. I cannot simply hire a hackney and return to my aunt's unescorted."

"I could take you."

"Then I would need a chaperone. In either case, I ruin the remainder of my sister's evening."

Michael pondered for a moment. "I was ready to leave rather than suffer a boring evening. What if I stay and suffer with you?"

To his surprise, Miss Philippa laughed and took his arm. "We can endure this together."

# TWENTY



Dry clothing. Phil breathed in the lavender scent Green added when laundering their clothes. Ever so much nicer than the essence-of-wine sauce she'd worn all evening. The sauce had been delightful, but smelling it for hours caused her to consider how a roast pig might feel.

Alex sat on the bed, rubbing lotion onto her stump. "I was surprised to see you return to the party with Lord Endelton. How did that come about?"

Phil was glad her sister had waited until they were alone to inquire about her entrance into the parlor. "I'm not entirely sure. He was leaving when I came down the stairs after trying to clean my dress. We had a conversation, and he stayed."

"I noticed he talked to you more than to any other lady there."

"How could you have noticed anything? Anytime I looked over, you were in conversation with somebody, usually Sir Rothy."

"He was rather attentive, wasn't he?"

"What is your first opinion of him?"

"He is rather desperate for a wife. I don't know. It entirely put him off when he noticed my cane. We shall have to see if he calls tomorrow. Now, about you and Lord Endelton."

"There's so little to discuss. I hoped he would be a good match for you. But he is determined neither of us will suit simply because of Father. Our friendship has only grown, which is creating difficulties as he doesn't understand it is not possible to cultivate friendships with the opposite sex at our age and still court others."

"Your feelings are deepening for him."

"I wish he would stay away. I tell myself it is only because he reminds me of William. But as much as I try to see him—"

"Lord Endelton is not our brother. "

"However, it is the only kind of relationship I can have with him."

"He asked about you at dinner."

Phil spun on her sister. "You are not helping matters. Tales of forbidden love never work out well, anyway."

"Romeo and Juliet?"

"Is a tragedy, not a romance. And it is not like he is forbidden to me. I am not good enough to be on his list."

"You could change his mind."

Tears stung Phil's eyes. She blinked them back. "The subject is closed, Alex. Even if I find him to be one of the most kind and fascinating men I've ever met, it will do me no good. The less time I spend in his presence, the better."

"You said the same after we went to the theater. Which is why I was so surprised you came in with him."

"Please, enough."

"Then what of Mr. Newcomb? You didn't tell me about your ride this afternoon."

Phil always wanted what she couldn't have. When she was younger, she wished to wear trousers like the gardeners. Then she wished to finish her education. And now she wanted for her sister to have a good match as well as her. What she was going to get was Mr. Newcomb.

Alex tugged on Phil's sleeve. She waited for an answer.

Phil searched her mind for something of interest other than their near-collision with Lord Endelton.

"Mr. Newcomb asked if Father was coming to Town."

"When did this happen?"

Phil sank onto the bed. "As we returned home. Do you think it is better I send him to Father or ask Father to come to Town?"

"Do you mean to accept him, then?"

"I don't see as if I have a choice. He has to be better than whoever Father chooses." Lord Endelton had been correct when he called the man supercilious. Phil did not look forward to long nights in the parlor hearing Mr. Newcomb expound on anything and everything scriptural. He'd missed his calling; he should have been a vicar. Fortunately, most wives could spend most of the day far from their husbands. And after children came, she would spend as much time with them as possible.

"You won't be happy with him. I saw you before you left today. You wore the same look you do whenever you had to haggle with the butcher and Father has yet to pay the bill."

"I will have a roof over my head and more pin money than I know what to do with. I shall be able to travel and see you. Mr. Newcomb has been clear on that point. I can visit you whenever I want."

"May I visit you?" asked Alex.

"Mr. Newcomb said he wasn't fond of visitors. But he didn't forbid them."

A knock on the door interrupted them.

"Come in," called Alex.

Their aunt entered the room. "My father arrived. I can't imagine what brought him at this hour. He asked to see both of you in the morning. I trust you will be up for breakfast at an appropriate hour?"

"Of course." They answered in unison.

"Good night." Aunt Healand nodded as if distracted and left the room.

Alex pushed a cork back into the bottle of lotion. "They must have moved up a vote. I didn't think Grandfather intended to come until nearer the end of the session."

"I wonder what brought him to Town." Phil had the uncomfortable feeling Grandfather's arrival had nothing to do with politics and everything to do with them.

After the Godderidge's party, Michael didn't go directly home. His mind was working too fast to rest. He walked several turns around the small park in the center of Grosvenor Square. Deborah whispered in his ear before he left, saying Miss Burke would not be a good choice. Michael had been grateful for a collaborative opinion for something he felt, but wasn't sure about. After all, Miss Burke seemed much like all the other debutantes. None of which had seemed right. The only enjoyable moments of the evening had been those spent with Miss Philippa. Had Richard struck her from his list in too much haste? Her father couldn't damage his reputation that much, could he?

That was the puzzle. Sir Lightwood didn't wield any political power and there were other men whose reputations equaled Philippa's father's, yet they moved about society with ease. Richard's father had been among them. The former duke went so far as to recognize his mistresses' son, Mr. Kenworth, as his own in the weeks before his death. The duchess' father forced Richard to marry, largely because of his father's reputation. One which Richard didn't follow in the least.

Picking up his pace, Michael contemplated other men of the peerage whose reputations were far from stellar. One only had to look as far as the Prince Regent for an example of someone who still held political power despite his own affairs. The only thing keeping him in his place was his birth and title. A viscount was nothing like a prince, but wouldn't his own reputation and title do more for him than the reputation of a father-in-law could hurt?

Turning off of the square, he continued his walk, passing others who were returning home from entertainments. Soon, he found himself at Russell Square across from Lady Healand's home. Lights still lit the upper windows.

A crested carriage was parked in front of her door. Michael drew closer until he could make out the letters and crest. Whitstone. Richard claimed the old earl rarely came to debate in the House of Lords and there wasn't a vote for at least another fortnight.

A few houses down, a door opened, and several people exited—among them, Miss Simesson and her mother. Michael stepped out of the lamplight. He didn't have a suitable answer for what brought him to this area of London and didn't wish to be quizzed. He waited for the carriages to leave before retracing his steps to his own home.

Sleep didn't come easy as every time he closed his eyes, he saw Philippa's. One of his last thoughts was to remind himself he had no right to drop the 'Miss' when referring to her, even in his dreams.

# TWENTY-ONE

As the first light of dawn penetrated their room, Phil and Alex gave up on any pretense of sleep. They forced themselves to stay in bed longer, knowing it would be two hours until an early breakfast was served.

Green brought in tea and helped them dress in their best morning dresses. She spoke less than usual and hid her yawns twice. Grandfather's unexpected arrival had likely deprived some members of the staff of more sleep than it had the sisters.

As Alex often did when around their grandfather, she opted not to use her cane. Phil kept her opinions about the matter locked away. It did no good to pretend to not need it, so Grandfather would feel less guilty. He hadn't caused the accident any more than anyone else had. And pretending to be better off than she was only resulted in her hip bothering her later.

They went to the breakfast room together and found the cook had put in extra effort this morning. Grandfather sat in the chair closest to the fire. "There are my lovelies."

They each greeted him with a kiss on his cheek.

"We didn't expect you to be in Town so soon," said Phil.

"I came earlier than I planned, so I could see you." Grandfather stood. "How grand you look."

Alex shook her head. "I am sure we are not the only reason. You came to scare off unworthy suitors, didn't you?"

Grandfather chucked. "Are there any I should scare off?"

Alex turned to Phil and raised a brow, leaving Phil to answer. "No one in particular. Alex isn't fond of my current caller. But I shall never want for a roof over my head."

Grandfather's brow furrowed. For a moment, it looked like he would speak. He waved to the food. "Let's eat while we talk."

They sat around the table near the window. Grandfather bowed his head and said a prayer over the food. Phil and Alex hurried to set down their spoons.

"I see you two have not been praying at mealtime. I know it isn't very fashionable, but the older I get, the more I wished I had paid more attention to God in my youth. Now, to the question of who is courting Phil. Tell me about him."

"Mr. Newcomb is supercilious." Phil covered her mouth. Not the first thing she intended to say. "I mean, his worst fault is— But he has a good fortune, and no one speaks ill of him."

"If he had no funds, would you marry him?"

"Of course not. He wouldn't please Father." Her quick answer surprised her.

"I made a mistake many years ago which I have been trying to rectify for over twenty years. Do you know what I did?"

Alex set down her spoon. "Was it with Mother and Father?"

"Yes. I pushed them together. I knew your father would inherit my title and lands through the entail. It seemed very logical to have one of my daughters marry him so my grandson could continue with the title. If only I'd known what my cousin understood when he gave up the title all those years ago. The title doesn't matter. I wonder how different things would have been if I had not pressured sweet Hannah to marry Felton. My wife cautioned me against such a match. Your mother understood most matches are played like a game of chess, sacrificing someone for an advantage. If I had known your father's gambling was as frequent as it has been these past years, or about his mistress, Marguerite, I would have never signed the marriage contract."

"You know about Marguerite?" asked Alex.

"I learned about her existence shortly before Philippa was born. I arranged for her to leave the area for some time. Unfortunately, when your mother died, she came back. And in the intervening years, your father became less careful than he once was."

Phil exchanged glances with her sister.

The color had drained from Alex's face. "Mother was so beautiful. How could he?"

They knew some men kept women other than their wives. One just didn't imagine one's own father having one when their mother had been so young.

Grandfather stared into his coffee for several long moments. "A very uncomfortable subject to discuss with one's granddaughters. And not why I am here." He sipped his coffee before continuing. "The only way I can atone for my mistake is to make sure you are not put in the same position your mother was and you are not forced to marry out of desperation. Philippa, word has reached me about your father's plan for your marriage. My solicitor has made inquiries into the man's suitability. And I'm afraid it is a terrible match. While I will not attempt to forbid you to accept it, I would counsel you to be very careful."

"Have no fear on that part, Grandfather. I know any man of Father's choosing is most likely not a wise choice for me."

Nor for any of her sisters. But how to prevent imprudent matches from being made on all of their parts?

Grandfather patted Phil's hand. "You are an intelligent girl. But for this supercilious person, after what your aunt tells me, I don't think you are being nearly as wise. You are only allowing him to court you because he is a better option than any man your father chooses. And your answer to the earlier question indicates you have no genuine affection for him."

Phil nodded in agreement.

"I much rather you marry a farmer or a chimney sweep you cared for, than a man with money to whom you have no affinity. And I hope I have made this possible."

Phil found she couldn't swallow. Aunt thought Grandfather might make some preparation for Alex, but for her?

"There are papers and deeds and such to show you. My solicitor will come by later this week. I purchased a townhouse in Bath, near the cathedral and Roman baths. I am leaving enough funds to pay for the upkeep and staff for fifty years. I had hoped to obtain five such residences so you each could know you would always have a roof over your heads without having to marry. However, the house is large enough you could all reside there. There is also the problem of any inheritance I leave the five of you being squandered by your father, which means the best solution is to give one home to Alexandra while I still live."

Phil looked at Alex, who seemed to have trouble finding a response.

Grandfather continued. "Next January, Alexandra, you will receive the deed to the home in Bath. I hope you two will continue to care for your younger sisters as long as necessary. I fear poor Jane will not find a match because of her shyness. A Season would be so painful for her. Although she might find some entertainment in Bath. I fear they will snatch little Rose up the first week of her first Season. As for Georgiana, she is the one most likely to marry a farmer and be content joining him in the fields. In any event, you will not be left to the mercy of your father."

"It is too much, Grandfather," said Alex.

"No, it is not enough. You need options other than becoming a companion to some old biddy with rotten teeth. Or caring for your father. There is little I can do to prevent the entail, but I can make it so you no longer are forced to keep his house."

"But won't Father claim the house as part of the entail?"

"He may try, but I purchased these with money from my own investments. My solicitor assures me I have written the bequeathment in such a way your father cannot claim them. If you choose to get married, the home remains in your name and you may do what you will with the property, providing your sisters may join you. I want to be sure all of my granddaughters are cared for."

Phil didn't know what to say. It was too generous, it was too much, and too unexpected.

"And if we are all wed?" asked Alex.

"Then you may sell the townhouse as you wish. The solicitor has structured it so the property will be yours, not your husband's."

"What of our aunt?" asked Phil.

"This home is, unfortunately, part of the entail. However, she holds the deed to the property in Lyme Regis, where she spends most of her year."

Alex sat back in her chair, food forgotten. "You have planned for all of us?"

"As well as I can. I have a plan which may change the entail, but it may leave you all unprovided for. I cannot allow my folly to force you into poor situations." Changing the heir to the earldom and the entail was practically impossible and required parliamentary intervention. Phil doubted that even Grandfather could orchestrate the feat.

Phil stared into her empty teacup and wondered what the tea leaves would say if she believed such a thing. "But Father has already made a match for me if this Season isn't successful."

"Then, you would marry this Mr. Newcomb?"

"That was my plan," answered Phil.

Grandfather slapped the table with the palm of his hand. "I am against it."

"But you haven't met him."

"I don't need to. Your first description of him was not a description a wife should ever have to give of a husband. A supercilious man would never listen to your wisdom. Does he listen to you?"

"I have little opportunity to talk when we are together."

Using his fork to punctuate his words, grandfather growled. "That will only get worse. I cannot see you living in a marriage where you never have a voice."

Alex picked at the bun on her plate. "Then I truly don't have to marry someone?"

"I have long worried about your situation and the effect your injury will have on your ability to make a match. I wish I had insisted you stay another day, or my coachman had checked out your carriage. Your mother had mentioned it rattled more than usual, but I thought it was the rain." Grandfather's voice quieted as he spoke.

Alex placed her hand on grandfather's arm. "It is not your fault."

"I should have insisted the coachman check the wheels."

Phil closed her eyes. Rehashing this conversation wouldn't bring Mother and William back. It wouldn't restore Alex's leg. She waited for her emotions to calm.

Alex leaned into her grandfather's side. "I've never blamed

you, and you have been more than kind my entire life. A townhouse in Bath is overwhelming. I've only visited once, and I know I'll love living there. I simply can't believe this is real. You are the kindest and most benevolent grandfather anyone could have."

Grandfather hugged Alex.

Phil let the matter drop for now. "Thank you for your kindness. Mr. Newcomb hinted he wanted to speak with Father. And I am glad I will not have to accept either proposal."

"My daughter indicated you might entertain interest from another front. True?"

Phil felt her face heat as she wondered what Aunt Healand shared. "No."

An early morning visit to his cousin might be the only way to calm Michael's mind.

He skipped all pleasantries when shown into the duke's study. "She isn't on my list."

Richard looked up from his papers. "It is standard to exchange a greeting."

"You hardly ever do." Michael sat in the chair his cousin pointed to. "Good morning."

"And what brings you here to disturb my peace, even before breakfast is served?"

"Miss Philippa Lightwood."

"Her father is an unsuitable connection."

"How is it that one of the two women you removed from my list of prospective brides is the only one I could even consider marriage to?"

"If you would cease to mingle with her. You would not think of her," grumbled Richard. "I told you to avoid her."

"I can't simply pretend not to know Miss Philippa."

"You could try."

"You mean give them the cut direct?"

"Precisely."

Michael stood and paced around a chair. "Wouldn't that diminish them in other's eyes?"

"Possibly."

"And hurt their chances of making a good match."

"Their chances were already low. If the duchess is correct, their chances are nonexistent."

"What did your wife say?"

"She heard Miss Lightwood has a clapper."

"A what?" Michael was more surprised by the use of the derogatory name for the prosthesis than by the revelation his cousin knew.

"A wooden leg. If the *on dit* is correct, a finely crafted one, as it makes almost no noise."

"Where did she hear such a rumor?" Michael felt he must stop the damage.

"She claims to have noticed it herself the night we were at the theater. But I think she heard last night at the soiree she dragged me to. Is it true?"

Michael pursed his lips. He'd made a promise.

"Your face says it all. That explains why Miss Lightwood was so injured at the duchess' ball."

"And what if she does?" Michael sat in the chair, defeated.

"It makes Miss Lightwood an unsuitable wife. The duchess is of the opinion she shouldn't be in public. Much less trying to secure a match."

"You are listening to your wife now?"

"It is hard not to. Have you not noticed how shrill her voice is?"

The duchess's voice seemed no different from most women's voices. "I haven't noticed, but I rarely speak to her."

"Consider yourself fortunate." Richard's voice was almost

a growl. Once, he had been jovial and fun to be around. The last year had changed him dramatically. "So is the duchess correct?"

"I am not in a position to answer."

Richard sat up, knocking papers off his desk. "She was right?"

"I said I couldn't say."

Richard shook his head. "Don't you understand? Your denial told me the truth."

"But I didn't answer you."

Richard stared at the ceiling for what seemed like an hour. He brought his arms down and clasped his hands in front of him. "We need to talk about another subject. Why are you here?"

"Miss Philippa isn't on my list."

"Between her father and her sister's deception, she doesn't belong on your list."

"None of the women on your list are matches for me."

"Why not?"

"Most of them are false and try to trick me. Others I don't understand at all. They only talk about hats, and if I don't respond properly, they are upset."

"All women do."

"Not Philippa."

Richard's brows raised at Michael's faux pas of using her Christian name. "You say you enjoy talking to *Miss* Philippa?"

"Yes. She talks like a person."

"She is a person." Richard's growl deepened.

"No, I mean, she talks about real things, not only the weather. She says things that make me smile."

Richard walked to the window and leaned against the sill. Michael waited for him to talk.

And waited.

And waited.

Finally, Richard turned to face him. "I don't think I am the proper person to give you advice. I suggest you talk to Edward."

"What are you saying?"

"My relationship with the duchess has jaded me. I had forgotten what it was like to have an amiable conversation with a woman. I forget not every woman is as conniving as the duchess. As for the Misses Lightwood, they have proven themselves by not entrapping you when they had the chance. And it is obvious you know whatever truth lies behind the eldest's limb. But I wish you would be careful. I never suspected I could be forced into an unwanted marriage, as I was. You deserve happiness. Perhaps I never did."

"I have heeded your warnings and I continue with caution. Although I don't feel I need to always be on guard with the Lightwoods."

"Remember, they are still women. Come, let us have breakfast. Mother should be down soon, and she would love to see you."

His aunt was the most amiable of women, but he had no desire to run into Richard's wife. She would ask him about Miss Lightwood's limb. Apparently, not answering was as good as telling the truth. According to his family, his lies were never convincing.

Richard dusted off his sleeve. "The duchess prefers to eat in her room, if that is giving you pause."

"Then I would be pleased to eat with you. I was curious about your opinion of some men who spoke during the debates last week."

"Politics and breakfast don't mix. Meet me this afternoon at White's, and we can discuss matters of state. I warn you, my cook's buns are not up to your usual standard."

And indeed they were not.

# TWENTY-TWO

Droplets clung to the blades of newly greened grass, sparkling in the rare ray of London sunshine. Phil tried to concentrate on anything other than the man walking with her. As soon as the rain stopped, Grandfather requested she take a turn with him alone in the park. His stride was not as steady as it had been last year. He waited until they were near the center of the park to bring up the reason he'd brought her out alone.

"Your aunt led me to believe you had a certain tendre toward the young Viscount Endelton." He paused. Phil was certain she was meant to say something, but found nothing to say. "Neither of you mentioned him this morning, despite his help when Alexandra was injured."

Phil chose her words carefully. "Lord Endelton has been most kind and is very amiable."

"And he brings a blush to your cheeks. Is he who you thought of at breakfast when you claimed there wasn't another man interested in you?"

"It was. But he cannot return my feelings."

"Does not or cannot?"

"I am not sure if he does. But at any rate, he cannot."

"Nevertheless, I am told he speaks with you often."

"He seeks out my company when we are at events together." Phil wouldn't contradict the truths he must have learned from her aunt. "I had hoped he would be a match for Alex. But like mine, her name was scratched off the list."

"List?"

"His cousin, the Duke of Aylton, helped draw up a list of suitable matches. Our names were removed because of our father."

"How did you come to know of such a list?"

"It fell out of a book in the Endelton library."

Grandfather stopped walking and turned to face her. "And you discussed this with this man?"

"Lord Endelton is somewhat like our William was. The subtleties of conversation and expression elude him. When he discovered I'd seen the paper, he asked for my help in choosing a woman who would suit. I know it was ridiculous, but I agreed. Of course it didn't work out."

"He still speaks with you?"

Phil's cheeks were all but on fire now. "He does. Most kindly. But there is nothing to do for it. The duke will never approve of tying father's name with his, even if Father is to inherit your title someday. Father's reputation preceded us. I despair of ever finding a match for Alex."

"Does Alexandra wish to be married?"

"She says not, but she used to." Dreams from before the accident were rarely mentioned now.

"Your sister is very practical. One of the reasons I purchased the townhouse in Bath for her." Grandfather's face was strained.

"It is a tremendous gift. I've often worried about her being stuck in Father's house forever. I didn't want to leave her to his mercy. I also know I can't depend on my future husband's kindness, either. Although I hope to find one who would welcome any of my sisters if necessary. Earlier, you said this would help me too. What is to keep Father from forcing a marriage onto one of us?"

"The law."

Couldn't he see the law wasn't enough to protect them? Threats and demands would weigh heavier. "What good is that? It cannot prevent his retribution if we say no."

"But society can, to an extent."

"Are you speaking of the entail?" Her father's fondest aspiration was to inherit the title of earl and the lands that went with it. Not a difficult thing to manage since he only had to wait upon Grandfather's death.

"With any luck, the Willows will never be in his hands. I have found a closer relative to take over the entailment."

"Where? How?" Phil's mind reeled. She and Alex had searched *Debrett's Peerage and Baronetage,* trying to understand the entail.

"My cousin, the one whose title I inherited, has a grandson."

"In America?"

"The grandson has agreed to a visit. Only with the war we are having with the Americans, he has not been able to come as of yet. Last week, I received news he is coming on the same ship as a delegation to the king."

"Does he know he would inherit the title?" Could an American even be restored to the peerage?

"I have no idea what my cousin has told him. But the grandson is unwed, and if he is a man of principle, as I believe him to be from my cousin's letter..."

"You wish one of us would marry him?" Phil hazarded a guess.

"Although I hope a marriage could result, I will not push any of you toward him beyond making an introduction. For all we know, he is balding and has no teeth."

Phil laughed at the ridiculous idea. "Do you wish me to meet him before accepting a proposal?"

"I wish for you to be happy. I am worried you will not be so with this Mr. Newcomb."

"I could be content." Or she hoped she could be.

"Your mother was content, at least for a while. She found joy in her children. Your aunt was happy. There is a vast difference between content and happy in their circumstances."

"What of Grandmother, was she happy?"

"Neither of us were at first. Ours was a marriage forged by our parents. We had barely met. It took us a while to build a friendship. And for her to help me understand, she had more of a purpose in my life than to provide for the heir and the spare. It wasn't until after your mother married I understood your grandmother was meant to be a good advisor to me. Some days I wish I could relive my life with all the wisdom I have learned in my seventy-six years."

"What would you do differently?"

Grandfather laughed. "I think I would run away to the colonies and join my cousin. The idea of creating a life from nothing is intriguing to me. Would I have the respect of others without a title?"

"I'd respect you."

Grandfather patted her arm. "Your father, like other men, sets a great store in titles. They are only masks for bad men to hide behind. I want to give you a warning. Word has reached my ears your Father has concocted a scheme to marry you off if you don't find a match. The man he has chosen, is not of good character."

Phil didn't point out her grandfather discussed the same over breakfast. To mention the subject twice, the match must weigh heavily on his mind. "I am wise enough not to trust any of my father's choices."

"I wish I could do more to protect you. As you have pointed out, you won't reach your maturity for two years. At my age, I am unlikely to be appointed your guardian."

"Your gift today is more than generous and provides us with a way out of our father's home."

"But what of Georgiana, Jane, and little Rose? I doubt I can live long enough to protect them."

"We will do our best for them."

"I know you will. Which is why I must do my best for you."

"You always have. Aunt told me you are funding much of our Season. And now we all have a safe place to go if we refuse the husbands Father finds for us."

They completed a circuit of the park's perimeter and stopped at a stone bench dried by the sun.

Grandfather sat, leaving room for Phil. "I would like your advice. I've thought of funding Rose's schooling. Something the other four of you were not gifted. Not because I didn't care for you; I didn't feel you should be separated. But since your father relies on your sisters to educate her, I believe the situation could grow untenable."

"We have managed so far. However, Father won't allow us to even give her lines as punishment when she refuses to work. Thus I worry her education is likely to be mediocre at best."

"I will have to think about it more. I don't believe she's reached an age to appreciate the opportunity."

"We don't often appreciate much in our lives until we can look back on them."

"How did you get to be so wise?"

"Alex says it is because I read too much." Phil believed it was because her time in the schoolroom had been cut short by Mother's death. What she wouldn't give to pay attention to the lessons she ignored or for a few more months of schooling.

He checked his pocket watch. "I intend to speak with your sister before I must deal with other matters."

When they returned to the house, the butler handed her a note from Mr. Newcomb. He would not be by, as he was leaving Town for four days. Just long enough to go to Gloucestershire and see Father.

Whites was more crowded than Michael liked. Having been informed the duke had not yet arrived, he wandered for several minutes before finding a quiet seat by a window. Michael had yet to talk with Edward, who had been called in by the Admiralty. Deborah was feeling indisposed and was no help either. He stared at the second page of the newspaper, allowing the words to blur before him.

Did he only like Miss Philippa because she was forbidden? When he'd been a child, Mother had often tricked him into eating something by telling him it was only for grownups. Occasionally, the forbidden food was just as he imagined, and the other times, it was as disgusting as tripe. He hadn't imagined their conversations or Miss Philippa's smiles. Neither was his desire to be near her. He hadn't imagined his reactions to her touch either. No, he would like Miss Philippa even if she was being thrust upon him. The only real objection to their relationship Michael could see was Sir Lightwood. If her father wasn't such a liability, would his friends approve?

"Pardon me," a footman interrupted. "The Earl of Whitstone has asked you to join him for tea."

Michael froze. He'd never been introduced to the earl. What was the rule to follow? What would Richard say? The earl out ranked him and was one of the oldest peers.

"Of course." Michael set aside his paper and followed the footman into a private parlor.

The powdered wig on the earl's head reminded Michael of his own grandfather, who had died when Michael was but a lad. The lines crossing the old man's face testified he smiled more than he frowned. "I am Lord Ryeland, the Earl of Whitstone, and I presume the footman was about his business, and you are Viscount Endelton?"

"Yes, my lord." Michael felt like a schoolboy again, unable to speak for fear of saying the wrong thing.

"Thank you for coming, Lord Endelton. I could have sought proper introductions, but those take time, and, at my age, time is not something I wish to waste. Do sit, please."

Michael sat in the only other chair at the small table.

Neither man spoke until the servants set out their tea and closed the door.

"I admired your father and your grandfather very much. We didn't always see eye to eye on the votes, but they were logical about their opinions. Your father was especially eloquent. Are you like him?"

"I wish to be." The comparison to his father would never put Michael on the better side. His father understood people and always seemed to know what to say to coax a smile to change a man's negative opinion. Michael seemed to create negative opinions of those around him.

"This is your first year in parliament. Observation is the best. No one expects you to stand out yet. And not all of us can be William Pitt and his son. Amazing orators they were." A sense of reassurance in the earl's tone softened what could have been harsh advice.

"I would have liked to hear them debate. My father spoke of both often."

The older man added an extra drop of cream to his tea. "I wanted to thank you personally for your kindness in rescuing my granddaughter, Miss Lightwood."

"Any gentleman would have done it."

"But not anyone did. And you kept your silence about the mishap. Which is to be commended."

Michael shifted in his chair. The earl seemed to know every detail. "I don't know if my silence helped. This morning I learned there are those who speculate about Miss Lightwood's limb. I do not know the source of the rumor."

The earl frowned. "I knew it would come, eventually. The Season is more than half over, so I guess it is time."

"I hope the gossip is isolated. My source takes a dim view on most things."

They ate in silence for a moment. Unlike most silences, it wasn't uncomfortable.

"I must commend your valet on his fine repair work. Is there any way I can reward him?" asked the earl.

"He was well compensated."

"Good. Good." The older man ate several bites.

The conversation and the food neared their end.

"You impress me, Young Endelton. I believe your father would be proud knowing you succeeded him. How is the hunt for a wife?"

If he had still been eating, Michael would have choked on his food. "The hunt for a wife?"

"Isn't that what you are about this Season?"

"It is my aim to find a suitable partner."

"Have you found someone to suit you?"

"Not one my cousin approves of."

"Your cousin?"

"His Grace the Duke of Aylton, Richard Thomas Kenworth."

"Ahh." The earl nodded. "There was much gossip around his marriage. Since his father recognized his bye blow as the successor after young Richard, it is hardly surprising."

"My cousin isn't like his father."

"I have heard as much. And the duke doesn't approve of your choice?"

"He worries someone will take advantage of me."

"I assume he was against the aid you rendered my grand-daughters."

Michael tugged at his cravat, too warm around his neck. "He was concerned."

"No doubt on my son-in-law's account. I wish it was not so. I still have some influence in my granddaughters' lives. If someone were to offer for them, the marriage settlement would be fair."

Unsure what to say, Michael nodded his head as he reviewed the conversation, sure he hadn't mentioned Philippa. It wasn't possible the man could have guessed his interests. Conversing about politics was much more comfortable than discussing the Earl's granddaughters. "Will you attend the House of Lords while you are in Town?"

The earl's full eyebrow raised, but he allowed the change of subject. "I believe I will."

As they finished their tea, they talked over the salient points of the current legislation. The earl pointed out counterarguments which Michael had dismissed.

When the teapot was empty, the earl stood. "It has been a pleasure meeting you. I hope we have a chance to speak again."

"Thank you." Michael bowed slightly and followed the earl from the private room. The earl crossed the larger parlor with a speed Michael would not expect from someone who spent three-quarters of a century on the earth.

The chair by the window Michael occupied earlier was now filled by men discussing the chocolate trade. Interesting thing, chocolate. He doubted it would ever become as popular as tea. Finding no one else with whom he wished to converse, Michael searched for a book in the library. If only all books about finding love were not fiction.

# TWENTY-THREE

Grandfather has arranged for me to meet with Mr. Potts about repairing Peggy." Alex's news was a welcome diversion from Phil's thoughts of the future.

"Do you think it can be repaired?" Phil poured the tea for their aunt.

The split in the wooden calf had grown since the night at the theater. And Alex now used her older, spare Peggy.

"I do hope so. The newer one was better weighted for me. I hadn't realized how heavy the old one was or how off-balance I felt when walking. The strap Lord Endelton's valet created is far more comfortable than any of the others I've had."

"When is your appointment?"

"Tomorrow afternoon. Aunt Healand is taking me."

"Tomorrow? Isn't that your at-home day?" Phil directed the question to her aunt.

Lady Healand set her cup back on the delicate saucer. "Unfortunately, yes. However, you can receive callers in my place."

"What if a gentleman were to come?" A high improbability, as Mr. Newcomb would have been pressed to travel to Gloucestershire and back in so little time.

"Father will be in the house." Aunt's answer wasn't entirely reassuring. Grandfather was as likely to sit in the parlor sipping tea for three hours as it was to pass an entire fortnight without rain in the late London spring. "If he believes, you need a chaperone or rescue, he has promised to join you."

"I am afraid I'll say all the wrong things."

"Have no worries, my dear. You have yet to make any serious faux pas during any of our calls and even fewer at our at-homes." Not entirely true. If Alex had not anticipated the rude remark Phil wished to make only last week and stopped with a reproving look, disaster would have occurred.

"I've never held an at-home day alone."

"No time like the present. Next year, you could be the hostess in your own home. If I did not feel you were up to the task, I wouldn't leave you."

"Couldn't Green go with Alex?" asked Phil.

"She already is." Alex leaned forward. "I could try to make another appointment—"

Although her sister's voice was hopeful, they both knew the reality. The appointment had only come to pass so quickly because the earl was in Town. The old prosthetic's clicking was more pronounced as she walked. The common nickname "clapper" truly fit the old wooden limb. At soirees and dinners, silent movement was a necessity to keep Peggy a secret.

Phil patted Peggy through her sister's skirt. "There is no need. It is only a few hours of conversation about the weather and the latest fashions and who was seen with whom in Hyde Park."

Lady Healand laughed. "Don't forget to notice their daughter's dresses and send compliments to the family."

"I won't."

"I'll make sure Cook has her best selection of cakes and sandwiches."

"She always does," said Alex. "If the Season doesn't end soon, I may have to let the seams out in my gowns."

Michael stayed at the club much later than usual, having joined in several political discussions. On his way out, he found Richard in front of one of the many fireplaces. "Why are you still here?"

"I am looking for you. I have come to apologize."

Michael sat in the seat across from his cousin. "Why do you need to apologize?"

"I have been overzealous in my advice. It is not my role to say whom you cannot marry."

"But I need your advice. I make so many mistakes where people are concerned."

"My advice is of little use. I am far from prejudiced against the fairer sex. Today you said something that made me remember a time when I wasn't. It is unfair of me to put my prejudices on you." His cousin stared into the fire, his face almost relaxed in a way Michael had not seen for years.

"I met the Earl of Whitstone today."

"He is here in London? What did he say?"

"We talked about politics and the Pitts and my father."

Richard's brow furrowed. "Did the earl seek the introduction?"

"Yes. He said he wished to thank me for my kindness in rescuing Miss Lightwood."

"Did he say anything more?"

"Not of import."

"You're sure? Sometimes you miss things others consider important."

Michael thought back on the conversation. "There was an odd moment. He said if someone was to offer for his granddaughters, the marriage settlement would be fair. But we were not discussing anything like marriage."

"You didn't mention Miss Philippa?"

"Neither of us did. Only the service I rendered to her older sister."

"Was any other woman mentioned?"

"No."

Richard was silent again. Michael hated it when his cousin thought for long periods of time.

A spider crawled its way down near the mantel. "She doesn't like spiders."

"Who doesn't like spiders?"

"Miss Philippa." Michael watched the spider for another moment. "Some people are like spiders. They have a plan to catch you."

"Michael, your description fits many people. It may be the truest observation of people you've ever made."

"Sir Lightwood is like a spider, isn't he? That is why you don't want me to have anything to do with his daughters."

"Unfortunately, most fathers are like spiders when it comes to marrying off their daughters." Richard's perpetual frown deepened. "But that does not mean their daughters are the same."

"Are you saying I can put Miss Philippa on my list?"

"We were wrong to give you a list. We were trying to help, but I am afraid it made it harder for you rather than easier."

"Richard, what are you telling me to do?"

"You need to choose for yourself, and we need to trust you can."

Michael slid forward in his seat. "You mean I can marry Philippa?"

"You might court her first, but I understand she has already been seen several times in Hyde Park with Mr. Newcomb."

"Am I too late?"

"Have her banns been read?"

The obvious question puzzled Michael. "No."

"Then you still have a chance."

"Then what should I do?"

"I believe talking to her is considered a good first step."

Michael hopped out of his seat.

Richard grabbed his sleeve. "Not now. It is far too late to make a social call."

He glanced at the mantle clock. "Tomorrow?"

"During proper calling hours."

Michael sat back down. "Yes, of course."

# TWENTY-FOUR

ater ran in rivulets down the window. Phil leaned against the window frame, watching carriages splash through the puddles. A footman hurried from the house next door and down the street. She'd been in London long enough not to hope the rain would keep callers at bay. It would lengthen the duration of the visits, as the ladies would hope for a break in the rain.

A tap on the door interrupted Phil's thoughts.

"The parlor is ready for your callers. Cook has prepared refreshments, as her ladyship directed," said the housekeeper.

"Thank you very much. I'll be down directly."

As soon as the housekeeper left, Phil checked her appearance in the mirror. She was presentable enough for callers, most of whom would be her aunt's friends.

On the way to the parlor, she stopped at the study. "Grandfather, will you be joining me to receive callers?"

"No. The last thing I want is some widow getting it into her head that I need a wife. If I see a gentleman come, I'll join you. I'd much rather discuss politics and the cost of tea."

"I am afraid the at-home shall be very dull, and Aunt has several friends who are widows." As yet, Alex and she had but a few friends. The Godderidges's at-home day was the same as Aunt's so she would hardly be expected to see them.

Grandfather laughed. "I will stay near enough to ensure they properly chaperone you until four thirty when I must leave. A maid will stay in the parlor during my absence."

"Mr. Newcomb has yet to return. I shouldn't need a chaperone."

"He can't be your only male caller, can he?"

"I am afraid he has been for several weeks now."

"The ton has been overrun by idiots if gentlemen are not lining up at your door." Grandfather looked properly affronted.

Phil laughed. "On the contrary, I am not the wealthiest, the prettiest, or titled. I am fortunate someone deems me of notice at all."

"Poppycock."

It felt good to have someone defend her. Pill settled into the parlor shortly before the first caller was announced. As she expected, most of the early callers were friends of her aunt's. After expressing disappointment Lady Healand was not in, they lingered exactly a polite fifteen minutes instead of their usual half hour. Phil did not feel slighted in the least, as she would have had difficulty filling more time with conversation.

Miss Abbott entered the parlor, followed by her mother. Phil hoped she masked her surprise, as they had never visited before. They looked around the room before taking seats next to each other.

Mrs. Abbott skipped the usual polite greetings. "Where is Lady Healand?"

"My aunt was summoned on an errand which could not be put off. I apologize for any inconvenience." Phil repeated the line she used a half dozen times already.

"And your sister? I so wanted to speak with her." Miss Abbott's voice lilted in a peculiar fashion, as if she was trying on a new cadence for the first time.

"Aunt Healand required my sister to accompany her." None of her aunt's friends had asked after Alex, but they had not been of the same age. "Would you like tea?"

Mrs. Abbott stood. "Come, dear, we have other visits."

Stunned by the Abbotts' rudeness, Phil's smile wavered. She hardly had time to wonder before the footman announced another mother-daughter combination. Phil could not recall having conversed with Lady Powell and her daughter before. And Lady Charlotte had never condescended to visit her aunt. They too asked after Alex but were polite enough to stay a full quarter hour before leaving.

Other debutantes came with their chaperones. The conversations with them were eerily similar. After general greetings, each asked where Miss Lightwood was, as if they were her sister's particular friends. Upon learning she was out with Lady Healand, they took their leave quickly. Since the rain had ceased, there was no reason for them to linger. Something unusual was going on, and Phil had no frame of reference. If only Aunt Healand were here.

Another two women had come and gone. Lady Endelton arrived with Moriah and Deborah. As friends, they were welcome. Surely they wouldn't react as the others had.

A moment later, Lord Endelton was announced.

Phil reached for her teacup, hoping the last few drops would alleviate the sudden dryness on her tongue.

"Welcome."

Lady Endelton and her daughters seemed amused rather than surprised at his entrance. Only then did Phil realize they had arranged themselves so the only seat for Lord Endelton was the one nearest her. Perching on the edge of the seat, Lord Endelton's knee bounced ever so slightly. Instead of studying her or the room as the previous guests had, Lady Endelton and her daughters watched Lord Endelton.

"How do you do?" His question wasn't as firm as his normal speech.

"Well, thank you. I apologize for Lady Healand's absence." For the first time that day, Phil mentioned the reason for her aunt's absence before she was asked. "She is accompanying my sister on an urgent errand."

"I am sorry we missed them," said Lady Endelton. The conversation turned to the usual topics, with Moriah bringing up the theater so often, Lady Endelton tapped her daughter's knee with her fan.

As the visit drew to a close, the Endelton women turned their attention to Lord Endelton, who'd not said a word since the opening of the conversation.

His knee bounced again. "You must wonder why I have come."

"Was it not to escort your sisters and mother?" asked Phil, as she didn't dare ask if he needed information for his list.

"Would you like to take a turn around the park?" The words rushed out of his mouth.

Moriah giggled.

"I would be delighted to. When?"

"Would a half hour be too soon?"

"Not at all. Our at-home hours are nearly to a close. And there is still some daylight left today."

Moriah giggled and was again hushed by her mother.

Lord Endelton stood, as did his mother and sisters, and bid the customary farewells.

Phil accompanied them as far as the parlor room door. The springs in the hall clock whirred as it prepared to announce the hour and the official end of callers. "Wait."

The entire family stopped and turned. She'd only wished to halt Lord Endelton. Heat warmed her cheeks. "If you will wait, but for a moment, I'll fetch my wrap, and we can take our walk now."

"As you wish."

In an act Aunt Healand wouldn't risk and shake her head at, Phil flew up the stairs in search of a wrap and a maid who could accompany them.

"Do you need information about someone on your list?"

"No." His answer was too clipped. Michael cleared his throat again, searching for words which wouldn't come.

"Is something wrong?"

"No." He'd talked with Philippa a score of times. Why was today difficult?

She stopped walking, her hand falling away from his arm as he took an extra step. "Lord Endelton, I am at a loss. We've circuited the park completely, and you've spoken no more than a few pleasantries. More than a half dozen visitors did the same this afternoon. Please tell me whatever has you so agitated and everyone acting so peculiar."

"I heard yesterday there was talk among the ton —"

Phil stepped closer, making it hard to concentrate. Michael offered his arm again, and she took it.

"Talk about us?"

"Your sister. I didn't say a word. You must believe me."

"What are they saying about Alex?"

He lowered his voice more. "She owns a prosthetic."

"May I ask how you heard the rumor about Alex?"

"The duke, naturally. From what he said, I don't think the story was known to be true." Michael didn't add that his bumbling confirmed the tale.

Philippa walked silently for a moment. "That could account for all the visitors today asking for her. There were several, including Miss Abbott and Lady Charlotte, who are not among our usual callers."

"Miss Abbott came here?"

"Yes." Phil hesitated. "Her mother is exceedingly rude. She is on your list, isn't she?"

"Not since last week. She told me never to call upon her again."

"How horrid."

"As Deborah would say, we didn't suit." He never would have approached her if not for the list.

"Our extra callers must have been seeking an opportunity to prove the existence of Alex's friend, Peggy."

It took him a moment to remember they referred to the wooden leg by name. "How would they do that?"

"Step on her toes, most likely. Kicking her in the shin would not be wise. Rose learned her lesson the hard way." Philippa laughed lightly.

"And for now, Peggy's existence will remain a mystery?"

"I suppose so. I only said my aunt and sister were out. You needn't have been so nervous to tell me. Especially when your family knows the truth."

"I never told Moriah, and I am not certain Deborah knows either."

"I have not confided in her, but Edward may have, assuming he knows the full extent of it. I believe Lord and Lady Godderidge know, so it stands to reason their children know some of the particulars of the accident."

Michael felt the need to defend his family. "Neither of my sisters would have started the gossip, I am sure."

"I don't think they did." The pressure of her hand on his arm increased. "You'll recall Lady Charlotte claimed to have seen it when we left the Duke's ball. There was an incident at the theater. She hit it loud enough people outside of the box could have heard. Alex's constant use of a cane could easily have fueled speculation. There are those who must always have a tale to tell."

"Why?"

"I don't know. Perhaps diminishing a person makes another feel greater. Or women believe they can eliminate the competition. Not that Alex was competing with any of them."

"No one has expressed interest—" Michael stopped. "Pardon my rudeness."

"Do not fret on Alex's account. She no longer needs to depend on a good match or our father for her future."

"How?"

"Our grandfather, the Earl of Whitstone, has been very generous and has found a way to secure her future and give us hope for our own."

This revelation didn't bode well for Michael. How would he ever convince Philippa to court him if she had no need for a husband? "Then you no longer need to marry?"

"I wish to, but I no longer fear having to choose a marriage simply to avoid my father's plans."

"What plans?"

"He has chosen a husband for me. A man who has five children. Since he is a friend of my father's, I have ample reason to avoid such a match."

"What of Newcomb?"

"Are you concerned on my part, my friend?"

The word friend, while once welcome, now stung Michael's heart. "Of course. He reminds me of our old priest, always lecturing on and on."

Again, her laugh lightened the air. "He does like the sound of his own voice."

It was Michael's turn to stop. "You are not serious about him then?"

"Mr. Newcomb has many fine qualities which make him a suitable catch in my Father's eyes, even without a title."

"Have you accepted him?"

"He hasn't asked."

Michael's lungs tightened, making it too difficult to get the next question out. "Do you mean to accept him?"

"I am trying to step around the subject, and you are not allowing me to. No, I haven't accepted him because he hasn't asked. Is your curiosity satisfied?"

The correct answer would be to say yes, but it would be a lie. Philippa hadn't said she wouldn't accept Mr. Newcomb if he offered. However, pressing her for the answer was outside of the bounds Mother set for conversation. "I don't have a list anymore."

Miss Philippa tilted her head, and the sunlight made her eyes sparkle.

Michael's mouth dried making it difficult to say the words he'd planned.

"Did you lose it? Rip it up?"

"I decided it wasn't for me. I should make my own choices."

She flung her arms wide and proclaimed to the sky, "Ladies of London! Lord Endelton's list is no more." Lowering her arms, she turned back to face him. "How are you enjoying your new freedom?"

"It is both exhilarating and intimidating." If he could get the words out to tell her how he felt it would be neither.

"I have full faith you will find what you seek. I always have. You don't need to be like the Duke of Aylton or the Lieutenant to make your way."

"But I might choose wrong."

"Whomever you choose, if she is your match, you cannot be wrong."

Michael swallowed. This was the moment he was waiting for. "Will you be attending the Simesson's ball this evening?"

"Will she be there?" It was a simple question, yet Philippa answered it with another.

"Who?"

"The person you have given up the list for. And don't tell me there is not someone you are hoping for."

"I hope—"

A carriage stopped in front of Lady Healand's home. The Earl of Whitstone's crest stopped Michael's next words.

Philippa tugged his arm. "Grandfather is back. Would you like to meet him?"

Helplessly, Michael crossed the street behind her. His opportunity to speak openly gone.

# TWENTY-FIVE

ord Endelton left the house when Alex and Aunt Healand returned. After seeing them settled, Phil entered the study. "Grandfather, have you met Lord Endelton before?"

The earl looked up from the letter he was reading. "We met at the club."

"Why did either of you not say so? Once I introduced you, it was obvious you had a secret. I expected you to burst out laughing at any moment." Phil sank into the settee.

"You did the introductions so beautifully, how could I have interrupted?"

"A balm to my foolish soul." Phil sighed.

"Dramatics. Have you been taking lessons from Rose?"

"No. I suppose I am out of sorts. It has been a very odd day."

"Odd? How?"

"There were many more visitors than usual during our at-home hours. Several of them were my age, whereas usually our visitors are Aunt Healand's friends—or Mr. Newcomb, of course. Each one asked about Alex, and upon learning she was out, abruptly left. The last visitor was Lady

Endelton and her daughters, and Lord Endelton. He came to warn me that Alex, or Peggy, had become the latest *on dit* among the ton."

The earl's bushy gray eyebrows rose almost high enough to touch his outdated powdered wig. "Warn you?"

"Lord Endelton said the talk was speculation, but he seemed worried. It does explain the extra visitors this after-noon."

"Only petty women who were jealous that their ankles are not as finely turned as Alexandra's."

Phil laughed in spite of her mood.

"There is my girl. I hate to see you down, especially when you still have a ball this evening."

"I cannot go. Aunt Healand returned with a headache so there is no one to escort me." There would be no coaxing Alex to go even if the day's events hadn't drained her.

Grandfather straightened his shoulders and lifted his chin. "Are you saying I am no one? I am a peer of the realm. Am I not a suitable escort?"

"You would attend with me?"

"Do you see another damsel in want of an escort?"

"No, but Aunt said you didn't care for the festivities of the Season."

"Not in the least, but I do enjoy seeing surprised looks on people's faces. And what bigger surprise could there be than me escorting my granddaughter to a ball?" He laughed. Though he had never been especially stern during her life-time, Grandfather was more jovial than he had been during visits of her youth.

Phil toyed with her handkerchief. "That would give the ton something to talk about."

Grandfather chuckled.

Awareness dawned. "You sly old fox, you are hoping they forget Alex."

"For tonight they will, providing you are properly turned out. Is there someone who can do your hair?"

"Green is very proficient."

"Then I shall await her handiwork."

Phil chose the last of her unworn gowns. The hem and bodice were embroidered with dozens of forget-me-nots. She'd saved her favorite dress for last, hoping to wear it for some special beau. Unlike some debutantes, she didn't have a new gown for every ball. However, arriving on grandfather's arm demanded she appear in her best.

They arrived in a short line of carriages. As grandfather predicted, there was a collective gasp when he was announced to the room. While the music didn't stop, for the length of a long breath, the talking did. Mr. Simesson couldn't bow deep enough. Phil worried he might tip over completely.

Mr. Newcomb was the first gentleman to approach her. He took her hand and stopped just short of kissing it. "Miss Philippa, you look delightful this evening."

"I see you have returned."

"Only just."

"Grandfather, may I present Mr. Newcomb? My Grandfather, the Earl of Whitstone."

Mr. Newcomb bowed appropriately. "I understand the third set is to start with a waltz. If it is not already claimed, may I have the pleasure?"

"I thought you did not approve of the waltz and never danced it." Phil could not refuse to dance with him, but she much preferred another set, perhaps one of the country dances.

"There are rare times when I feel it is appropriate." The gleam in his eyes sent a shiver down her spine.

It seemed her suspicions might be correct, and Mr. New-comb did intend to declare himself soon. "Yes, you may."

As soon as he left, Grandfather snatched up Phil's dance card. "Put me down for the supper dance, will you? I am of the mind to dance once with the prettiest girl in the room."

Phil wrote his name in with her stubby pencil. Before she crossed the room, every dance was full, and Mr. Newcomb was the only man in the group she'd ever danced with before. Not at any ball had her card filled so quickly. Was it Grand-father or further curiosity about Alex? She wouldn't know until the conversations started. Spotting Lady Godderidge and Isabel, Phil angled toward them. Grandfather greeted Lady Godderidge as an old friend. They had not spoken for long when Lord Endelton appeared.

After greeting everyone in the conversational circle, Lord Endelton addressed Phil. "I wonder if you might have a dance I could claim?"

"I am terribly sorry. My card is full." Phil desperately wished she could erase all the names from her list.

Grandfather cleared his throat loudly. "I had claimed the supper dance for myself, however after watching these youthful dancers, I don't know if I could keep up. Would you mind taking my place, Endelton?"

"It would be my honor." Lord Endelton's smile was the largest she'd ever seen.

Phil bobbed the slightest of curtsies. "I look forward to it."

The first set was announced, and Lord Endelton left.

"I think I shall go to the card room. With your dance card full, I dare say there is little trouble you can find." Grandfather squeezed her hand as he left and her dance partner arrived.

The first set was a lively country dance. Her partner wasn't particularly bad, nor was he good. The conversation wasn't stimulating. Then again, she didn't expect it to be with the number of turns and switches. Was she imagining it or were there more whispers than usual as she passed? Grandfather's appearance caused more of a stir than she expected.

Her partner for the second set was no more remarkable than the first. Although he seemed to be trying to step on the toe of her right foot. At first, she thought it a mistake, but his aim was far too precise. Phil sidestepped enough, other dancers looked at her in askance.

There was a short break after the set for the musicians. Phil took the opportunity to drink a cup of punch and listen to Isabel's latest intrigue.

While Phil listened, a hand grasped her upper arm and spun her around. "Ouch!"

Mr. Newcomb did not release his vice-like grip. "Is it true?"

"Is what true?"

"Your sister. Does she only have one leg?" He made no effort to temper his voice.

"Let go of me this instant." Phil squirmed, but his grip was too strong.

Conversations around them ceased.

"Is it true?"

"Please. Unhand. Me." She raised her hand to slap him. As her hand reached his face, Mr. Newcomb fell back. Phil caught nothing but air and had to step quickly to keep from falling over.

"Miss Philippa asked you to let her go." Lord Endelton and the Duke of Aylton stood on either side of Mr. Newcomb.

The man shook them off. "It is true. I see it in your eyes. I made an offer to your father last night. I was willing to overlook your paltry dowry, but I won't be shackled to a lying—"

"What is the meaning of this?" Grandfather's voice boomed.

The onlookers parted, allowing him a clear path. Mr. Simesson followed behind. Isabel gripped Phil's hand giving her strength.

The duke growled, but it was Lord Endelton who spoke. "This man has forgotten his manners. My cousin and I were about to show him out."

Mr. Simesson spoke. "No need, your Grace, my Lords, I will show him out myself."

Mr. Newcomb shrugged off the men holding him. "It is no matter. No self-respecting man would align himself with you or your crippled sister."

The duke growled again. Two footmen appeared. Mr. Newcomb cursed and left.

Heat flooded Phil's cheeks. She looked for some way to escape, but she was hemmed in on all sides.

The duke stepped forward. "Am I mistaken, or did your dance partner abandon you?"

Phil willed her voice not to shake as every inch of her seemed to be. "He has left, your Grace."

The duke whispered something to Mr. Simesson.

"It would be a shame if I didn't dance at least once. Would you do me the honor?" The duke extended his hand.

Phil couldn't run, neither could she refuse, so she set her hand on his arm as an answer. Conversation resumed around them as he led her to the floor. The musicians quickly tuned their instruments. The caller announced the minuet.

The man behind them complained loudly. "I thought it was to be a waltz."

Other voices echoed his sentiment, but no one left the floor.

"Keep your chin high."

"Why?" Phil whispered the word as the dance started. "Why rescue me?"

"Because you have proven yourself these past several weeks. You have integrity. Which is more than I can say for most women."

"But he said I lied." Anything with the intent to deceive was a lie. Mother had taught them that.

"You didn't, did you? Not once did you ever claim your sister was hale and healthy to him."

"No, but we—"

"Attended functions?"

She waited until the forms of the dance brought them closer together to speak. "Yes."

"To which you were invited?"

"Yes."

"Did anyone ever ask you about your sister's cane?"

"No." They stood face to face, much too close for a dance given out of pity. Phil wished to step away, but she would never embarrass her rescuer.

"If a man offered for your sister, would she have—" the duke didn't finish the question.

"Of course."

"Then you have proven my point. Which means you are worthy of this dance. It will not stop the tongues from wagging. But for tonight, it will keep you from being cut. I only wish I could do more."

"It is more than I ever expected, your Grace." A dance with Duke Aylton would have every person talking. "You asked the dance to be changed, didn't you?"

"Clever girl." His tone carried no hint of condescension.

For the first time, Phil perceived the duke was not as imposing as she had first believed. She dared to answer him back. "Wise man."

The music came to a close. The duke bowed at the end before escorting her back to Lady Godderidge and her grandfather.

"Whitstone, you have lovely granddaughters." Laying particular emphasis on the plural, the duke's pronouncement was loud enough for all nearby to hear. "I am done with dancing. Would you join me in a game of cards?"

The men walked off leaving Phil with Lady Godderidge.

"Oh, Philippa, your mother would be proud of you."

Phil looked at the crowd who all seemed to be studying her and wondered if the Lady could be wrong.

The supper dance was a quadrille, affording almost no conversation with one's partner if one was to follow all of the intricate steps. Michael assumed the hostess had designed it so the dance partners could talk while dining. How much longer would he have to wait to tell Philippa she was his choice? If only Deborah hadn't cautioned him against his usual way of declaring what was on his mind, Michael would have made his feelings known in the park. He wished his sister was in attendance, but she begged off of the festivities at the last moment, claiming she was ill.

All he could do was offer a smile each time he met Philippa after a turn. Thankfully, she returned his smile. The exercise and the lights of the chandelier intensified the sparkle of her eyes. When they married, he would make sure to look at her often under the chandelier in the ballroom of Terrace Hall. Would it be in the budget to have so many candles? Perhaps the chandelier could be converted to gas and burn long and evenly. Preposterous. Gas lights would endanger the entire household. Michael shook his thoughts away as the music ended. At last, he would have a word with her.

"The Simessons hired excellent musicians, don't you agree?"

"Yes." All about him people pressed too close for a private conversation.

"I don't see the duchess, do you think she left with your cousin?"

"His Grace came with me. I believe the duchess is at the theater."

"Will she be annoyed to learn he danced with me? People are saying he hasn't danced with anyone since opening his own ball at the beginning of the Season."

There were still far too many ears listening to them talk. "That would be the duke's affair."

"Yes, yes, of course." Philippa fell silent as they proceeded to the tables remarking on the food as if they hadn't eaten in weeks. Or as if they had never eaten at a ball before. With as many conversations as he could hear, it would be unwise to say something of a personal nature during the meal.

"It was lovely to see Moriah today. Does she often accompany your mother on calls?"

"I couldn't say." When he asked Deborah to call with him on Lady Healand, he'd hardly expected the entire family to join him, making the visit more awkward.

Philippa paused eating, her fork suspended over her plate. "Are you sure all is well?"

"Yes. I should ask you the same."

"If you are referring to the moments leading to my unexpected waltz-turned-minuet partner, I do not know. Such an odd turn of events. Father will not be pleased."

"What will he do?"

"I don't know. The loss of Mr. Newcomb's fortune will be a huge blow."

"Were you going to accept him?"

She kept her voice low. "No. You were right. I couldn't live with the man, no matter how much it would please my Father."

Warmth filled Michael's chest. Perhaps there was a chance for him.

"What about you? Your supper dance was wasted on me. Have you had an opportunity to dance with the woman who enticed you to abandon your list?"

"Yes." He answered truthfully.

"If I was not a very good friend, I'd inquire after your dance partners. I'm afraid I didn't notice your dances at all."

"You didn't?"

"The first set, I was too busy protecting my toes. I'm quite sure he was trying to step on them."

Michael laughed more at her expression than the words.

"The second set, I was far too conscious of people whispering and looking in my direction. The third, which should have included a waltz—I'm grateful your cousin changed it to a minuet—I was much too preoccupied. I assume you danced with her during the third, since you, like every other gentleman, was hoping for a waltz."

"She danced with someone else."

"Oh, I am sorry."

"I am not."

"Well, since it was a minuet, I suppose you were the other person in the room not disappointed. You must thank the duke for me. I had thought him rather austere, but he is very kind. He kept me from receiving the cut direct by everyone in attendance."

"He is the best of cousins. I am sure he is happy he could be of service. I did warn you about Newcomb." Michael finished the last bite of his food.

"I hope the duchess isn't put out. I suppose I'll remain a subject of talk for a few days, but it won't all be Newcomb's rejection."

"The duchess is likely to laugh over it." At Richard's expense. Under the table, Michael clenched his fist. Richard had performed more than one kindness that evening. It was he who overheard Newcomb in the cardroom as the man's fury had grown. If Richard had not followed him to the floor and motioned for Michael to join him, they would not have been in a position to rescue Philippa.

"Thank you also for your part in removing Newcomb."

Michael's gaze fell to her arm, there was a faint purpling above her glove. He traced it with his index finger. She shivered. Michael pulled back his hand. "Did I hurt you?"

"No. Not you."

"I want to call him out."

"Don't. Please. There is already enough talk. And it would ruin your chances with whomever she is."

Around them people stood and returned to the ballroom.

Michael stood and assisted Philippa to rise. "I danced the supper dance with her."

Philippa turned to him, eyes wide. "Me?"

A fullness in his throat prevented him from answering, so he nodded his head.

She looked everywhere but at him before whispering, "But you can't."

"Why not?"

"The list, the duke, my father…"

"Gone, approves, doesn't matter."

They walked toward the ballroom where they must separate for the next dance. With only seconds left before someone came to claim her for the next set, the question he'd wanted to ask all night rushed out of his mouth. "May I come call on you tomorrow?" The words, even to his own ears, sounded much more like "May I chew on marrow?"

Philippa blinked a couple of times before smiling. "Of course."

"At two?"

"Please."

The Earl of Whitstone stood near the ballroom door. Philippa stopped to speak with him. Unsure if he should stay or leave, he nodded to the earl and walked on. Minutes later, he noticed the earl leaving the ball with Philippa. Michael cursed himself for not lingering so he could have told her goodbye.

# TWENTY-SIX

Alex walked the length of the corridor and returned to their bedroom. "This new Peggy is the best yet. I don't feel the need for a cane. I still cannot believe he had it nearly finished when we arrived."

"Will you try to dance?" asked Phil.

"No. I wouldn't dare. But I shall not draw so much attention to myself if I do not need my cane." Alex sat on the bed and pulled up the hem of her dress. "With the extra hinge, the ankle is not so finely turned. And I will need a heavy stocking to hide it. This one is much too thin."

"I will see to it right away," said Green. "His lordship will be so pleased you like your new prosthesis."

"Thank you, Green. Do you think it will be possible to find some today? We are likely to have callers."

"I'll go myself." Green hurried from the room.

Alex turned to Phil. "Now she is gone, you can finish telling me your tale."

"There is nothing more to tell. Grandfather asked we leave, so we did."

"Yes, there is more to tell. How do you feel now Lord Endelton declared himself?"

"It may not have been his intention. You know he doesn't always understand what is said."

"That may be true, but he does understand what he says. Now tell me all."

Phil sat on the bed next to her sister. "Last night my nightmares and my dream happened at the same time in the same room. I hardly know if I am awake now or if it truly happened."

"The bouquet in the parlor testifies something occurred. Lord Endelton has never sent you flowers before."

"Therefore, I am cautious in my optimism."

Alex gripped Phil's hand. "I am more hopeful. I have seen how his countenance changes when he speaks with you. He is quite enamored."

"I am not so sure. What if he only likes me because his cousin tells him not to. Like the toy our nurse would put on the highest shelf. Then, when she pulled it down, we found it was no different than every other wooden horse in our collection, and she had only used it to convince us to do her bidding. What about when he realizes I am not so special?"

"Impossible. Because you are. There is one part of your story which puzzles me because it made you blush. Why did you blush when he asked if Mr. Newcomb had hurt you?"

"It is nothing." Phil willed the heat in her cheeks to recede.

"Liar. You are blushing again."

Unconsciously, Phil touched the spot above the bruise. "Lord Endelton touched me with his ungloved hand. And —" As silly as it sounded, her sister would not give up until she told. "—it tingled. Not like when a spider crawls on me. It was pleasant."

"Is this the first time?"

Phil thought back on her interactions with Lord Endelton.

"No, but I have been trying to not think of anything other than friendship. I don't know if I dare hope for more."

At precisely two o'clock by the chiming of the nearest church tower, Michael knocked on the door of Lady Healand's townhouse. A butler opened the door, but instead of showing him into the parlor, Michael was directed to the study where he found the earl behind the desk.

"Right on time. Good, good. Have a seat young Endelton."

Michael sat in the straight-backed chair near the desk.

"I have received word, my son-in-law is traveling to London. Since he rarely comes directly to Town, I expect you have two or three days before he arrives, and then the madness ensues."

"Whatever do you mean?"

"Unless the news reaches him first, Sir Lightwood will expect to find his daughter engaged to the odious Mr. Newcomb. My son-in-law's temper is of a violent nature. My first priority is to keep my granddaughters safe. If you are not pursuing my darling Philippa in earnest, then I ask you leave now so I may make a provision to protect them."

"My … my … suit is in all earnestness. If she will have m-me." Michael couldn't recall ever stuttering in his life.

"I will do all I can to assist. Go. She is waiting in the parlor with her sister. We can see the whole of the little park from the windows if you wish to talk privately."

Michael's head hurt. Was the earl pressuring him to propose? Not today. Surely it was much too soon according to what Deborah told him. A footman led him to the parlor. The ladies sat working some sort of needlework as they spoke.

Lady Healand gestured to the chair nearest Philippa. "Welcome, Lord Endelton. I'm glad to see whatever my father said when he waylaid you did not scare you away."

"I do not think he meant to scare me." Michael sat in the indicated seat.

"Should I order tea now or after you and my niece take advantage of the sunshine and take a turn around the park?"

Everyone seemed insistent he go to the park. Not a bad idea as it was the only place to talk privately. He turned to Philippa. "I believe they want us to leave."

"So it seems. Perhaps they find watching people circle the park a form of entertainment."

"Is a walk in the park agreeable?" asked Michael.

"Quite. I'll fetch my bonnet." Phil and Michael stood at the same time.

"No need. Green left it with the footman. Go on now." Lady Healand waved them out of the room as one would shoo cats.

It was a shame she had to wear a bonnet. It hid her eyes from him and shadowed her smile. Although the blue bonnet did make her eyes all the bluer. Michael offered his arm and they crossed the recently cleaned street. Safely in the park, they looked back at the house to see three figures watching from the window.

Phil turned away first, tugging at his arm. "I apologize for my aunt. I don't believe she meant to oust us from the house."

"Your grandfather also advised a turn about the park after informing me he could see the entirety from his window."

"So he can. They are pleased you have come to call."

"Are you pleased?" He held his breath waiting for her answer.

"Not pleased." She smiled at him. "Delighted."

"May I continue my suit?"

"I'd like nothing better."

Michael returned her smile. They walked in amiable silence around the next corner. "I am not sure what I am to do next."

"I believe it is customary for us to talk as often as possible so we may determine if we suit."

Of course they did. He didn't need more walks to determine that. "Do you think they will always push us out of the house when I come?"

"Not if it is raining."

"What else must I do?"

"We could go to events together, perhaps the menagerie at the Tower."

"Oh, yes. Deborah mentioned it was a good place to court."

"Taking a turn about the park is pleasant as well."

"Should I take you for a ride in Hyde Park?"

"That depends."

Michael tilted his head.

"If you are driving the curricle, I say no. You do not enjoy driving it, and I would not enjoy worrying we might crash."

"If I had a coachman drive?"

"Then definitely."

"Would you like to go to the theater again?"

"That would be delightful."

"I will ask Richard for his— That reminds me." Michael dug the folded paper out of his breast pocket. "This is for you from the duchess."

Phil broke the seal and read the invitation. "Do you know what this is?"

"Yes, she is holding one of her musical nights. It is short notice. Are you already engaged?"

"No, but I am expected to perform. I am not skilled at playing."

"Didn't you once say your sister played, and you sang?"

"For family and the Godderidges. This is very different. Grandfather has been having Aunt plan such an evening as this. I am sure ours will not be as grand."

"You may decline." He hoped with all his heart she would not.

"I'll have to ask Alex before I can accept."

"Lady Healand and your grandfather are included in the invitation."

Phil was silent for several paces. "She isn't upset with me and trying to exact her revenge for my dancing with the duke, is she?"

"No. Why would she do that?

Phil laughed. "Because she can. Neither you nor your cousin ever call her by name. Which makes me think she could be vindictive."

"I don't understand."

"Neither do I. Not every person's motives are understandable."

Movement in the windows of Lady Healand's townhouse caught his attention. "We are still being observed. I thought they would grow tired of watching us walking."

"Of course they are watching. We are out without a chaperone," said Philippa.

"And they are curious."

"Did your mother and sister come yesterday as our chaperones?"

"I asked them to come in case there were many visitors. Since there were none, they were good chaperones."

They completed the third side of the block and rain drops began to fall. "Would you like to come in for tea?"

"Philippa."

"What?

"Your name. I was thinking about it, and it came out."

She moved closer to him. "When we are alone you may use my Christian name."

"Mine is Michael."

"I know. I heard it once."

"Will you say it?"

"Michael."

The sweetest sound he'd ever heard was his name on Philippa's lips as her eyes met his. Lips he had the urge to kiss despite the audience in the widow. A raindrop landed on her nose reminding him he should be indoors.

# TWENTY-SEVEN

The carriage slowed to a stop in front of the Duke of Aylton's residence. There were not as many lights burning as there had been at the ball. Grandfather and Aunt Healand exited the coach first, followed by Lord Endelton and his mother. Phil clutched the sheet music as she descended behind Alex who for the first time in years had left the house without her cane. Although grandfather wielded one if she were to have need.

Liveried footmen directed their group to the music room. Still in the doorway, Phil's lungs froze. From the neat rows of chairs, the *small* gathering sat more than sixty people. They had never performed to more than a dozen, the Godderidges being their only audience.

The Duke of Aylton stood stiffly next to his wife, greeting guests.

"Miss Lightwood and Miss Philippa, I am so delighted you could join us. Since you are a late addition to our little event, I have placed your performance last save one. Lady Charlotte will perform the final number."

"Thank you, your Grace," Alex answered for both of them.

The duchess appraised Phil from head to toe. "Not an incomparable or even a great beauty. I fail to understand what possessed my husband to dance with you."

Not wanting to cross the Duchess, Phil answered meekly. "It is a mystery to me as well."

The answer earned her a careless nod, and the duchess waved them past. For his part, the duke spoke not a word beyond the obligatory greetings.

Lord Endelton found them seats together and arranged to sit next to Phil with Alex at her side. As it turned out, the program was rather short with only five ladies performing other than the sisters.

While the first three performances were executed well, none of them outshone the others or displayed extraordinary talent. The panic enveloping Phil upon entering the music room dissipated. While they wouldn't outshine the others, neither would they disappoint.

After the fourth performance, which was a violinist accompanied by her brother, the panic returned. The pair played exceptionally well. Mediocrity after the siblings would draw undue attention.

Alex gripped Phil's hand. "Imagine Mother can hear us."

The simple words were all Phil needed to gather her wits and walk with Alex to the dais upon which the piano rested. Alex navigated the two steps without assistance. Phil so intently watched her sister, she didn't notice a ripple in the carpet and stumbled a half step but didn't fall. She took an extra moment to help Alex arrange the music before taking her position on the other side, where she would sing.

The two songs they'd chosen were familiar, taught to them by their mother years ago. Alex had composed the piano solo between them in such a way to show off her own skills without putting aside the singing. As soon as the first notes played, a calm settled over Phil and she could almost imagine her mother sitting next to her grandfather and aunt. Grandfather's smile grew with each passing stanza. Phil didn't dare look for Michael's reaction until she completed the first song and Alex played the piano bridge. As she had hoped, his face glowed with adoration. He had not been disappointed. Another face caught her eye, the duchess did not seem pleased. Perhaps the versions on the country tunes were not as acceptable as if they had been played by Handel or another revered composer.

Alex played the notes leading into the second song, a love ballad. Phil looked first at Michael, then feeling heat rise in her cheeks, then to her aunt, who resembled her mother enough to cement the illusion in her mind. The first note swelled within her and came out thankfully in tune. Their piece concluded to general applause. Phil curtsied from her position, and Alex from next to the pianoforte as she had practiced at their home. Phil gathered the music and followed Alex to the platform.

Lady Charlotte stood at the bottom step, not waiting for them to take their seats as others had before. She reached out her hand and touched Alex's elbow as if to congratulate her. To Phil's horror, Lady Charlotte grabbed her sister's elbow and propelled her off the step. Alex caught herself with her good leg and would have remained upright, if Peggy hadn't snagged on the rumple in the carpet. As her sister stumbled, Phil dropped the music sheets and jumped off the platform. Instead of helping Alex to her feet, Lady Charlotte used the toe of her slipper to raise Alex's skirt past her knees exposing Peggy to all.

There was a collective gasp.

Phil dropped to her knees as Alex rolled over and they both fixed Alex's skirts.

"Only my pride is hurt," whispered Alex.

Phil stood and helped her sister to rise.

Lady Charlotte smoothed a triumphant smile from her face. "My apologies."

Since her hands were occupied helping Alex, Phil couldn't slap the lady's face.

Alex gained her footing but still held to her sister's arm. She faced the murmuring crowd. "I understand the *on dit* among the ton is I'm not in possession of all my limbs. I assure you, I own all of them, and I have three more at home. The finely turned ankle you glimpsed is the creation of Mr. Potts who has created many prosthetics for those of our brave soldiers and their commanders who have need of them."

With her head held high, she released her grip on Phil and walked to her seat. A maid handed the music sheets to Phil, and she followed her sister in stunned silence.

Just as it would have been impolite to applaud Miss Lightwood's pronouncement, jeering Lady Charlotte's inept performance was simply not done. Michael wondered if there were others who wished they could break the rules of polite society. When the final note of the pianoforte mercifully fell silent, the duchess stood and directed everyone to the refreshments.

Michael turned to Miss Lightwood who took the seat next to him as she had reached their row before Philippa. "Are you injured this time?"

"Not as I was last time I visited this house. I am quite able to walk." She smiled at all of their small group. "Truly, I am well. I am glad grandfather insisted Peggy be replaced."

The look of concern on the earl's face faded. Philippa's worried forehead did not.

"Shall we see what the duchess prepared for refreshments?"

Miss Lightwood turned to her sister for assistance to stand before Michael could offer it.

As they proceeded, a retired general joined the earl in conversation. Michael found himself wondering which of the ladies he should escort. His mother was of higher rank, but Miss Lightwood might need more assistance, and in truth, he'd rather be at Philippa's side. The earl beckoned his daughter and granddaughters to join him in his conversation, solving Michael's quandary. His mother took his arm and they followed the others out of the room.

As usual, small groups formed and the conversation grew. In the corner of the room, the Abbotts spoke with the duchess. Michael led his mother in the opposite direction.

Richard joined them. "I have a book in my study I think you would enjoy."

"What is the subject?" At the rate he'd been purchasing books this spring, he may already have it.

Richard pursed his lips.

Michael's mother leaned close. "Go with your cousin, I have others to visit."

Ah, there must not be a book. Michael asked a new question. "Do you have time to show it to me?"

When they reached the study, Richard closed the door.

"There isn't a book, is there?"

"I have many books. They are not the reason why we are here."

Michael slumped into a chair. "Why did you ask me to come?"

"Did Lady Charlotte push Miss Lightwood? From where I stood I could not see clearly." Richard sat in the chair opposite.

"I am not sure. Phil— I mean Miss Philippa— almost tripped there too, on her way up. I assume the carpet had a bump in it."

"Not a bump. A candle under the carpet. I caught the footman removing it."

"It was deliberate then? Will you sack him?"

"He is not one of ours. He works for the Abbotts. The duchess had him on loan for the evening."

"Then it was planned?"

"It appears so. Mrs. Abbott is the duchess's cousin of some sort as is Lady Charlotte, and my wife has been seeing to Lady Charlotte and Miss Abbott's advancement among the ton. I shudder to think this could be the duchess's plan." Richard ran his hand through his hair.

"Why would she do that?"

"Why does she do anything?" Richard lifted his hand to run his fingers through his hair then dropped his hand before he could ruin his valet's work. "I don't know. I understand my wife less and less each day."

Michael found little comfort in his cousin's admission, he didn't understand people either.

Richard rose from his seat. "Thank you. I will have to look into the matter. Will you apologize to the Lightwoods on my behalf? I cannot risk angering the duchess further. As her next plot..."

Micheal waited a moment before answering. "I understand."

"We best return before we are missed."

The ride back to Lady Healand's was full of conversation, none of it concerning Miss Lightwood's fall. Michael wished they had taken a separate carriage so he might talk with Philippa. But if they had taken one, he would be with his mother and Philippa with the earl.

As the coachman pulled to a stop, Michael realized he would not have the moment alone he'd hoped for with Philippa. He could hardly leave his mother in the coach for even five minutes. He had yet to compliment her on her singing or her sister on her playing.

When they arrived, Michael took advantage of being nearest the door and assisted Lady Healand out and bid her farewell.

He extended his hand to Miss Lightwood. "I never got to tell you I enjoyed your playing."

"Thank you."

"I hope I may hear from you again."

Miss Lightwood smiled and removed her hand from his, joining her aunt and grandfather near the door.

Everyone watched as he handed Philippa out of the couch. "Your singing was delightful."

Her eyes lowered and her long lashes brushed her cheeks. "I'm glad you enjoyed it."

"More than anything."

One of the horses snorted.

"May I see you tomorrow?" he asked.

"Of course."

Reluctantly, he relinquished her hand.

# TWENTY-EIGHT

A new novel in hand, Phil retreated to the small private garden at the back of the townhouse. For a moment, she needed to find some quiet. Not five minutes later, she slammed her book shut. Unlike the garden at Kellmore Manner, her aunt's garden was not peaceful. The rumble of carriages echoed from the nearby streets. The spring flowers could not mask the stench of horse dung and coal smoke permeating the air. The combination drove her back indoors.

Alex sat at the small pianoforte in the corner of the parlor. "Did it start to rain?"

"No. London drove me indoors. I can't believe we once longed to come here." As girls they'd played 'getting presented to the queen' more times than either would admit.

"I've heard it is even worse during the winter months."

Phil perched on the settee. "That is difficult to imagine."

"I feel for the families who live here year-round."

"Poor souls."

Alex settled in one of the well-stuffed chairs. "I wish I would never have to come here again, but with three more sisters to find matches for, I am afraid I am doomed to return."

"Why?"

"Father will ask me to chaperone—since after last night, I will have no other use. I couldn't be more firmly on the shelf if I were covered with dust and filled with pickled herring."

"Not true. You could still marry."

Alex raised her brows. "You are always my champion, but you must be realistic. No man wants three-quarters of a wife."

"I think your math is off. Less than a tenth of you is made of wood. It could be much worse. Some of the gentlemen I have met seem to have wood for brains."

Alex laughed and the mood lifted. "I am thinking of returning home early."

"Please don't. I'd be lost without you."

"No you wouldn't, and it would be much easier to steal a private moment with Lord Endelton if I wasn't about all of the time."

"Nonsense. There would be a chaperone anyway."

"Speaking of which, I promise to be heavily involved in my book on the opposite side of the room when Lord Endelton comes." Alex's smile was more teasing than reassuring.

"If I look at the cover, I am sure I'll find it upside down as you are straining to hear our every word."

Alex looked at the clock. "He should be here soon, shouldn't he?"

A knock on the front door answered her question. They only had to wait a few moments for him to be shown into the room. Phil handed Alex her book and looked pointedly at the chair in the far corner. Alex stood.

"There is no need to leave, Miss Lightwood."

"A good chaperone doesn't linger too close."

"True but I wish to speak to both of you for a minute."

Alex retook her seat.

"You will pardon me asking, but Richard is most anxious to know if you were pushed last night."

Alex turned the book over several times. "Pulled. If it hadn't been from the folding in the carpet I could have avoided the fall. It's not entirely Lady Charlotte's fault."

Deep lines appeared in Michael's brow. "It was not a fold in the carpet. A candle had been placed under it."

"Deliberately? I nearly tripped on it," said Phil. "Any one of us could."

"Richard is most displeased and is trying to find out who placed it there."

"It doesn't matter. No one was injured," said Alex.

Michael shook his head. "It exposed you to ridicule."

"There is nothing for it. The story was already circulating. Since the truth is known, they'll move on to something else. I suspect fun is in the speculation." Alex's practical answer didn't surprise Phil. "If there is nothing else, you two are interrupting my quiet reading time. I am going to remove to the chair in the corner."

Alex crossed the room, and Michael joined Phil on the settee. "She is very pragmatic, isn't she?"

"I suppose."

"I'm still in the room, and I can hear you. Talk quieter, or I'll be forced to play the piano." Mirth laced Alex's voice.

Phil inched closer to Michael. "Does the duke think the duchess had something to do with it?"

Michael nodded.

"I'd hate to think Alex was hurt because of me."

"You don't know the duchess well. She would expose anyone for anything to make sure the talk stayed off of her—unless of course she wants it to be focused on her."

"I don't understand how the duke could have married such a woman."

Michael looked out the window. "I don't know what I am at liberty to tell you ... but he was forced into it."

"As you have said."

His hand slid across the brocade of the settee between them until their fingers touched. A pleasant warmth spread from Phil's fingertip to her elbow and eventually her heart.

"I did enjoy your singing last night. Why didn't you tell me you could sing?"

"It's been years since I've sung in company. Although even my mother said I sang well, I am never sure I do."

His fingers moved to cover her hand. "I do wish to hear from you again."

"That can be arranged."

"Soon?"

"Should I ask Alex to play?"

"She didn't want to be disturbed."

A voice came from across the room. "Yet, you are disturbing me."

Phil slid her hand out from under Michael's and angled herself to better see her sister. "You are a terrible chaperone."

"I think not. I have done nothing to separate your tête-à-tête or remind you to put on gloves."

"Then come play something." Phil turned to Michael. "Do you sing? Alex has some duets. George always tries to pitch her voice low but it never quite works."

"I have sung with my sisters."

They rearranged themselves around the pianoforte. Michael's voice was strong and usually on key. Alex played a selection of children's ditties. Soon they were laughing so hard, Grandfather came into the room. "What is all this ruckus?"

"Music. Would you like to join us?"

"No, but I'll have tea and listen."

Phil looked about the room. Her grandfather's smiling face, her sister's laughter, and Michael's tender gaze. Oh, if she was an artist and could capture the moment to remember forever.

According to the clock, Michael had stayed longer than customary. Since he was expected at the House of Lords in less than hour, he would have to end the visit.

"Endelton, are you off to listen to the debates?" asked the earl.

"Yes, I was about to take my leave."

"May I ride with you?"

"Of course."

The older man stood. "If you wait while I have my valet make sure I am presentable?"

Michael nodded.

At the door the earl turned. "Alexandra, I almost forgot, I need to show you a sketch my solicitor sent over."

Miss Lightwood left the room, closing the door all but a hand's span.

Philippa's cheeks bloomed into a blush. "Forgive my grandfather; he is not very subtle."

Nothing to forgive, the man knew how much Michael wanted to be alone with her. "It was kind of him to give us a few moments."

Michael reached for Philippa's hand, and she freely gave it to him. "I've read my sister's books, and they were of no help. I don't know what to say."

"What do you mean?"

"I need to say things."

"Such as?" She stepped closer causing the words in his brain to scramble.

*I love you. I want to ask for your hand.* "It seems I should give a speech about your eyes." He touched her cheek with the back of his finger. Remembering he should not, he dropped his hand. "Or say something grand."

Her free hand took his. "Perhaps you are asking permission to speak with my father?"

"That is how it is done, isn't it?"

"I believe so."

"Then we have an understanding?"

Her smile calmed all his fears. "Yes. We have an understanding."

Her gray eyes held a new depth to them as their gazes locked. Michael leaned forward, uncertain if he should tilt his head to the left or right. He'd seen Deborah kiss her husband often enough, it couldn't be difficult. Not wanting to bump her nose, he raised their clasped hands to his lips and placed a kiss on her knuckles.

Her eyes followed his every move. A tear formed in them. What had he done wrong?

She blinked and the tears disappeared.

He stepped back, unsure what to do. Footfalls in the corridor saved him from making another mistake.

Miss Lightwood opened the door but didn't enter. "Grandfather is waiting at the entryway."

Philippa dropped their clasped hands and stepped back. "When will I see you again?"

She still wanted to see him. His heart leapt; perhaps he'd been mistaken about the tear. "Tomorrow?"

She nodded and whispered, "Tomorrow."

He crossed the parlor and found the earl, who said something Michael didn't hear. Michael nodded and answered the only word he could think of. "Tomorrow."

The earl's laughter accompanied them all the way to parliament.

# TWENTY-NINE

Dinner was a quiet affair. Grandfather sent word he'd been invited to dine elsewhere, so it had only been the three of them. They retired to their aunt's sitting room where Phil and Alex took turns reading while their aunt worked on a needlepoint still life of fruit.

At the end of the chapter, Phil took the book from Alex and moved closer to the lamp. Three sentences in, someone pounded on the front door of the townhouse and yelled loudly for admittance to the house.

Phil dropped the book, Aunt Healand dropped her tapestry needle, and Alex dropped her jaw. They all focused on the doorway as they heard the rushing footsteps of the footman.

"Where are my daughters?" The unmistakable voice of Father boomed through the townhouse.

Phil looked at Alex. Her sister's eyes must've been as wide as hers. Phil took Alex's hand, wishing the two of them could hide.

Moments later, the butler appeared at the sitting room door. "Mr. Lightwood is here to see his daughters."

"See him to the parlor. We will be down momentarily." Aunt Healand waited for the servant to leave before she spoke again. "There's no need to rush girls. We will all go calmly after we pray."

Phil stood on shaky feet. Alex gripped her arm with all the force of a drowning woman. Father couldn't have possibly heard about the duchess's musical evening disaster so soon.

Aunt Healand smoothed her dress and raised her chin. "Come now. We will not cower in the corner. This is not your father's house."

Father paced the length of the parlor. He stopped as he noticed them come in and opened his mouth.

Aunt Healand cut him off. "Felton, what is the meaning of this intrusion? Why do you disturb our peace? The entire street must've heard you bellowing out there."

"Is this how you are introducing my daughters to society? By lazing around your home? You should be attending a ball or something."

Aunt Healand settled into the largest and most regal of the chairs. Her spine straight, she somehow managed to look down on Father from her lower position. She signaled for Phil and Alex to take the settee. "As you may remember, there are rarely events on Monday nights among the ton. But I am not the one who needs to justify his actions. I ask again—why are you here?"

"I have come to remove Alex home. I have heard rumors her leg has ruined any chances Phil has of a proper match." He pointed an accusing finger at Alex.

"Hurting Philippa? Surely not. Well, there was one addle-pate, but she was best rid of him anyway," said Aunt Healand.

Phil squeezed Alex's hand. Their aunt was brilliant. A queen couldn't be more regal than their aunt appeared at this very moment.

Father spun to face Phil. "Is this true?"

Taking a cue from her aunt, Phil answered her father without wincing. "Have you not heard? Mr. Newcomb no longer requests my hand."

"Mr. Newcomb? He has eight thousand a year and a growing business. What did you do?" Father's voice rose.

"Absolutely nothing." That was the truth of the matter.

"You are lying." For a moment, Phil feared Father might slap her with the back of his hand.

"Mr. Newcomb must have written to me if you refused him. I have been in Borehamwood for the last several days."

Phil recognized the name of the village. Margarita lived there. The household accounts would likely need adjusting again, depending on how much Father lost in one of the gambling hells. "You didn't tell us you were so near Town."

"I saw no reason to tell you. Mr. Fry, the man I wrote you about, is there. I put him off on account of your pending proposal, but if Mr. Newcomb has declined ..." Father rubbed his chin. "I shall have to think about this. Healand, I require a room for the night."

Aunt frowned deeper at his informal use of her name. "You will need to seek it elsewhere. My father is in residence and is occupying the last of the rooms."

"The earl?" Father's face paled for a moment before he could mask his surprise.

"The Earl of Whitstone is the only father I have."

"Don't tell me. He came to defend poor Alex's reputation. Like he can make her peg leg disappear. Words and his title can't make the truth go away. She is a cripple not fit for society and unfit to be a wife. There are men who will overlook her scarred face, and some who would find a one-limbed wife a great curiosity..."

"Stop!" Phil jumped to her feet. "She is your *daughter*. Why must you speak of her as if she is worthless?"

"Worthless? All a daughter is good for is the connections she can make through marriage. If your grandfather had not wanted the connection, he never would have allowed your mother to even look at me. I have five daughters. Only three of you are worth the investment I've put in to your upbringing. Jane is—"

"Enough!" boomed Grandfather from the doorway. "Leave this house at once."

"You can't expel me from my home."

"It is not yours as long as I still live."

Father stood nose to nose with Grandfather. "It can't be long, old man."

Grandfather didn't flinch. "Leave now."

Father turned to Alex. "Be prepared to leave in the morning. You will not further endanger your sister's chances of a match. I should have never allowed you to come."

He left, the clank of the lock of the door echoing through the house. Alex leaned into Phil's side.

"Why did you allow him in?" asked Grandfather.

"He is their father. I can't deny him from speaking to his daughters."

Grandfather sank into a chair, his bravado gone. "Unfortunately, that is true. I don't like him removing Alex from London."

"Felton mentioned a Mr. Fry. Do you know him?" asked Aunt Healand.

Grandfather shook his head. "I can send out inquiries."

"Father's anger will lessen by morning; it always does." Alex's observation, while true, unless Father drank, was of little comfort. "If I am harming Phil's chances, I should leave. I've had a lovely time. Five weeks was an adequate Season for me knowing London is not for me."

"I will not have you leave until my solicitor can speak with you. I will send for him first thing. You only have a few months before your maturity, and you must be protected."

Alex sat up straight. "What is to protect everyone else? Phil is safe as long as Father believes she is of value, but George and Jane are old enough to marry off. George will fight for herself, but Jane…"

"George will fight for her too," said Phil. The twins' closeness kept them safe.

"They are not old enough. I cannot give them independence, but there is one thing your father craves above all else, and that is money. I will have a plan by morning." Grandfather marched out of the room.

Aunt Healand stood. "We need time. I will do all I can to delay Alexandra's departure. Do try to get some sleep. I know how difficult the journey will be for you."

Phil and Alex clung to each other as they left the room. Phil's mind raced. Something had to be done.

How early was too early? Michael looked at the clock in the study again. The minute had barely moved since he returned from breakfast. He'd spent the morning drafting a letter to Sir Lightwood as the earl suggested. It would take at least four days to travel to Kellmore Manor and back on the fastest of journeys. With the vote drawing close, Michael couldn't leave Town for a week. A letter would have to suffice.

Michael read it again. Was he too eager? From what little he knew of Sir Lightwood, the title of viscount would hold as much sway as the lands and fortune behind the title. While not as large as Mr. Newcomb's holdings, the Endelton name was free of debt.

Folding the letter, he didn't seal it. Perhaps he should ask Edward or Richard if the letter was good enough. He'd been careful not to write any of the flowery sentiments floating through his mind.

He pulled another paper from his drawer.

Dearest Philippa,

I have written to ask your father's permission. Oh, that I could have a bird fly the missive to him and have an answer this very hour.

Michael poured out all the words he'd been unable to find yesterday onto the paper. When he finished writing, he sealed the letter and went in search of a footman.

"What is the fastest way to deliver a message to Russell Square?"

"A street messenger is almost as fast as a messenger on horseback. Would you like it delivered, my lord?"

A thought struck Michael. It might be too early for a call, but if he delivered it himself, he may see Philippa. "No. Will you prepare my horse?"

Ten minutes later, he entered Russell Square. Two carriages stood in front of Lady Healand's townhouse. One bore the crest of the earl, and the other was older and unmarked. Footmen swarmed around them, loading trunks and boxes. Michael stopped behind the carriage. A footman he recognized took the reins of his horse and handed them to a stable boy.

"What is happening?"

"You'll need to ask his lordship or her ladyship, my lord."

Michael hurried up the steps and waited at the open door as a maid passed through with a large basket. The butler recognized him and hurried over. "Lord Endelton, his Lordship is— No, perhaps I should have you wait in the parlor. This way, please."

The familiar room was silent. Michael watched at the window. The rush of servants in the corridor was the loudest sound in the house.

"Michael?"

He turned to Philippa's voice. Her eyes were red rimmed. "Are you leaving?"

"Father is taking Alex." Her voice caught. "Grandfather was unable to stop them."

"Where? When?"

"Home. Now."

Michael reached for Philippa's hand and led her to the settee. "Can you tell me more?"

"Last night, Father came. He was already furious, but then he discovered Mr. Newcomb declined to continue his suit. He insists Alex is at fault. He wants me to marry Mr. Fry. I won't."

"Why two carriages?"

"Grandfather is sending his so Alex can travel more comfortably. He refuses to allow Father in it." Philippa gave a strangled laugh.

"Where is your father?"

"I don't know. I heard him yelling at Grandfather earlier. Grandfather had taken Alex to his solicitor. Father is upset to learn Grandfather gave her a home in Bath when she turns twenty-one."

"Does your father know about our understanding?"

"I haven't had a chance to speak with him."

"Maybe if I go declare my suit to him, your father will allow her to stay."

"You would do that?"

"I wrote him a letter asking for your hand this morning. It would be better in person." Michael stood. Philippa didn't release his hand. "I'll be back as soon as I can."

She walked him out of the room. "I'm going up to help Alex. Have a footman send for me."

The butler led Michael to the study. Michael waited outside while the butler announced him. The butler exited and held the door for Michael to enter.

The earl stood from behind his desk. "Endelton, welcome. Allow me to introduce you to my son-in-law, Sir Lightwood."

Michael went through the niceties. Sir Lightwood barely acknowledged him.

"Felton, I suggest you listen to what the young viscount has to say." Lord Whitstone emphasized the title.

Sir Lightwood's eyebrows raised in interest. "Viscount?"

"Viscount Micheal Endelton." Michael bowed again. "I have come to ask for Miss Philippa's hand."

"Rather convenient timing." Sir Lightwood glared at the earl.

"Not my doing, Felton. In fact, I believe I should go check on the carriages." The earl exited the study leaving Michael alone.

"You wish to marry my daughter?"

Michael swallowed. "Yes, sir."

"Why?"

"Because we are a good match, and she makes me smile."

"Stupidest reason I've ever heard." Sir Lightwood sneered. Michael couldn't recall being treated so disrespectfully since Harrow. "You know she has only a small dowry."

"I am aware."

"You have the means to care for her, give her the pin money she requires?"

"Yes."

"Do you know about Alexandra's defect?"

"I am aware she wears a prosthesis. She is also one of the best pianists I've heard this Season."

"I am surprised you have heard her play."

"And I have heard Philippa sing. Her voice is enchanting."

Sir Lightwood leaned forward, his eyes narrowed. "You are enamored with her."

"Yes, sir."

"Have your solicitor contact mine to draw up the agreement."

"Then I have your blessing?"

"If the agreement suits. I am not just losing a daughter, I am losing the person who keeps my house running."

Michael used a line Richard told him. "I'll leave the negotiations to our solicitors."

Sir Lightwood nodded. "As you wish. Now if you will excuse me, we must be leaving."

"Can't Miss Lightwood stay?"

"Is that the game? No, she cannot stay. When you get married, Alexandra may attend the ceremony. I need a daughter to run my estate." Sir Lightwood didn't bid any farewells when he exited the room.

Michael found the family in the entryway. Philippa and Alexandra embraced near the door. Michael stayed in the shadows, allowing them time. He watched until the coaches left. Phil reentered the house and walked into his arms and cried.

# THIRTY

hin up. It won't do for our callers to see you gloomy."
Lady  Healand stood behind Phil as her Abigail fixed
Phil's hair in Green's absence.

"Better?" Phil's smile felt foreign to her face. Despite using one of Green's face creams, her eyes still showed signs of last night's restless sleep. The thought of Alex traveling alone for days haunted her. Since the accident, they had always traveled together. The nightmares which woke her early in the morning were all of Alex and another accident. It didn't matter that she knew Alex was in Grandfather's well-maintained carriage and with both Green and her husband. She would not be able to rest until she received word Alex arrived at Kellmore safely.

"You'll have to be more convincing during our at-home hours. I know you miss your sister. Try to think of other things. Perhaps your understanding with a very handsome viscount?"

Phil watched her cheeks color in the mirror. "I haven't said I had one."

"You must have, or my father would have never allowed you ten minutes in the parlor with him yesterday after your sister left. Unchaperoned."

Grandfather's direction giving Michael permission to calm her in the parlor without a chaperone was unusual, now she thought about it, and rather telling. She sobbed in Michael's strong arms for several minutes before gaining control of herself. He hadn't tried to push her to be happy or cheer her. Somehow, he understood platitudes people usually gave wouldn't help. Or he was incapable of saying them to begin with. He'd left shortly after, with a promise to meet tonight in Almack's assembly rooms. "Grandfather is unusually understanding."

The mirror reflected Aunt Healand's knowing smile. "That did the trick. Your expression is much more joyful. And that style is very becoming."

To Phil's eye, her hair didn't look much different than what Green usually did for day wear. Nevertheless, she smiled and thanked her Aunt's Abigail.

A tap came to the door, and the upstairs maid entered. "The butler asked I fetch you directly."

Aunt Healand took the calling card the maid offered and her face blanched. "Come, Philippa."

"Who is it?"

"Countess Lieven."

"One of the patronesses of Almack's?"

"Yes, this cannot be good news. She is well before calling hours."

Phil hurried down the stairs after her aunt. Outside the parlor door they stopped as her aunt took a deep breath before entering.

"Lady Lieven, what an unexpected surprise. Shall I ring for tea?" A remarkable calm that Phil could have never managed filled Aunt Healand's voice.

"Tea will not be necessary. I shall not be here long enough." Lady Lieven's accent added a harshness to her words. "I have come to revoke your nieces' vouchers. After the dreadful display at the duchess's soiree, we simply cannot risk their attendance. If you will go get your voucher, and your sister's as well."

Since the countess stood in the center of the room, no one sat. Aunt Healand laid her hand on Phil's arm. "Only Philippa had a voucher. We did not apply for one for Miss Alexandra."

Lady Lieven's brow raised. "We are pleased you did not try to hoodwink us in that regard. The voucher?"

Aunt released Phil's arm, and she scrambled out of the room as quickly as she could. Phil startled a maid when she entered the room. The coveted square paper voucher lay in the dressing table drawer where she had left it after attending the assembly rooms last time. The voucher wouldn't be a total loss as she would have an excuse to avoid the overcrowded rooms. When she returned to the parlor, Lady Lieven stood closer to the doorway.

"At last." She held out her hand for the voucher.

Phil handed it to her, not sure what to expect.

With one quick move, Lady Lieven tore the card in half, dropped it on the floor, and exited without looking at either of them.

"Of all the pompous—" Aunt Healand didn't finish the sentence as a maid swept in and cleaned up the papers.

For a moment, Phil wanted to keep the remnants, but there could be no good come of holding on to a poor memory.

"Would you mind singing for me until it is time for callers? And don't tell me Alex isn't here. You can play well enough to accompany yourself."

"Something fun and daring? I know a few sea shanties."

Her aunt laughed. "Why not?"

Grandfather joined them halfway through the second tone. "What is this my little Philippa is singing?"

"Tunes to make us laugh. Would you like to join us?"

"Do you know "Lavender Blue"? I haven't heard it in ages."

It took Phil a couple of false notes to find the tune until they sang together.

The clock in the hall struck the hour as they sang the last chorus.

"Thank you, my dear. I am off to the club so you ladies can receive your callers." Grandfather left.

Carriage after carriage passed the townhouse without stopping. The hall clock chimed. An hour passed, and not even Aunt's usual friends came. Phil turned the last page of her book and set it on the table. Her stomach rumbled loudly enough Aunt looked up from her needlework. At quarter to five Lady Healand ordered tea.

"History does repeat itself."

"Whatever do you mean Aunt?"

"When I decided to marry Mr. Healand, word spread like wildfire. All of my supposed friends abandoned me. It wasn't until after he died, when I resumed using the title which is my right as an Earl's daughter,  did I become marginally accepted again. Years later, no one remembers my fall from society, or at least claims to." Phil bit into one of cook's special biscuits. One advantage of no one visiting was she could have the best of the tea cakes for herself.

"All of this because Lady Charlotte tripped Alex at the soiree. Shouldn't she be censured for her actions?"

"Fairness isn't the purpose of the ton."

"What is their purpose? Why do they think themselves so important?"

"That, my dear niece, I have never quite figured out. However, it is the way of things, and if we are to get on in our world, we must follow their rules."

A knock sounded on the door. Isabel and Moriah, accompanied by a harried looking maid, entered the room. The girls sat on either side of Phil.

"Please forgive us for not coming earlier," said Isabel, her face flushed. "We also bring our mothers' greetings."

Moriah fidgeted, and the light caught the stain of a tear on her cheek.

Alarmed, Phil looked closer at Isabel, who also seemed distressed. "Whatever is wrong?"

"It's Deborah—" Moriah's voice cracked.

Isabel grasped Phil's hand. "Deborah is in a terrible way, and both of our mothers are with her."

"As is the doctor. I'm so afraid." A tear escaped Moriah's eye.

Phil handed the girl her own handkerchief. "Why ever did you come then?"

"Deborah didn't want you to think everyone had abandoned you and begged Mother to send us here." Isabel was much more composed than Moriah; still her voice shook.

Aunt Healand rang for a second round of tea. Fortunately, most of the best confections remained.

Contrary to what every English woman claimed, Phil knew tea did not cure all ills.

Sometime in his youth, Michael learned punctuality was a prized virtue. Being late to anything bothered him. Tonight, he was nearly an hour late to meet Philippa at Almack's. It couldn't be helped. Edward needed him after being banned from his own house. There was naught for Michael to do for his brother-in-law but to keep him occupied until word came. Deborah lost the child she carried. He could only listen as Edward raged at the blow until he was allowed to see his wife.

According to the doctor, Deborah required rest to return to full health.

If not for the chance to talk with Philippa, Michael would not have come. Hopefully, she and her aunt would be persuaded to leave quickly. He had no stomach for dancing.

He searched room after room, unable to find either Lady Healand or Philippa. Had she left because he failed to arrive? Michael walked a wide path around a group of debutantes, the last of which was Miss Abbott. He pretended not to notice them. They, however, noticed him.

Miss Abbott tapped his arm with her fan. "Lord Endelton, what a surprise to see you here."

"Excuse me, I must…"

"Must what? Find the Misses Lightwood?" Her mocking laughter caused him to stop.

Michael nodded and scanned the room beyond.

"He hasn't heard," whispered one of the women. Her comment unlocked the mouths of the others who bombarded him with answers.

"They aren't here."

"Their vouchers were revoked."

"The duchess saw to it after such an embarrassing display at her home."

Michael searched their faces to know the truth. Miss Abbott laughed again. He spun on his heel and left, his quick action ending their laughter.

The hour was well past the time of making proper calls, yet lights still burned in the front parlor of Lady Healand's residence, so Michael took a chance and knocked. The butler opened the door and showed him into the parlor.

Philippa held a book in her lap as if keeping her place. Lady Healand worked on a piece of needlework. The earl sat closest to the fireplace looking over a chess set. "Do you play?"

"Tolerably well."

"Good. I cannot figure out the next, best move."

Phil placed a ribbon in the book and closed it. "Do be warned. Grandfather has been studying his move for ten minutes, hoping to find a way to not allow me to win. I picked up this book to pass the time."

"You play too?"

"Passably." She rose and stood next to him. "I'm sorry I didn't send word we would not be at Almack's tonight. The topic slipped my mind during Moriah's visit. Is there any word on Deborah's health?"

"We are assured she will recover."

Lady Healand sighed. "Poor dear. Please tell her I've been praying for her."

The sentiment caused Michael to pause. Most people didn't speak of prayers as if they meant it, but Lady Healand did. "I will pass on the message."

The earl moved a knight. "Confound it. I think that was still the wrong move.

Philippa didn't bother to sit at the table as she captured the earl's knight with her rook. "Checkmate."

"I should have never taught you this game."

"You mean you should have never taught Alex."

Lord Whitstone stood. "I suppose you would like a few minutes to speak with my Philippa. Come, daughter, let us give them a quarter hour. Mind you, I'll send the burliest of my footmen in if you are even one minute beyond the quarter."

Michael watched in awe as, once again, he was left alone with Philippa, though the door was not fully closed.

"He likes you. And trusts you to a point." She led him over to the settee.

"You have been banned from Almack's?"

"Yes, I shall never have to suffer the crowded rooms and watery lemonade again." The laughter in her smile didn't make her eyes sparkle. "I am very sorry I didn't send word. Once Moriah came with the news, my not being able to dance seemed rather unimportant."

He picked up her hand and laid it on his. "I understand. I should have sent word I would be delayed."

Philippa shook her head enough that a curl bobbed, and she pulled her hand away. "Have you told anyone of our understanding?"

"No. I suspect my mother has guessed."

"That is well. I fear I must end it."

"Why?"

"You have aspirations. It is not only my father which would hold you back. It is me. Today Aunt Healand didn't receive a single caller until your sister and Isabel came. My voucher is gone. The ton does not easily forgive."

"It doesn't matter."

"We do not suit." Her words were said without the malice Miss Abbott used.

"But I love you."

She took a deep breath and turned, looking into the dying fire. "But I do not love you."

Michael jumped to his feet. "Philippa? Please don't lie."

She turned enough so he could see her profile. "It is time for you to leave."

"Why?"

Philippa stepped to the bellpull and raised her hand.

"Stop, I'll go." Michael slowly walked to the entryway without making eye contact with anyone as he exited the house. It wasn't raining. It should have been, as his insides were drenched with tears he couldn't shed.

# THIRTY-ONE

Why had Philippa lied?

The question kept Michael awake most of the night. Her words had to be a lie, else she would have looked him in the eye. The one woman he had thought was incapable of falsehood, proved him wrong. Michael had no one to turn to for advice. Edward and Deborah were rightfully occupied with their own problems. They had also drawn in his mother and were occupying her time. Richard's opinions he'd heard a thousand times, and last night's rejection only proved him right.

Michael wandered into the small library in search of distraction. *The Mysteries of Udolpho* still sat on the small table next to the lamp where Philippa left it five weeks and four days ago. Instead of returning it to the shelf, it had been dusted around. He should have never instructed the staff to leave his books where he set them. The urge to chuck the book through the window caused him to flee from the room. Violent outbursts were not becoming to a viscount, nor were they something he was unaccustomed to in himself.

Michael left the house with no destination in mind. When he passed White's, he pondered going in, but the early hour stopped him. A few doors up the street, the man he least expected to meet walked or rather staggered toward him.

"Endelton." Sir Lightwood's words were less slurred than expected given his condition. "Do you have a fiver you could loan your future father-in-law?"

Michael managed to leave his home without even a tuppence in his pocket. Even if he had a five-pound note on him, he would not give his money to an inebriated man. "No, I do not."

"Come now, son." Mr. Lightwood drew himself up.

"I am not your son, nor will I be."

"You said you'd marry her."

"She wouldn't have me."

"How dare she!" The news brought Sir Lightwood to his full facilities. "Ungrateful brat. Defying me at every turn."

Too late, Michael realized his mistake. "I intend to ask again. It has become fashionable to refuse the first offer."

"Fashionable? Foolish. I should have never allowed her to come to Town with her sister. This entire problem would have been solved if not for the crippled chit."

For the second time that morning, the overwhelming desire to punch something, or rather someone, filled Michael. He took a step back, wondering how to extricate himself from the conversation.

A man exited the door to his right. "Lightwood!"

Philippa's inebriated father stumbled in the direction of the voice.

Michael made his escape, returning home by the fastest route. His mind cleared with the brisk walk. He would allow his solicitor to complete negotiations with Sir Lightwood's, and he would propose again. It wasn't until he was safely ensconced in his study that he wondered why Lightwood was in Town when he was to be traveling home with his daughter.

Phil pulled the blanket over her head to block out the light creeping over the windowsill. It had been an easy thing to plead a headache when the maid came in to commence the day. Between mourning the words she told Michael and the emptiness Alex left behind, she'd had no sleep. In the dark hours of the night, her imagination had worked images worse than any nightmare—Father forcing her to marry Mr. Fry to keep her younger sisters from the same fate. Alex not arriving safely at Kellmore Manor. Michael being cut by the ton despite her actions to keep him safe. Each thought plagued her in turn, each scene becoming more dire as the night wore on.

News of Alex's safe journey home could not arrive sooner than another two days. Father couldn't possibly hear she had refused Lord Endelton in less than a week. And she wouldn't know if Michael had been shunned by his peers for much longer. There was little point in remaining in London. Traveling by post would be the most economical way to return to Kellmore. Unfortunately, news of Alex could not reach her on the post. And if there had been an accident she could well pass it.

Waiting for news was best.

Staying was too difficult.

Leaving would be the best course to take.

Phil punched her pillow. Before the maid returned with a breakfast tray, Phil fell into a fitful sleep.

# THIRTY-TWO

The clock in the church tower welcomed the noon hour. Philippa threw off her coverlet. Staying in bed all day proved to be more difficult than she had imagined it would be. Partially because Grandfather kept sending maids to check on her. She dressed in a simple day dress she often wore at home and wound her hair into a twist at the nape of her neck.

Aunt Healand sat in the morning room at her desk. "Are you feeling better?"

"My head still aches."

"What of your heart?"

She'd said nothing about her conversation with Michael the night before. "What do you mean?"

"I heard from the butler that a very disgruntled Lord left the house before his fifteen minutes were over." Aunt Healand moved to a small couch and patted the spot next to her.

"Sometimes I forget how much is noted by your staff." Not to mention reported.

"Do you want to talk about what happened?"

"There is nothing to talk about. I released him from our understanding before his name was also damaged." Phil sunk into the closest chair.

"Very gallant of you. Did he want to be released?"

"He will see the wisdom of it." At least, she hoped he would. Michael didn't see the world as others did, although he tried his hardest.

Aunt Healand's lips pinched together. "Hmmm. Have you eaten yet today? The maid said you didn't touch your tray."

"Is everything I do in this house reported to you?"

"Only those things that give the staff occasion to worry. No one has ever reported to me about what novel you are reading or if you had butter or jam on your scone."

"What a relief." Phil didn't mask the sarcasm in her tone.

"Shall I order tea?"

"You might as well. We must discuss my return to Kellmore Manor." As much as she was loath to admit staying in London was no longer an option. There would be little chance for her to avoid the marriage her father planned.

A day and half. Time had never dragged on as slowly as it had since Philippa ended their courtship. Invitations for upcoming events sat on the corner of Michael's desk. He'd already relayed his acceptances; now he dreaded going. At least tonight, like last night, he could sit in the House of Lords and listen as men discussed the upcoming vote. No one would know his assumed attention masked thoughts of his own.

Perhaps there would be something diverting at White's. Before Michael finished clearing his desk, his mother entered the room.

"There you are. I've had a note from Edward. Deborah is in terribly low spirits, and he wonders if it might be within our means to send them back to the country early."

"The journey would take more than two days. Is she up to it?"

Lady Endelton frowned. "Not that distance, at least not for several weeks. Lord Godderidge's holdings are no closer."

"I am off to White's. I shall ask Richard if he knows of anything I might let within a day's easy drive."

"You are the best of sons and brothers." Lady Endelton patted Michael's cheek, an action he endured only because she was his mother.

Since the sun was shining, Michael walked to White's, which would only take a few moments more than by hackney if the lanes were crowded. Two blocks from his destination, he spied a carriage marked with the crest of the Duke of Aylton.

The carriage stopped, and Richard stepped out. "You're off to White's earlier than usual."

"Matter of fact, I was in search of you."

Richard raised his brow as a reply. Briefly, Michael explained Deborah and Edward's loss. "Mother feels it would be best if she could leave the city to recuperate, but the arduous journey to our country home would be more than she could bear at present."

"I have a small lodge near Egham that I haven't visited for some time. It is completely closed up. If you have mind to leave this afternoon, we could arrive before sunset and see if it would suit."

"Splendid."

"I'm afraid we may have to spend the night at the inn, as we are likely to find the place in want of every comfort." The men stopped near the corner of an alleyway.

"Could we not stay at the house?" asked Michael.

"If it suits, I will hire people to prepare the home this very evening. Unless you are skilled with the broom and mop, we would be in the way."

"I am not opposed to helping where I am useful."

"I need to speak with a couple of men before I leave." Richard turned to the club. "Can you meet me in two hours? We can take my coach."

Michael agreed and turned back the way he came. A shadow in the alley caught his eye. Not a shadow. A man. The same who had called to Sir Lightwood yesterday morning. Michael shook his head; he had to be wrong.

"You are wanted in the parlor, Miss." The footman disappeared from the morning room's doorway as quickly as he appeared.

Phil set aside her book. She'd acquiesced to her Aunt's wishes and agreed to remain in London for another fortnight and had no need to pack. Therefore, all that was left was to read and answer mysterious summons from the staff.

Aunt was out making calls and taking what she called an "assessment of the damage." Grandfather would have called her to the study if he wanted to talk further.

The man standing in the parlor with his back to the door was easily recognizable.

"Father? Why are you here? Where is Alex?"

Her father turned. A large purple bruise covered the right side of his face. "Oh, my dear Philippa, your sister is why I have come. She needs you. We must leave at once!"

"What happened? Is she ill? Injured?"

"Yes." Father's words brought to life her every nightmare.

Phil rang the bell, and the same footman appeared. "Is my grandfather here?"

"His Lordship left a quarter hour ago."

"My sister has been injured, and I must go to her. Can you send a maid to my room?"

"Yes, miss."

Phil whirled to face her father. "I will be ready in a few minutes. Do I need any bandages or salves? Is Green with her?"

"Green is doing her best. Bring only a bag. You can have your trunks sent later. Do you need to tell anyone you are leaving?"

"The staff will inform my aunt and grandfather."

Father adjusted his coat. There was a rip in the sleeve. "What of your suitors?"

"I have none." Father didn't need to know the details. He would work out for himself soon enough that Lord Endelton was no longer a prospect.

"Hurry then."

Phil flew up the stairs. She debated about changing into suitable traveling clothes for only a minute. The dress she wore would suit well enough, and she could put the sturdier dress in her bag.

Father stood outside, next to his carriage. A balding gentleman conversed with him. As she hurried down the front steps, the gentleman left.

"Father, who was that?"

"No one you need to concern yourself about. Hurry, we must go."

Phil whispered a prayer as she sat in her father's well used coach, both for her sister and for the journey.

The lodge belonging to the Duke of Aylton, would have been better described as a cottage. Still, it was large enough for Deborah and Edward and a couple of servants. The elderly caretaker had not had it cleaned since his wife passed the previous summer. Each of the rooms showed signs of neglect. A crack crossed one of the panes in the parlor window. Richard added it to the list of minor repairs. Outside, flowers dotted the grounds, and the trees and lawn had been recently trimmed.

After a thorough cleaning, the place would be cozy and peaceful. "I believe my sister will enjoy it here."

"I asked the caretaker to bring in a staff. He assures me his daughter is a fastidious housekeeper." Richard left in search of the old man while Michael continued to inspect the house.

A large cat had taken up residence in the parlor. Michael assumed the cat kept the mice population down, as there were few signs of rodents. The cat eyed him suspiciously.

"Have no fears; you'll like my sister better than me as long as you don't give her your catches."

The cat yawned and closed his eyes.

In the corner, a spider resided on a large web. "You'll have to move out." He couldn't help but wonder at what Philippa's reaction to such a large web would be.

A square pianoforte lay under one of the dust covers. Deborah would enjoy that.

Richard's boots clicked on the dusty floor. "I am assured this place will be ready for occupancy by Saturday night."

The nearby village must hide an army of maids for such a prediction to be met. Not that Michael knew much of housekeeping.

Richard adjusted his gloves. "Come. Let us find rooms for the night and dine."

They'd timed their visit well. The last rays of sun disappeared in the western sky as they reached the inn. The proprietor gave them what he claimed were the two finest rooms. Michael's room was clean and had a large window. The boy who showed them to the room opened the sash high enough to let in a much-needed breeze.

Returning downstairs, the men found the dining room overflowing with travelers waiting for the post coach to continue its trip to London. Richard suggested a pub where he'd eaten the last time he visited the town. A rider passed them as they walked down the street. Michael was sure it was the same man from the alley this morning.

"I think we were followed from London." Michael nodded his head in the direction of the man.

Richard turned to look. "Nonsense. If he had followed us, he would have been to the cottage and come from the other direction."

Michael tried to dismiss the idea. There was no reason to follow either of them. He repeated the thought over and over again until he almost believed it.

# THIRTY-THREE

The coaching inn was nothing more than Phil expected her father to use for her sister's comfort. Ivy covered walls hid most of the ancient building. Likely the linens hadn't been changed, and she would need to be on the lookout for mice. She could see no other alternative inn, so perhaps this was the best this particular hamlet had to offer.

Father led her through the side door and up a set of squeaky stairs to the bedrooms. At the third door, her father thrust a key into the lock and opened the door to a musty chamber, lit only by the moonlight from a single window.

"Alex?" Phil crossed to the bed expecting to see her sister. The bed was empty.

Behind her, the door closed and the key clicked in the lock.

Rushing across the room she tried to turn the handle. It wouldn't budge. "Father?"

She looked around the bed chamber. What was her father up to? A bag sat on a chair next to the wardrobe. It was not her sister's. She traced the initials carved in the handle. M.N. It was the same bag she'd seen Michael's valet use to smuggle Peggy to her. What was this bag doing here?

She inspected the bag closer. There was no mistaking it was the same luggage, though why Lord Endelton would leave Town she couldn't fathom.

Phil closed her eyes and groaned. Father meant to force Michael into marrying her. What better way than to have them found together in a dingy room someplace between London and Gretna Green?

No, no, no. Michael was too good of a man. She had to get out of the room now.

Even if she was as proficient as George, a hairpin in the lock would risk Father hearing her attempted escape. The chamber was too small to have a concealed servant entrance.

Phil flew across the room to the window. The vines clinging to the building were old and thin. Hopefully, they were strong enough to support her escape. A drop to the ground would likely break a bone, and then she would be of no help to Alex wherever she was. Phil reached for the nearest vine and found it thicker than she'd first thought. A solid tug didn't budge the twisted stalk. She took one rueful look at her pale primrose dress before shimmying out the window. The cloth would be ruined by the time she reached the ground. The creak of the stairs beyond the door spurred her on. Being found in a man's room, even if it wasn't Michael's, was the worst of all her alternatives.

A moment later, she discovered her lot could be worse. Spiders.

Dinner left a sour feeling in Michael's stomach. On the other side of the table, Richard negotiated with a roofer about checking for leaks at the cottage. Wishing for sleep, Michael returned to the inn alone. Using the side door, he mounted the stairs to his room. He slowed his step as two men stepped out of the room at the end of the passageway.

The lamplight reflected off the familiar man's balding head and illuminated Mr. Lightwood's contorted face. "There you are, you bounder. How dare you abscond with my daughter!"

"What do you mean, sir?"

"I heard her calling out from inside that room." Mr. Lightwood pointed to Michael's door.

He should have waited for Richard and returned together so at least Michael would have a witness.

"I demand you open this door this minute."

Michael drew the key from his pocket, hoping there would be some explanation if Philippa were there. Surely she would proclaim his innocence loudly enough to break through the din of the coaching inn's parlor and dining room.

Silence met him as he opened the door. The lumpy bed remained as it had been when he brought in his bag. Had the bag moved? He was sure it had been on the chair, not the floor. The chair had been moved next to the open window. In the dim moonlight, he could not be entirely sure he was alone.

Mr. Lightwood elbowed his way past Michael and into the room. His companion held a lantern high, illuminating the small space. "Phil—" The words died on his lips. "She is here. I know it!"

Philippa's irate father crossed the room to the wardrobe and threw open the door.

Empty.

Michael forced himself not to smile as the men turned over the lumpy mattress revealing nothing but the sagging ropes of the bedframe and thick layers of undisturbed dust on the floor. If Philippa had been in the room, she managed an escape. Hopefully to safety.

Cheeks red with rage, Mr. Lightwood bellowed, "What have you done with my daughter?"

"Sir, I have not seen your daughter for two days. I must ask you to leave."

The innkeeper appeared in the doorway. "Problem, gentle-men?"

Mr. Lightwood pointed to Michael. "He has my daughter."

The innkeeper's brow creased. "Lord Endelton? Impossible. He arrived with the Duke. Come along and leave his lordship alone. Your daughter must be someplace else."

"But … but I know she was here." Mr. Lightwood looked around the room as the innkeeper and the other man ushered him out.

Michael waited until he heard the sound of feet descending on the stairs before rushing to the window.

# THIRTY-FOUR

Snap. Phil's foot broke the vine, and she tightened her grip, both grateful and saddened she wore gloves. They would have to be replaced. She looked over her shoulder, finding the distance still too far to jump down. Blindly, she searched for another foothold, and then another. She froze when her hand landed on a partially destroyed spider web. She needed to be away from the vile spider-infested vines. The authors of the novels she'd read never included spiders in the vines when the hero climbed up to save the damsel in distress. Phil pushed the thought out of her mind. She could check for spiders later.

Hands closed about her waist and pulled her from the wall. "Caught you! What are you doing sneaking into the inn?"

"Let me go. I was escaping—" Phil struggled free and turned to face her accuser. "— y-your Grace." Her clumsy curtsy could not have been worse than the front of her dress. Phil swiped dead leaves from it, refusing to consider the number of spiders that could be hiding in the folds and under her skirt.

"And what were you escaping from?" The duke held her elbow firmly, making a second escape unlikely.

"Philippa?" The shout from above caused them both to look up to see Michael leaning out of the window she had exited.

"Unhand my daughter, you blackguard." Her father's voice came from the doorway of the inn.

The duke loosened his hold. Phil turned to face the two men storming from the front of the building, her father in the lead. "The Duke of Aylton was assisting me."

"Duke?" Her father stopped short, causing the other man to barrel into him.

The duke gave Phil a sideways glance and raised a brow.

"Your Grace, my father, Sir Felton Lightwood, and the answer to your previous question as to what I was escaping from. Father, may I introduce you to his Grace the Duke of Aylton."

"You escaped?" sputtered Mr. Lightwood. Phil had seen that look in her father's eye. She needed to say something quickly before he found a new plan to entrap her.

"Yes, from the room you locked me in claiming Alex needed me. Where is my sister?"

Michael burst from the front door of the inn and wove his way through the onlookers gathered at the edge of the conversation. His gaze swept over her dress, and then over her face. Phil hoped her hair had survived the climb better than the dress. Hopefully, there were no spiders— A shiver wracked her body at the thought.

Michael passed her father and offered his arm. "You're freezing. Let's get you inside."

Phil laid her hand on his offered arm, relishing the support. Would this be the last time? Once he learned of Father's intended deception, she would likely receive the cut direct from both him and his cousin. Then all of her father's hopes for her future would be dashed.

Something tingled on her back.

Spiders.

Her body shuddered. She answered Michael's concerned look with the truth. "Spiders."

"Spiders?"

"In the ivy."

The crowd parted, and he led her to a small private parlor. The duke and her father followed. The innkeeper blocked the others from following, including the man who had been with her father. The innkeeper addressed her. "I'll send in my wife with some tea."

"Thank you."

The four of them stood silent for a moment. Phil knew she should sit first, but the thought of sitting on a spider caught in her skirt kept her upright. What she wouldn't give for a change of clothes and a hairbrush and to be anywhere other than facing what must surely be her last tribunal.

Under different circumstances, the parlor might have been considered cozy. Michael wasn't sure who he wanted answers from first. His cousin glared coldly at Mr. Lightwood. As for the man destined to become his father-in-law, Michael was sure whatever would come out of his mouth would be a deception. As for his lovely Philippa, the state of her dress and hair begged an explanation. Ladies didn't climb out of windows for sport.

The innkeeper's wife entered the room with a steaming pot of tea on a tray. She set it on the small table. She addressed Philippa. "Is there anything else you need, love?"

"Do you have a private place where a maid might assist me? I'm afraid I–I have spiders in my gown!" She shuddered violently.

"I'm afraid we are full up for the night, Miss, but I can help you in my private rooms."

Michael produced his key. "The lady may have my room. I'll not be needing it tonight."

The innkeeper's wife took the key. "Come, love, let's get you sorted."

Philippa followed the woman from the room.

Sir Lightwood lifted his chin.

Richard spoke first. "You never answered Miss Philippa. Where is Miss Lightwood?"

"Alex … er … Alexandra is safe at Kellmore Manor."

"I presume you brought Miss Philippa under the guise of your eldest daughter's request. As I recall, Miss Philippa is unusually devoted to her sister." The duke's statement begged an answer.

"What do you know of my daughters?" The fight hadn't gone out of the man. "What business are they of yours?"

If he wasn't worried about Philippa, Michael might find the interrogation more entertaining. "His Grace is my cousin. He has been introduced to your daughters on a number of occasions."

For the first time, uncertainty flashed across Sir Lightwood's face. It was replaced by something altogether different. "Your Grace, surely you must understand how distraught I was to discover my daughter in a man's arms in such a state. What was a father to think?"

Richard leaned forward. "That depends on where you last saw her. Upstairs, perhaps? In Lord Endelton's room, I presume."

Sir Lightwood shifted his weight and a sheen of sweat glistened on his brow. "When I saw her last, she was not in a disheveled state."

The duke stepped forward, crowding Sir Lightwood. "A state she claims came from climbing from an upper story window. Seeing as your daughter did not fall to her death, the question remains. How did she arrive to be here at this inn and locked in an upper room which, if I am correct, was not let to her?"

Philippa's father narrowed his eyes. "It is highly unusual for a man I've never met to know so much about my daughters' affairs."

"As I said, I am looking out for my cousin's welfare. I have been keeping an eye on several women who might seek to entrap him into a less than desirable marriage. So far this Season, my watchful eye has prevented him from three such traps."

"What? You never—" Michael ceased his protests at Richard's raised hand.

"Later." Richard responded to Michael only to quickly return to speaking directly to Sir Lightwood. "However, the one woman whom I thought would trap my cousin from the very first day had yet to make a move. I knew she would, she was exactly the type, desperate with an even more desperate father. Still, I waited and my concern grew as I realized my cousin growing ever more partial. He shunned my every warning. Then she rejected his proposal to save his name. I didn't think a woman was capable of such a thing."

Sir Lightwood's face grew red. Michael had little doubt the man would take his wrath out on Philippa the first chance he had.

"Imagine my surprise when I saw her scaling the ivy out of the inn, in an apparent attempt to escape the room above." Lord Richard studied his tea. "I had not expected that. Miss Philippa is all my cousin claims—a woman who risks her own life, wardrobe, and reputation rather than sully someone else's. I didn't think such a woman existed. My apologies, Michael. And not that it matters, but you have my blessing." Richard turned to Michael and slowly bowed his head.

"His blessing?" Bellowed Sir Lightwood. "What about mine? No contracts have been signed."

"Considering what occurred here tonight was of your doing, I don't think it would be wise to do anything other than give your consent if marriage is what your daughter wants. As for the marriage contract, Michael and I use the same solicitor." There was no mistaking the threat in Richard's voice was as clear as the growl of a caged lion.

"I intend to have Philippa for my wife, if she will agree. All of her sisters will be welcome in our home. However, sir, whether or not you are depends entirely upon your daughter's opinion. May I put that in the marriage contract?" Michael addressed the question to his cousin who answered with a nod.

Sir Lightwood sidestepped the duke toward the door. "I'll get my daughter then."

"No," said Michael. "You will allow her to come down on her own terms. What you will do is prepare your coach—"

"Have you seen Sir Lightwood's coach?" interrupted Richard. "Most uncomfortable, I assume. Might I suggest Sir Lightwood go about finding a spinster or some other suitable companion to accompany you and Miss Philippa back to London in my coach? That will give me time with Lightwood and his accomplice, assuming he has not abandoned this place, to come to an agreement or two."

"Agreement?" Sir Lightwood and Michael asked in unison.

The Duke of Aylton's lips thinned. "Yes, I want to be sure his other daughters have a fair chance on the marriage mart. Which means Sir Lightwood needs to change his ways."

The color drained from Sir Lightwood's face.

"Endelton, you need not worry about us. Just send my coach back when you return to London. Lightwood, you must secure a chaperone post haste for your daughter's welfare."

Sir Lightwood scrambled from the room.

Michael blurted the question that had been on his mind. "You believe Philippa did not mean to entrap me?"

"When I first saw her climbing the ivy, I thought she was trying to get into your room. However, once she pointed out she had scaled down the wall, it was easy to see the trail of broken vines descending from your window. She must think very highly of you to risk falling to the ground to prevent you from being ensnared."

"I hope she does." Michael prayed he was correct. He could not endure another refusal to his proposal.

The innkeeper's wife gave Phil's dress another shake. "Oh, and there is another one of the little creatures. That's only three, Miss. Spiders are not my favorites at all, and the ivy be full off them. Why did you do a fool thing like climbing down the wall?"

"My father wanted to force a man, a viscount, to marry me." Having stripped to her chemise, Phil shook out her stays. No spiders appeared. There had been one on her shoe and none on her stockings.

"Don't you like this Lord?"

"I do, very much, but I won't force his hand. What kind of marriage can you have if it started by trickery?"

"I don't rightly know. Mine was started by a wee bit of devilry in the hayloft, if you know what I mean." The innkeeper's wife didn't even blush at her comment. "I suppose we all do what we must to get us a man. With all these wars, the good ones are in short supply. I'd take him any way you can. I'll check your back next."

Phil stood as still as possible as the woman lifted the back of her chemise.

"I don't see any more of the little crawlies. But in my opinion, you have more than enough inside y'er shift to keep a man happy. He wouldn't mind if he was tricked into marriage with ye."

Phil's face heated. The conversation was worse than having spiders crawling on her. "I have a bag with another dress and my hairbrush in it, only I do not know where it went."

"I'll go and fetch it for you." The innkeeper's wife left with her dress.

If she did want to trap Michael, she was certainly dressed for the part. Phil rubbed her arms to warm herself and sat at a rickety table and pulled the pins and twigs out of her hair. She didn't feel anything crawling along her scalp as her fingers combed. Her hair had been the first place the innkeeper's wife had checked, declaring it free of spiderwebs or moving creatures. Thank heavens she'd not participated in George and Jane's contest to grow her hair out. Jane's fell well below her knees. It would be impossible to finger comb it all out.

A tap on the door announced the return of the innkeeper's wife. "Your dress will need a good soak to come clean. Your father's coachman gave me this bag. Is it the one you wanted?"

"Yes, it is."

"Have you eaten?"

"No."

"I'll fetch you a bite of supper while you see to y'er hair." The innkeeper's wife left again.

Phil found her brush and worked on her hair. Satisfied that she was ivy- and spider-free, Phil plaited her hair and wound it into a simple bun.

Phil eyed the window. An escape to the barn might be best, but then how to return to London? Father must have left her here. She had no money for the mail coach. Imposing on the Duke or Lord Endelton would hardly be proper—providing they came in a coach. They could have easily ridden.

The innkeeper's wife didn't knock when she let herself back in.

"Here is a bite for ye." The woman set a plate of cold meat, cheese, and bread on the table with a cup of tea. Not an elegant meal, but enough to satisfy. If Phil's mother watched from heaven above, she would have yelled at her daughter to take small bites and not wolf her food down like one of the hunting hounds.

"Best hurry up now and put on y'er other dress. Don't want to wait too long. When men talk too long, they come up with plans. Plans never work out for us women folks now, do it? Look at parliament. If women were in there, things would be different."

Phil was startled at the idea. Women would run the country differently. However, she had enough of her own problems to attend to tonight. Men talking must mean Father was still here. Perhaps she had a way back to London. "What men are talking?"

"The gentlemen, of course. Me husband is serving them in our best parlor, he is." She tightened the stays a bit tighter than how Phil preferred them.

Anxious to get downstairs, Phil didn't have the innkeeper's wife readjust them. The old gray dress Phil had in her bag hid the stains on her petticoat. Tying fresh stockings in place, Phil looked up at the innkeeper's wife. "Thank you for your help. I'd give you something, but I was dragged from my home without even a tuppence."

"No worries, his lordship slipped me husband a half crown for my help. And the duke paid me husband a crown more. Don't know who you are, but you may not need trickery after all."

Phil followed the woman down the stairs, wondering exactly what she did need.

Only Lord Endelton and Duke Aylton sat in the small

parlor when she entered. They both stood at her entrance. Phil glanced in all the corners. "Where is my father?"

The duke bowed slightly. "He is securing an escort for your ride back to London. I am going to check on his progress. You'll leave in five minutes." He swept out of the door leaving her alone with Michael.

Phil took a step to the door. She hadn't climbed down a trellis of ivy to have the duke leave her in a compromising situation in the private parlor of a coaching inn. "Please don't go. We are unchaperoned."

The duke smiled and closed the door behind him.

"I asked for five minutes with you privately. I hope you don't mind." Lord Endelton gestured to a chair so she might sit.

Phil remained standing. "But it isn't proper."

"It is if what I intend to ask is for your ears only."

Phil's hand flew to her chest, and she took the offered seat. It was the only way to keep her rapidly beating heart from flying away. Could he mean to ask for her hand again? Despite her father? Despite all that transpired tonight? She couldn't form any words, so she sat at the end of the small sofa, signaling her willingness to stay.

Michael sat next to her and took the hand not holding her heart in check in his own. "You braved spiders for me."

Still unable to speak, Phil nodded.

"No one has ever braved spiders to save me. I know you love me. Philippa, please marry me. I love you. I want you. I need you to tell me when I am being foolish, correct me when I am wrong, and love me when I need forgiveness. Please be my wife?"

"But my father—"

Michael shook his head. "—is of no consequence. Please?

"You love me?"

"Ardently." He lifted her soiled glove to his lips.

"Truly?"

"Deeply." Michael moved closer and lowered his voice. "And if you don't answer me soon, I'll pull you into my arms and kiss you with such passion that when my cousin opens the door, he will force us to marry."

Phil giggled. The idea he would force her hand was the most insane thing she'd ever heard. She bobbed her head. "I love you too. Yes."

Michael's lips touched hers. She leaned into him and dropped the hand holding her heart in place to his chest. His heart beat as rapidly as hers, like a mighty bird trying to flee its cage. His lips danced over hers. She gasped, and he trailed kisses along her jawbone. His lips returned to hers, and she matched his movements. If Phil had known such bliss was ruination, she might have tried it earlier.

The door thumped open against the wall, causing them to jump apart, although Michael retained his grip on her hand.

The duke leaned against the door frame. "I assume she agreed to have you. I really don't want to have to polish my dueling pistols."

Michael stood, helping Phil rise with him. It would have been hard to do otherwise, as she wanted to be as near as she could to him. "She said yes."

One of the Duke's rare smiles graced his face. "You are sure, my dear? He is a terrible bore, and he has been known to try to cheat at cards."

Phil couldn't contain her smile. "I think I will be quite content with that. I only see one problem."

"What is that?"

"I will have to put up with a cantankerous and conniving duke as my cousin. I do hope you don't show up at the break of dawn often. I simply won't put up with your yelling."

Michael pulled her into his arms. "Yet another reason to make you mine." He kissed her again, ignoring the stomping of the duke as he left the room.

# EPILOGUE

The loveliest of fall days blessed The Willows. A few trees hinted at the change in color to come in the next weeks. Friends and family lined the drive greeting the new viscountess and her husband from the church. As Michael helped Phil out of the open carriage, he whispered in her ear. "Lady Endelton, it seems our friends don't want to leave us in peace."

"Don't be rude," she whispered back. "Grandfather went to much trouble to host our wedding. After the wedding breakfast is over, you can whisk me away and then we can have our peace."

"Promise?"

Phil placed her hand over his heart. "Always."

They greeted and mingled and ate as they were expected.

Lady Endelton hugged Phil and kissed her on each cheek. "It seems I am the Dowager Viscountess now. I've never been happier to change my title. I have decided to stay with Deborah at the cottage since Lieutenant Godderidge is gone back to sea. I'll keep Moriah with me so the two of you will have the whole of Terrace Hall until we descend upon you at Christmas."

"You will be most welcome any time."

"Mother says we should leave newlyweds alone for two months altogether."

"Moriah." A tone of good-natured warning filled the dowager's voice.

"Are you going on a tour?" asked Deborah.

"Grandfather has tasked us with visiting his many holdings, and Michael has several friends who have invited us for a few days here and there. Enough of a tour for me. Will you come at Christmas as well?"

"Lord and Lady Godderidge have asked me to come live with them from Christmas until Easter." Deborah nodded to the place across the hall where Isabel Godderidge stood with her parents.

"I should speak with them. You are also welcome to come visit any time it suits you. Michael is ever so fond of you." Phil turned to Julia. "And you as well. You must bring your daughter for a visit. Babies are always welcome."

"Not so much at weddings, although I miss her very much. We will leave soon after the two of you. I have never had a desire to stay at home as often as I have this past month."

"Then Michael and I must hurry our farewells." Phil didn't need to search the room to find her husband; some indescribable link told her he was behind her and to the left.

Moriah giggled and her mother tapped her with her fan.

Phil moved on, both wanting to hurry and slow time all at once.

At last, Phil found a quiet corner with Alex, the farewell she'd saved for last. "My only regret is I am leaving you to manage Father on your own."

"I won't be alone. I have George and Jane and only four months until my freedom from Father's home. There is a great deal of planning I must do." Alex looked across the room where their youngest sister flitted from person to person. "Only five days until she leaves for school. I hope she learns the manners our influence has failed to teach. We shall all get along without you, though we will miss you terribly."

Phil nodded to where their father drank another glass of wine—or perhaps something stronger. Grandfather stood near frowning. "I can never thank Grandfather enough knowing you have an escape. I worry Father will only become more difficult."

Michael joined them. "Alexandra, you and your sisters are welcome any time in our home."

"Thank you."

"No, thank you. If not for you, I would have never spoken with your sister."

"The thanks lie with Peggy." Alex tapped her false foot on the floor, her infectious laugh spread among the three of them.

Michael tucked his new bride next to his side and whispered into the ticklish spot behind Phil's ear he'd located the other night. "Ready, darling?"

Phil forgot about being ladylike for a moment, stepped closer to her husband, and lifted her lips to give him a chaste kiss. Michael responded by wrapping his arms around her and pulling her close. Even as cheering erupted around them, Phil could not end the kiss. Michael pulled back. "Does that mean yes?"

Phil laughed and they made their way out of the room with his arm still about her. Most of the party followed in their wake.

The Earl's butler opened the heavy door wide. A weary young man in wrinkled clothing stood on the doorstep. Poised to knock.

"Beg your pardon. Does Mister Whitstone, Earl of Ryeland live here?" The man's accent sounded odd to Phil's ear as did his confusion of the proper form of address.

The butler raised his chin. "This is the residence of Lord John Ryeland, Earl of Whitstone."

"Ah, that is what I meant. Titles are most confusing."

"Come back another day when you aren't interrupting his granddaughter's wedding."

The man didn't budge. "Will you inform him Johnathan Whittaker, grandson of Nathaniel Whittaker, born Nathaniel Ryeland, heir to the sixth Earl of Whitstone, is here from Massachusetts to fulfill my grandfather's last request?"

Everyone in the hall grew silent and parted for Grandfather to come forward. Phil and Michael stepped to the side.

Grandfather extended his hand. "You came at last."

## THE END

# HISTORICAL NOTE

I almost didn't include a historical note, since the note has more to do with Alex than it does Phil.

Alexandra's last "Peggy" is based on the the famous Anglesey Leg. A groundbreaking prosthetic device invented for Henry Paget, the Marquess of Anglesey, who lost his right leg during the Battle of Waterloo. This artificial limb was created by James Potts, a skilled London-based limb-maker who had previously worked as a watchmaker. Potts' background proved invaluable in designing a more advanced and functional prosthetic than what was available at the time. The Anglesey Leg featured articulated knee and ankle joints. The design incorporated a combination of wood, steel, and catgut strings, mimicking the actions of tendons which allowed for more natural movement and improved mobility compared to the rigid peg legs, sometimes called clappers, used by amputees of that era.

Despite significant contributions to the field of prosthetics, James Potts is barely mentioned in historical records. I only wish it had been named for him instead of the famous user of the device. The success of the Anglesey Leg led to increased demand for Potts' services, and he eventually moved his business to Chelsea to be closer to the military hospital there.

The design of the Anglesey Leg was used widely with few improvements for more than 150 years. I wish to give Mr. Potts a shout out for his invention. In my mind, Alex received an early prototype which, as a fiction writer, I could give her.

Of course I had to give homage where homage was due. *Pride and Prejudice* was published anonymously in 1813 with the front cover stating "By a Lady". Jane Austen (1775-1817) wrote the novel, but she did not use a male pen name.

# ACKNOWLEDGMENTS

For almost two years this book has been sitting in my computer waiting for the right time to be published. It has been read, and reread by my friends as they encouraged me to return to historical fiction.

As always, thanks to Tammy, Nanette, and Julie who are so willing to help make all my projects better and to read for all my mistakes. I would never make it through a day without Mara whose messages keep me on task. Thank you wonderful ladies.

Big thanks to Maria for the excellent edits. And to my excellent proofreaders who are not to be blamed for any remaining errors. Thank you all!

My husband encourages me every crazy step of the way and puts up with all my messy spreadsheets, and lack of cooking as my imaginary friends eat better.

And all gratitude to my Father in Heaven for putting these wonderful people, and any I may have forgotten to mention, in my life. I am grateful for every experience and blessing I have been granted.

# ABOUT THE AUTHOR

Lorin Grace was born in Colorado and has been moving around the country ever since, living in eight states and several imaginary worlds. She holds a degree in graphic design which comes in handy with creating book covers. Currently, she lives with her husband, and a dog who is insanely jealous of her laptop.

When not writing, Lorin enjoys creating graphics, visiting historical sites, museums, painting furniture, and reading. Three of her books, her debut novel, *Waking Lucy* (2017), *Mending Fences* (2018), and *Not the Bodyguard's Baby* (2020) have won Recommend Read awards in the League of Utah Writers Published book contest.